Crimes Across the Sea

Crimes Across the Sea

Edited by John Creasey

Preface by Herbert Brean

The 19th Annual Anthology
of the Mystery Writers of America

1964

HARPER & ROW, PUBLISHERS
NEW YORK, EVANSTON, AND LONDON

FIRST EDITION

LIBRARY OF CONGRESS CATALOG CARD NUMBER: 64:18074

G-O

Acknowledgments

"The Deveraux Monster" by Jack Ritchie. Copyright © 1962 by Flying Eagle Publications, Inc. Reprinted by permission of Larry Sternig Literary Agency and the author.

"A Question of Honor" by Ellery Queen. Copyright 1953, 1954 by Ellery Queen. Reprinted by permission of the author.

"Sea of Troubles" by Henry Slesar. Copyright © 1963 by Henry Slesar. Reprinted by permission of the author.

"The Unlocked Room" by John F. Suter. Copyright © 1960 by Davis Publications, Inc. First published in *Ellery Queen's Mystery Magazine*. Reprinted by permission of the author and Davis Publications, Inc.

"Murder Delayed" by Josephine Bell. Copyright © 1961 by Josephine Bell. Reprinted by permission of the author.

"The Hoofs of Satan" by Edward D. Hoch. Copyright © 1955 by Columbia Publications, Inc. Reprinted by permission of the author and Columbia Publications, Inc.

"Something White in the Night" by Herbert Brean. Copyright 1950 by Herbert Brean. Reprinted by permission of the author.

"Three Ex-Soldiers" by James McKimmey. Copyright © 1962 by The Greenleaf Publishing Co. Reprinted by permission of Harold Matson Co., Inc., and the author.

"United Nations Murder Case" by Lawrence Treat. Copyright © 1957 by King-Size Publications, Inc. Reprinted by permission of the author and King-Size Publications, Inc.

"Fear and Trembling's" by Michael Gilbert. Copyright © 1962 by Michael Gilbert. First published in the U.S. in *Ellery Queen's Mystery Magazine*. Reprinted by permission of the author and *Ellery Queen's Mystery Magazine*.

"The Frightened American" by Bill Knox. Copyright © 1961 by Bill Knox. Reprinted by permission of the author.

"The Dynamics of an Asteroid" by Robert Bloch. Copyright 1953 by the *Baker Street Journal*. Reprinted by permission of the author and the *Baker Street Journal*.

"Castle in Spain" by Julian Symons. Originally appeared in the London *Evening Standard*. Reprinted by permission of the author.

"(Untitled)" by Fred Levon. Copyright 1955 by Mercury Publications, Inc. First published in *Ellery Queen's Mystery Magazine*. Reprinted by permission of the author and Mercury Publications, Inc.

"The Frantick Rebel" by Lillian de la Torre. Copyright 1948 by Davis Publications, Inc. First published in *Ellery Queen's Mystery Magazine*. Reprinted by permission of the author and Doubleday & Company, Inc.

"The Man Who Hated Scenes" by Robert Arthur. Originally published in *The Mysterious Traveler Magazine* as "The Hint." Copyright 1952 by Grace Publishing Co., Inc., Copyright assigned. Reprinted by permission of the author.

"Love Will Find a Way" by David Alexander. Copyright © 1960 by David Alexander. Reprinted by permission of the author.

Contents

Preface: A Note About Mystery Writers of America

You will not need a magnifying glass, or fingerprint powder complete with feather duster, or even spectroscopic analysis to detect that this volume consists entirely of mystery and suspense short stories. Many noted authors' names, not excluding that of Editor Creasey, will tell you as much.

But you may like to be reminded that, since it is what it is, this book is a part of the youngest and certainly most vigorous art form in world literature. Others, such as the drama, the poem from quatrain to narrative, the novel, the tale long or short, have been with us for centuries or even millenniums. But the detective story, in its absolute form, came into being a mere 123 years ago.

That was when Edgar Allan Poe published *The Murders in the Rue Morgue* and thus became, among other things, the patron saint of the Mystery Writers of America.

He did considerably more, though. Poe invented the classic pattern of mystery-detective story, complete with crime, clues and solution. He fathered a gradually growing breed of followers, admirers and, each in his own way, imitators.

Most important, he started something which in the relatively short span of its life has become a familiar instrument for the creation of excitement and entertainment throughout the world. Call it mystery, thriller, suspense story, spy story, detective story, whodunit (ugh!) or what you will, the *genre* that Poe brought into being with one stroke of genius is now read and revered not only in the United States, where it originated. Or in Britain, which received it with welcoming and nurturing arms. Or in France, where it appealed at once to the Gallic appetite for reason and intellectualization.

It is today read and known almost everywhere—an international commodity. Japan, for example, has a tremendous appetite for mysteries; the Latin countries love them, as does Canada; and they are to be found on bookstands from South Africa to Scandinavia. The Iron Curtain is the last major area on the face of the globe where the mystery is actually frowned on. Russia has long regarded it as a capitalist invention that could encourage resistance to state authority. Even so, mysteries are pirated and read in Russia, though their foreign authors receive no royalties.

Ironically enough, royalties will not be paid to the authors of the stories in this book either, but for a different reason. They are all members of the Mystery Writers of America.

And who is that?

The Mystery Writers of America comprise a professional writers' group, more than 500 in all, who number in their ranks most of the big names in mystery writing and who have now existed as an organization for almost two decades. MWA's purposes are varied: to improve the quality and status of the mystery, to improve contractual terms for its authors, to provide the means for social companionship and the exchange of professional knowledge and techniques among people who, living from coast to coast and often overseas, share one thing: dedication to the mystery.

To maintain its treasury MWA gives an annual dinner on Poe's birthday at which "Edgars" are awarded for the best mystery of the year, the best first novel, and for a number of other mystery categories. We also run an annual workshop class in mystery writing (Fred Levon, represented in this volume, is a graduate). And we publish anthologies such as this one, all proceeds of which go to the treasury.

You've contributed to it, incidentally, by buying this book, for which our thanks, and our hopes that you enjoy it.

Enough of this. Crime marches on, so please march with it, into what Philip Guedalla called "the normal recreation of noble minds," the detective story.

HERBERT BREAN

Foreword: Who Knows Enough?

When the theme of *Crimes Across the Sea* was first mooted there was much enthusiasm but one small voice of caution: did enough American writers know enough of England and Englishmen to write convincingly about them? And did enough British writers know enough about America and Americans to present them effectively to that most discerning of the *genus* reader: the crime story *aficionado?*

The evidence in this book gives the answer, I hope. There were enough who knew enough, which in two short paragraphs is quite enough enoughs.

It did not always promise well. I am told that each succeeding editor of the anthology lives for months in a nightmare of foreboding that too few stories will come from even fewer members. There is no unreadiness on any member's part to offer a story, if only it could be any old story, preferably the author's current favorite; but a story to fit a specific theme—oh dear, oh no, not I; the cupboard is bare.

On a day of determined optimism all those responsible for this particular collection met together late in September, with only a third of the book yet gathered, and so little time to harvest more. Catherine Barth, who is responsible for so much of MWA's coordination, tried hard to reassure Anna May Wells, Winfred Van Atta (by proxy), and me that all would one day be well; that the spark of hope in a short story offered by one of the most famous as well as the doyen of the art, would one day become a flame.

I must admit to misgivings when I read American anglicisms and anglicized Americanisms; the ear and the eye did not always coordinate even in the mighty. Back in England, offerings came sporadically through the letterbox with a thud and a thump reminding me nostalgically of the bad old days of rejections by the dozen. On one such morning I became almost dizzy with a new kind of heady wine: the wheel had turned full circle, and here was I editing my peers. At first the notion exhilarated me; then it troubled me; next it horrified me; and finally I began to comprehend, though only vaguely, the misery of doubt and indecision which must haunt every editor for life.

One by one, however, came stories which my advisers (bless their broad shoulders and their open minds) not only liked but recommended and—marvel of marvels—which fitted the chosen category. True, for the sake of variety we stretched that category a trifle, but the day dawned with too many wholly suitable stories actually in hand. When I had to send some of those back, I nearly cried, and probably would have but for the exquisite relief of knowing that duty was done and no honor infringed.

There is a school of thought which opines that an editor should explain his reasons for selecting each particular story. I am not of this school. Each story in this book is here because I like it. I hope you'll like them all, too.

JOHN CREASEY

Crimes Across the Sea

The Deveraux Monster

BY JACK RITCHIE

"Have *you* ever seen the monster?" my fiancée, Diana Munson, asked.

"No," I said. But I had. A number of times. I smiled. "However everyone seems to agree that the Deveraux monster rather resembles the Abominable Snowman, but with a coloring more suitable to a temperate climate. Dark brown or black, I believe."

"I wouldn't take this at all lightly, Gerald," Diana said. "After all, my father *did* see your family beast last night."

"Actually it was dusk," Colonel Munson said. "I'd just completed a stroll and was about to turn into the gate when I looked back. The fog was about, yet nevertheless I clearly saw the creature at a distance of approximately sixty feet. It glared at me and I immediately barreled toward the house for my shotgun."

Freddie Hawkins summoned the energy to look attentive. "You got a shot at it?"

Colonel Munson flushed. "No. I slipped and fell. Knocked myself unconscious." He glared at us. "I did not faint. I definitely did not faint."

"Of course not, sir," I said.

Colonel Munson, recently retired, and his daughter Diana had come to our district some eight months ago and purchased a place at the edge of the village.

As a subaltern fresh from Sandhurst and bursting for a good show, he had joined his regiment on November 12, 1918, and subsequently initiated a remarkably consistent career. In the Second World War he sat in England during Money's North African campaigns. When he finally wrangled a transfer to that dark continent, he arrived in Cairo three days after Rommel's command disintegrated. He fretted under the African sun during the invasion of Europe and when at last he breathlessly landed in France, the fighting had moved on to Belgium. He still fumed at a training depot near Cannes when our forces joined the Russians in Germany. In the 1950's he set foot in Korea just as the cease-fire was announced and during the Suez incident he was firmly stationed at Gibraltar. It is rumored that his last regiment's junior officers—in secret assembly—formally nominated him for the Nobel Peace Prize.

Freddie sighed. "All I have at my place is a ghostly cavalier who scoots about shouting for his sword and cursing Cromwell. Rather common, don't you think? Haven't seen him myself yet, but I'm still hoping."

Diana frowned in thought. "Who, besides Father, has seen the Deveraux monster recently?"

"Norm Wakins did a few nights ago," Freddie murmured lazily.

I smiled. "Ah."

Freddie nodded. "I know. Norm hasn't gone to bed sober since he discovered alcohol. However, he has always managed to walk home under his own power. As a matter of fact on Friday evening he was quite capable of running. Norm left the village at his usual time—when his pub closed—and his journey was routine until just north of the Worly Cairn when 'something made me look up.' And there he saw it—crouching and glaring down at him from one of those huge boulders strewn about. His description of the animal is a bit vague—he did not linger in the area long—but from what I was able to piece together, it was somewhat apelike, with dangling arms, a hideous face, and glowing yellow eyes. He claims that it was fanged and that it howled as it pursued him to his very cottage door."

I gazed out at the gathering fog. "I shall have to carry a revolver loaded with silver bullets."

"Only effective against werewolves," Freddie said. He stretched. "During the last ninety years the monster has been seen dozens of times."

Diana turned to me. "Gerald, just how did your family ever *acquire* this monster?"

"There are the usual dark rumors, but I assure you that there is *no* Deveraux monster."

Freddie scratched an ear. "Gerald's grandfather had a brother Leslie. This Leslie was always a bit wild and just before he disappeared . . ."

"He went to India," I said. "And eventually died there."

". . . just before he *disappeared,*" Freddie continued, "Leslie seemed to grow a bit *hairy.*"

I remembered a few paragraphs of the letter my grandfather had left to his son—a letter which had been passed on to me by my father.

I first became aware of what was happening when I accidentally came across Leslie at the Red Boar. It is not my usual pub—when I do choose to go to pubs—but I was in the vicinity after seeing my tailor and thirsty for a pint.

When I entered, I recognized my brother's back at the bar. I also could not help noticing that the other patrons seemed to shy away from him and that the barmaid, in fact, was quite pale.

When Leslie turned at my approach, I stopped in shock. I had seen him less than two hours before and yet now I scarcely knew him!

His eyebrows had grown thick and shaggy, his hairline was almost down to his eyes, and his complexion had turned a dark brown. He leered when he saw me, revealing stained yellow teeth.

"According to legend," Freddie continued, "Gerald's great uncle never did go to Africa, or India, or some beastly place like that. His brother was finally forced to keep him confined. In the east room on the third floor, wasn't it, Gerald?"

"Somewhere about the house," I said. "Though if you have a monster, I should think that the most logical place to keep him might be in one of the cellars."

"Too damp," Freddie said. "And you must remember that your grandfather was rather fond of his brother. Even in his final condition."

Diana's eyes were wide. "You don't mean that . . . ?"

"Oh, yes," Freddie said. "Leslie is supposed to have turned into the monster."

"How ghastly," Diana said dutifully. "But *why?*"

Freddie shrugged. "Heredity, possibly. The monster eventually escaped. Bit through his chains, I believe. The Deverauxs always did have good teeth." He glanced at me. "Either that or he was let out periodically for a constitutional?"

"My grandfather would never intentionally release a monster," I said firmly. "Matter of honor."

Freddie began calculating. "If this monster is human . . . I mean solidly animal . . . then it should be about ninety years old—considering Leslie's age at the time of his metamorphosis. Rather decrepit by now, I should think. Did you happen to notice its condition, Colonel?"

Colonel Munson glowered at the floor. "Seemed spry enough to me."

"I know that people have *seen* the monster in the past," Diana said. "But is it *dangerous?*"

Freddie smiled faintly. "Eighty-five years ago one Sam Garvis was found dead at the foot of some cliff. His body was frightfully mangled and his neck broken."

"Packs of wild dogs roamed this area in those days," I said. "Garvis was unfortunate enough to meet with one of them."

"Possibly. Yet fifteen years later your grandfather was also found dead at the base of a cliff."

"He fell," I said. "Broke his neck."

"Undoubtedly while being pursued by the monster," Freddie put in equably. "It had been seen just before he died. And then there was your father himself, Gerald. Died of fright practically at his front door."

Colonel Munson came out of his private reverie. "I did not *faint.*"

"My father did not die of fright," I said. "Weak heart plus too much exercise." I glanced at my watch. "I'll have to be running along now, Diana."

Freddie rose too. "Mother's expecting me. Besides, Gerald needs an escort across the wild moors. Someone by nature fearless."

The colonel saw us to the door. He was a short, broad-shouldered man with a military mustache in gray prime. "I'm going to hunt the beast," he told us.

"Best of luck," I said.

"I'll need it," he muttered morosely. "Hunted tigers in Malaya, leopard in Kenya, grizzly in Canada. Never got a blasted one."

Freddie and I said our good-byes, adjusted our collars against the chilly mist, and began walking.

"I rather envy you," Freddie said.

"No need to. I'm perfectly willing to give you the monster."

"I mean Diana."

"Quite different."

Freddie brooded mildly. "Of course I can't court her now. You do have some kind of a definite arrangement, don't you?"

"We intend to marry in June."

He sighed. "My only hope is that the monster might conveniently slaughter you before then."

"No assists, please."

"Wouldn't think of it. After all, we've known each other since time immemorial, so to speak. We served in the same regiment. I saved your life."

"Barely."

"I'm fumble fingers with bandages and the like. Besides, I never could remember where the pressure points are supposed to be."

We walked silently for a time and then he smiled wryly. "You don't believe there is a monster, do you, Gerald?"

"Of course not."

We parted at the branch in the path and I continued on toward Stonecroft.

My way took me through lichen-covered boulders and I paused for a moment at the remains of the huts. They were low roofless circles of stones now, but once they had been the dwellings of a forgotten, unwritten race. Perhaps they had been men erect, but I have always entertained the feeling that they might have been shaggy and that they crawled and scuttled by preference.

I wondered again what had happened to them. Were they all really dead and dust or did their blood linger in our veins?

The moor wind died and I glanced up when I heard a faint rustle. A dark figure moved slowly toward me out of the swirling wisps of fog.

After a moment I recognized Verdie Tibbs.

Verdie is simple—quite simple—and he has no profession or avocation but aimlessly wandering the moors.

He seemed a little disappointed when he saw that it was me, but still he smiled.

"Hello, Verdie."

"I thought it was my friend," he said.

"Your friend?"

Verdie nodded. "My friend. But he always runs away."

"Why?"

Verdie frowned. "I don't know. He has fur."

"Fur?"

"Brown fur," Verdie said. He shook his head slowly and wandered back into the dusk.

I reached Stonecroft ten minutes later. No one seems to know just how old my home is. It began its existence as a modest stone cottage in a distant time, but generations of Deverauxs had added to the original—the last substantial addition being in 1720. My contribution has been the installation of plumbing, electricity, and the telephone. At the present time I occupy only the central portion of the three-story structure and very little of that.

When I reached the front steps, I heard the great key in the lock and the bolt being drawn. The massive door opened as I ascended the landing.

I stepped inside. "Well, Jarman, taken to locking the doors?"

He smiled fleetingly. "It's my wife who insists, sir. She feels that it would be wiser at the present time."

"I've never heard that the monster enters buildings."

"There's always a first time, sir."

Jarman, his wife, and their twenty-year-old son Albert are my only servants. I could perhaps do without Albert, but it is family history that the Deverauxs and the Jarmans stepped over the threshold of Stonecroft at approximately the same moment. Turning out a Jarman was unthinkable—equivalent to removing one of the cornerstones or snatching away the foundation of Stonecroft.

The next morning at late breakfast, I noticed that Jarman seemed preoccupied. When he brought the coffee, I spoke to him. "Is there something troubling you, Jarman?"

He nodded slowly. "It's Albert, sir. Yesterday evening he went to the village. He didn't return by ten thirty, but my wife and I thought nothing of it at the time and retired. This morning we found that he hadn't slept in his bed at all."

"Probably spent the night with one of his friends."

"Perhaps, sir. But he should at least have phoned."

Five minutes later, Freddie Hawkins wandered in from the garden and took a seat at the table. "Thought I'd drop over and see if you're tired." He helped himself to bacon. "Sleep well last night?"

"Like a top."

"No sleepwalking?"

"Never in my life."

"You appear a bit hairy, Gerald."

"I need a haircut and I haven't shaved yet. Bachelor's privilege."

"Do you mind if I examine the bottoms of your shoes?"

"Too personal. Besides, if I roamed the moors last night as the monster, I surely wouldn't have worn shoes."

"There is the possibility that you are a monster only from the ankles up, Gerald." He considered the scrambled eggs and took some of those. "I imagine you'll be dropping in at the Munsons this morning?"

"Of course."

"Mind if I toddle along?"

"You're frightfully infatuated with Diana, aren't you?"

"Fatally. We male Hawkinses are invariably lanky, tired, and muddle-headed, but we are always attracted to the brisk, practical woman. The moment I saw Diana and learned that she had once taken a course in accounting, I experienced an immense electrical reaction. Why don't you step out of the picture, Gerald? For an old comrade-in-arms?"

"Not the thing to do."

He nodded glumly. "Of course. Not gentlemanly. It's the woman's prerogative to break up things like this." He buttered toast. "Gerald, last night Diana saw the monster."

"How do you know? Have you been over there this morning?"

"No. But Diana phoned my mother and told her. The two of them seem to get along remarkably well." He put down his coffee cup. "Just after Diana retired, she thought she heard a noise outside. She went to the window and there in the moonlit garden she saw the monster crouching beside a rose bush. By the time she roused the colonel and he found his shotgun, the creature had scampered away."

I lit a cigar and took several thoughtful puffs.

Freddie watched me. "I don't know what to make of it either, Gerald."

After I shaved we walked to the Munson place.

Diana met us at the door. "Gerald," she said firmly, "I'd like to talk to you in private for a few moments, please."

Freddie waved a languid good-bye. "I'll continue on to the village. If anyone needs me desperately, I'll be at the Red Boar."

When we were alone, Diana spoke. "Really, Gerald, I simply cannot accept a monster."

"But Freddie is really very . . ."

"I mean the Deveraux monster."

"Oh, that. Diana, if the animal exists, I believe that it is actually benign."

"Benign, my foot! That thing is dangerous."

"Even if it is, Diana, it seems that only the male Deverauxs actually have anything to fear. You are perfectly safe."

"Gerald, I'm looking at this from the practical point of view. I cannot have you murdered after our marriage, especially if we have children. Do you realize that the death duties these days would force me to sell Stonecroft? I might even have to go to London to find some employment. And I do not believe in working mothers."

"But, Diana . . ."

"I'm sorry, Gerald, but I've been giving this a good deal of thought. Especially since last night. And I've come to a decision: Gerald, I'm afraid that I'll have to terminate our engagement."

"Diana," I said, "is this your decision because there is actually someone else?"

She thought for a moment. "I'll be frank with you, Gerald. I've been examining Freddie. He does seem to be in need of management."

"Freddie has a family specter too," I pointed out. "That cavalier who runs about looking for his horse."

"His sword. But he is entirely harmless. He's tramped about the grounds since sixteen forty-three and has never yet harmed anyone—which is more than I can say for your monster."

"Suppose he finds his sword?"

"We will cross that bridge when we come to it."

I went to the window. "That cursed monster."

"It's your own fault," Diana admonished. "You Deverauxs should have watched your genetics and things like that."

I said my good-bye and went to the Red Boar in the village.

Freddie was rather pale and he finished his pint as I entered. "I just heard a moment ago," he said. "Jarman's son, Albert, was found dead on the moor about a half an hour ago. Head bashed in."

I frowned. "Does anyone know who did it?"

"No, Gerald. But I'm afraid that people are talking about the Deveraux monster." He then smiled weakly. "Gerald, I know I've given you a rather hard time about the monster and I apologize. Let me say that you just need a haircut and that's all there is to it."

I returned immediately to Stonecroft, but the Jarmans had evidently gone on to the village.

I went upstairs to the east room and unlocked the chest. I removed the envelope and reread my grandfather's letter.

. . . I believe that the expression on my face gave Leslie considerable pleasure. I pulled myself together and was about to ask for some explanation, but Leslie took my arm and led me outside. "Later," he said.

We mounted our horses and rode out of the village. After half a mile, Leslie pulled up and dismounted. He removed his hat and then I watched a transformation. He pulled at his forehead and the coarse hair forming his low hairline came away in his fingers. His bushy eyebrows disappeared in the same manner. "And, my dear brother," he said, "my complexion can be washed away and a good tooth brushing will remove the stain from my teeth."

"Leslie," I demanded sternly. "What is the meaning of this?"

He grinned. "I'm creating a monster. The *Deveraux* monster."

Then he put his hand on my shoulder. "Bradley, we Deverauxs have been here since the dawn of history. We were here before the

Norman invasion. Deveraux is not French, it is simply a corruption of some prehistoric grunts applied to one of our ancestors. And yet, Bradley, do you realize that we are not *haunted* by anything or anyone?"

He waved an arm at the horizon. "The Hawkins family has its blasted cavalier. The Trentons have their weeping maid waiting for Johnny to come back from the fair, or some such thing. Even the Burleys, *nouveau riche,* have their bally butler drifting through the house looking for the fish forks. But what do we have? I'll tell you. *Nothing.*"

"But Leslie," I said, "those are *authentic* apparitions."

"Authentic, my Aunt Marcy! They were all *invented* by people with imagination to add to the midnight charm of the homeplace. People are not really repelled by ghosts. They actually *want* them. And so when they do not tell outright lies about seeing them, they eventually *convince* themselves that they have.

"Bradley," Leslie continued, "I am *creating* a Deveraux monster. We must remain in style. And what better way than this? The villagers actually *see* me turning gradually into an ugly apelike creature. And in a week or so more, I, the human Leslie Deveraux, will disappear entirely."

I blinked. "Disappear?"

"Bradley, I am the younger son. I cannot possibly remain at Stonecroft the rest of my life waiting for your demise. You seem remarkably healthy. I suppose I could poison you, but I'm really quite fond of you. Therefore the only course open to me is to go abroad and seek fame, fortune, and all that. But before I go—as a parting present, so to speak—I am endowing you with the Deveraux monster. I will be seen wandering about the countryside—in full costume—and pursuing a passerby here and there in the next few days. I have had a complete ape suit constructed in London, Bradley, and now it is locked in a chest up in the east room. I will wear it during my midnight excursions."

Of course I immediately and vigorously launched into argument condemning his scheme as ridiculous and mad, and, at the time, I thought that I succeeded in convincing him to give up the entire affair. But I should have known Leslie and that half smile when he finally nodded in agreement.

Leslie roamed the moors in his Deveraux monster suit the next week—though I did not learn about that until later. It seems that people were reluctant to bring the creature's existence to my attention.

And then Leslie disappeared.

It was not until a year later that Leslie finally wrote to me from India—but in the meantime I had had no answer to those of our friends who cautiously inquired about his disappearance. In a fit of pique one day, I declared that actually I kept Leslie chained in the east room. It was an unfortunate remark and my words were eagerly taken at face value by a number of people who should have known better.

I might have exposed the Deveraux myth when Leslie's letter finally came, if, in the meantime, this district had not enacted the mantrap laws.

I have never scattered mantraps about my grounds. I feel that their jaws are quite capable of severing, or at least mangling, a poacher's leg. But I *have* nourished the *impression* in the countryside and at the village that I was particularly liberal in strewing them about my property. That had always been quite sufficient to keep most of the poachers off my land.

But then—as I mentioned—the mantraps were outlawed, and if I have a reputation for anything, it is obeying the law and the poachers hereabouts know that. They immediately descended upon me with their snares and traps, causing untold depredations to the quail and partridge I had been protecting.

I tried everything to stop them, of course. I appealed to the authorities, I hired a gamekeeper, and I even personally threatened to thrash any poacher I apprehended on my property.

But nothing availed.

It was in a moment of total desperation that a wild idea descended upon me. I gathered up the house keys and went up to the east room. I opened the chest Leslie had left behind and found the Deveraux monster costume neatly folded inside.

It fit me perfectly.

I believe that I have never since enjoyed myself as much as I did in the next few weeks. At night I would slip into the costume and flitter about. I tell you, my son, that it was with the most delicious pleasure that I pursued—with blood-chilling howls—the elder Garvis to the very door of his cottage.

The elder Garvis did not poach again—to my knowledge—but it

is unfortunate that his experience, or his telling of the experience, did not make an impression upon his son. He persisted in poaching and eventually toppled off one of the cliffs and broke his neck.

It is widely believed that his demise occurred while the monster pursued him. That is not true. I never met Sam Garvis, Jr., on the moors. But I have done nothing to discourage the legend. As a matter of fact, the monster has been "seen" a number of times when I did not leave the house.

And so, my son, when I depart, I leave you the Deveraux monster. Perhaps you too will find some use for him.

Your loving father,
BRADLEY DEVERAUX

My own father had added a note.

Gerald, it is remarkable how persistent the Garvis family is. Each Garvis, apparently, must learn about the monster from first-hand experience before he refrains from poaching and I have found the occasions to provide it.

I pulled the costume from the chest and put it on. At the mirror I gazed at the monster once again.

Yes, he was indeed frightening, and the good Colonel Munson *had* fainted.

Norm Wakins had seen the Deveraux monster, and the simple Verdie Tibbs, and Diana.

But Albert Jarman? No.

After I had let Diana catch a glimpse of me, I had returned directly home. I had met no one on my way and I had gone straight up to bed. And slept soundly. Except for the dream.

I removed the head of my costume and stared at my reflection. Did I need a shave again?

I was at the window at dusk when I saw the Jarmans returning to Stonecroft. I met them at the door.

Mrs. Jarman was a spare woman with dark eyes that stared at me as though she were thinking something she didn't want to believe.

"Mrs. Jarman," I said, "I'd like to extend my most sincere . . ."

She walked by me and disappeared into the back hall.

Jarman frowned worriedly. "Mrs. Jarman is very upset, sir. We both are."

"Of course."

Jarman was about to pass me, but I stopped him. "Do the authorities have any idea at all who might have killed your son?"

"No, sir."

"Is there any . . . any talk in the village?"

"There is talk about the Deveraux monster." He sighed. "Excuse me, sir. I should go to my wife."

Before turning in for the night, I opened the bedroom windows for air. The rolling hills of the moor were almost white with moon and in the distance a dog howled. I felt the drift of the cool wind and shuddered.

A movement in the shadows below caught my eye and I watched the spot until I could make out a crouching figure. It moved again and then stepped into a patch of light.

It was Verdie Tibbs. He glanced back at the house without seeing me and then disappeared into the darkness.

That night I dreamed again. I dreamed that I left the house and crossed the moor until I found the circle of stones. I remained there for a long time, silent and waiting. For anyone.

Albert Jarman's funeral took place on Thursday and I, of course, attended. It was a dark gloomy day and at the graveside the mist turned to light rain. Most of the countryside seemed to be in attendance and I was conscious of a great many eyes covertly examining me.

Freddie Hawkins appeared at Stonecroft the next morning while Jarman and I were going over the household accounts.

He sat down. "Another death. Frank Garvis was found dead in his garden this morning. Strangled. Several tufts of hair . . . or fur . . . were clutched in his fingers. Definitely not from a human, according to the inspector."

Jarman looked up for a moment, but said nothing.

I rubbed my neck irritably. "Freddie, just what do *you* make of all this?"

"I'm completely puzzled. Perhaps some ape has escaped from a circus or something of the sort."

"The papers would surely have carried a notice."

He shrugged. "Could there actually *be* a Deveraux monster? What do you think, Jarman?"

"I have no opinion, sir."

Freddie grinned faintly. "Perhaps Gerald rises in the middle of the night, gripped by some mysterious force, and goes loping about the hills searching for a victim." He seemed to consider that and then shook his head. "But I guess that's out. I hardly think that he would grow fur just for the occasion. Or does he slip into a monkey suit of some kind?"

Freddie regarded me for a few moments and then changed the subject. "My mother told me about your break with Diana. Dreadful sorry, Gerald."

"Thanks. I think that she rather fancies you."

He flushed suddenly. "Really?"

"No doubt about it. She's impressed by your intelligence and drive."

"No need to get nasty, Gerald."

After he was gone, I went upstairs to the east room and unlocked the chest. I pulled out the Deveraux monster and examined him. Tufts of hair had been torn from both of the arms.

That evening I was in my study with a half-empty bottle of whiskey when Jarman entered.

"Will that be all for today, sir?" he asked.

"Yes."

He glanced at the bottle and then turned to go.

"Jarman."

"Yes, sir."

"How is Mrs. Jarman?"

"She is . . . adjusting, sir."

I wanted to refill my glass, but I decided not to while Jarman was watching. "Do the authorities still have no suspects for your son's murder?"

"None, sir."

"Do *you* have any . . . ideas?"

His eyes flickered. "No, sir."

I decided to pour the glass anyway. "Does your *wife* have any ideas? Does she think that the Deveraux . . ." I drank some whiskey and my next words were undoubtedly inspired by the alcohol. "Jarman, I want you to lock me in my bedroom tonight."

He raised an eyebrow. "Sir?"

"Lock me in my bedroom," I snapped.

Worry seemed to creep into his eyes.

I came to a sudden decision. "Jarman," I said firmly, "follow me. I have something to show you."

I took him to the east room, unlocked the chest, and put my grandfather's letter in his hands. "Read this."

I waited impatiently until he finished. "You see, Jarman, there is no actual Deveraux monster."

"No, sir."

"Jarman, I wouldn't tell you what I am going to now if it weren't for the present circumstances. I must have your word of honor that you will not repeat my words to a soul. To no one at all, do you understand?"

"You have my word, of course, sir."

I paced the room. "First of all, you do know that the poachers have been plaguing us again?"

"Yes, sir."

"Well, Jarman, I have been wearing the Deveraux monster. I am the one responsible for chasing Norm Wakins to his door. I wanted him to spread the story that the monster was roaming again. Another night I met poor simple Verdie. Accidentally, I assure you. He is not a poacher. He actually tried to make friends with me and I was forced to flee."

Jarman smiled faintly. "Is Colonel Munson a poacher?"

I flushed. "That was a spur of the moment thing. A lark."

He raised an eyebrow ever so slightly. "A lark, sir?"

I regarded his half smile and decided that I might as well come out with the entire truth. "Jarman, you are aware that the colonel and Diana Munson came here only eight months ago? And that within two months I found myself engaged?"

"Yes, sir. Rather sudden."

I agreed. "I don't quite know how it happened, though I'm sure Diana is clear on that point. I was committed and I am a gentleman . . . a man of my word . . . but still . . ."

Jarman helped me. "You found yourself not quite as happy as you thought you should be?"

My flush deepened. "I happened to see Colonel Munson while I was in the monster suit and suddenly it occurred to me that if the colonel, and perhaps Diana herself, should see the monster, they might not be so eager to . . . join the family."

"I understand, sir. And I am sure that Miss Munson will be quite satisfied with Mr. Hawkins."

"Jarman, I have frightened a number of people, but I have injured no one. I am . . . positive . . . that I did not kill your son." I stared down at the Deveraux monster in the chest and at the bare spots on the arms. I began to perspire.

Jarman's voice was quiet. "Do you still want to be locked up for the night, sir?"

I rubbed my forehead. I wasn't sure now.

There was silence in the room and when I looked up I saw that Jarman was studying me.

And then he spoke. "Sir," he said. "I *know* that you didn't kill Albert."

"You *know?*"

"Yes, sir. Last night Verdle Tibbs came to the back door and spoke to me. He had been a witness to Albert's murder." Tired lines appeared in Jarman's face. "Albert was returning from the village when apparently he came across a set of poacher's snares or nets. According to Verdie, Albert was bending over them and he seemed to be tearing them apart, when suddenly a figure leaped behind him and struck him with a rock."

"Who was it?"

Jarman closed his eyes for a moment. "Frank Garvis, sir."

"But why didn't Verdie go to the authorities?"

"Verdie was afraid, sir. He's heard talk that he might be sent to an institution and he wants nothing to do with any public officials. But even if he had gone to the police, what good would that have done, sir? It would have been the word of simple Verdie against that of Frank Garvis."

"But then who killed Garvis last night?" I looked down at the Deveraux monster again and wondered if I had been only dreaming when . . .

"Sir," Jarman said, "the Jarmans and the Deverauxs have been together ever since the beginning. There are no secrets a Deveraux can keep from a Jarman—not for long, at least." He smiled faintly. "My grandfather also left *his* son a letter, and that son passed it on to me."

He brought a key out of his vest pocket. "This unlocks the chest too, sir, and the Deveraux monster fits me—as it did my grandfather and my father whenever they chose to wear it."

He gazed at the key and then put it back in his pocket. "I would have preferred to remain silent on the whole matter, but I saw that you were beginning to fear that you were responsible for the death of my son and possibly Garvis too, and so I had to speak." He sighed heavily. "Now that you know, I will put my affairs in order and go to the police with a full confession."

"Jarman, what have you told your wife?"

"Only that Garvis killed Albert. Nothing more yet, sir."

I paced the floor for a bit and then faced Jarman. "I really fail to see that any . . . any *good* . . . can come from your going to the police and giving yourself up."

"Sir?"

"The Deveraux monster murdered Garvis," I said. "I think it is much, much better if we just leave it that way."

Jarman's voice was rather choked with emotion. "Thank you, sir."

I pulled the Deveraux monster from the chest. "However, I believe that we ought to destroy this, don't you, Jarman? After all, someone might just manage to compare it with the tufts of hair Garvis had clutched in his fingers and we'd all get into trouble."

Jarman draped the monster over his arm. "Yes, sir. I'll burn it right away." At the door he looked back. "Is the Deveraux monster dead, sir?"

A sudden gust of wind whispered around the shutters.

"Yes," I said firmly. "The Deveraux monster is dead."

When he was gone, I happened to glance at the mirror.

I rather needed a shave again. I seemed to be getting a bit hairy lately.

A Question of Honor

BY ELLERY QUEEN

It wasn't every day that Ellery found himself meeting a policeman who was a minor authority on Shakespeare, and he shook the hand of Inspector Queen's British visitor with interest. It was a hard hand attached to a squared-off torso, satisfying the professional requirements; but above the neck Inspector Burke of New Scotland Yard took an unexpected turn—broad forehead, pale skin, and the bright, sad eyes of a scholar.

"Over here on a case, Inspector Burke?"

"Yes, and then again no," said the Scotland Yard man dourly. " 'All hoods make not monks,' as Katherine points out in *Henry the Eighth.* I'm here hunting a bad one, right enough; but the thing is, he's waiting for me—and, what's more, when I catch the blighter I'm going to have to let him go."

"Why?" asked Ellery, astonished.

"Seems like a long trip, Burke," grinned Inspector Queen, "for mere exercise."

" 'Necessity's sharp pinch,' gentlemen." The Englishman's sad eyes turned sharp. "It's rather a yarn. A certain young woman in London —daughter of someone very highly placed—is shortly to announce her betrothal to a man very much in the international eye. The principals are so distinguished that—well, the match couldn't have been made without the consent of Whitehall, which is all I'm free to say about it at this time.

"A year or so ago this girl, who is charming but headstrong and overromantic," continued the British policeman, "wrote seven highly indiscreet letters to a man with whom she was then infatuated.

"Now the position of the girl's fiancé is such that, should those letters get to him or become public knowledge, he would be forced to break the engagement, and the resulting scandal would almost certainly create a nasty diplomatic situation in an extremely sensitive political area. 'Great floods from simple sources,' you know!

"When the girl's . . . family learned about the letters, they took immediate steps to retrieve them. But there was the rub. The man to whom they'd been written no longer had them. They had just been stolen from him."

"Hm," said Ellery's father.

"No, no, Queen, he's above suspicion. Besides, we know the identity of the thief. Or rather," said Inspector Burke gloomily, "we're positive he's one of three men."

"Parties of our acquaintance?" asked Ellery.

"Undoubtedly, Mr. Queen, if you've browsed through your Rogues' Gallery recently. They're all Americans. One is the international jewel thief and society impersonator, William Ackley, Jr., alias Lord Rogers, alias le Comte de Crécy; another is the confidence man, J. Phillip Benson, alias John Hammerschmidt, alias Phil the Penman; the third is Walter Chase, the transatlantic cardsharp."

The Queens exchanged glances; Ackley, Benson, and Chase were three of Centre Street's incurable headaches.

"When the matter was turned over to the Yard, very hush-hush, I was placed in charge, and I bungled it." Inspector Burke's sensitive face flushed. "Word leaked out that something big was in the wind, and all sorts of mugs with guilty consciences ran for cover before we could tighten our lines. Among them were Benson, Chase, and Ackley —all three got away to the States. One of them—exactly which one we haven't been able to determine—subsequently made contact, with demands and instructions, and I'm here to pay him off."

Inspector Queen clucked. "When and where, Burke?"

"Tonight, in my hotel room. I'm to hand him twenty thousand pounds in American dollars—in exchange, of course, for the letters. So tonight I'll know which of the three he is—and much good will it do me." The Englishman rose, tightening his lips. "And that's my tale of woe, Queen. I must ask you not to go near any of the trio—really my chief reason for stopping by. We can't risk another slip. Those letters must be repossessed and returned to England to be destroyed."

"Can we give you any help?"

"No, no. Unless I botch it again—in which case," said Inspector Burke with a twisted smile, "you might offer me a job sweeping out your office. I shan't feel very happy about going back. . . . Well! Gentlemen, wish me luck."

"Luck," said the Queens in sober unison.

They recalled the bitter twist in Burke's smile the next time they saw him, which was in his hotel room the following morning. A chambermaid had found him. He had been seated slackly in the armchair beside the neatly made bed, a bullet hole in his powder-burned right temple. He had been dead since the night before. No shot had been heard; it was an ultramodern hotel, with soundproof walls. The gun lying on the carpet below his right hand had already been checked in the police laboratory against the slug dug out of his head by the medical examiner.

The room was the picture of peace. A Gladstone bag was spread on the luggage rack, undisturbed. The night table held Burke's pipe and tobacco pouch and a dog-eared copy of Shakespeare's plays with Burke's signature on the flyleaf. A dispatch case initialed *L. B.* lay, open and empty, on the bed.

"Poor Burke," muttered Inspector Queen. He handed Ellery a sheet of hotel stationery. "Found on the writing table. It has a couple of his fingerprints on it, and it's his handwriting—we've checked."

The script was even and unhurried, as if the brain directing the hand that had written it had reached a decision:

Mine honor is my life; both grow in one;
Take honor from me, and my life is done.

—LESTER BURKE

"Epitaph by Shakespeare," murmured Ellery. "What went wrong, Dad?"

"Apparently his man came last night with the letters, as agreed, but while Burke checked them over—probably turning away slightly—the rat sapped him; Doc says there's a slight contusion toward the back of Burke's head. Then the doublecrosser took the money *and* the letters, and skipped. Guess he figures those highborn pash notes are good for at least one more transatlantic squeeze when the heat dies down, and meanwhile he's got some fifty-odd grand to tide him over. And when poor old Burke came to and realized what he'd let happen—and all it meant—he couldn't face the disgrace and committed suicide."

"There's no doubt it is suicide?"

"You name it. Bullet fired in contact with Burke's temple, angle of entry checks for righthanded man, slug from Burke's own gun found in the body, Burke's prints on the stock. Suicide note in Burke's authenticated handwriting. Letters not here. Money taken. It's suicide, all right—the only question is which one of those three cuties crossed Burke up and drove him to it . . . Ackley, Chase, or Benson."

Benson, a gray-haired, dapper little man with a Florida tan, was located in a barbershop on Park Row having his nails manicured. The confidence man looked like a Wall Street broker or a corporation executive. He seemed annoyed.

"Don't know what you're talking about, Inspector," Benson snapped. "I can account for every second of my time all day yesterday until well after midnight. I was up in Westchester looking over some property with two associates of mine, we had dinner and spent the evening discussing the deal at the home of one of them in White Plains, and the other one drove me back to my apartment in town—dropped me off a few minutes past one A.M. Their names? Certainly!"

Benson's associates turned out to be two confidence men with slightly lesser reputations. However, they corroborated Benson's story, which was all Inspector Queen was interested in at the moment.

Chase was located in a midtown hotel at the tail end of an all-night poker game—a big, soft-spoken rancher type of man, whose drawl and slow movements ingeniously drew attention from the smooth lightning of his long white hands. No pigeon was being plucked: Chase's companions were professional gamblers.

"Relaxation," smiled the cardsharp. "Man gets tired playin' with rank amateurs. Last night, Inspector? Why, I've been right here since we started our game four o'clock yesterday afternoon. Haven't left this room. Have I, boys?"

Four heads shook emphatically.

That seemed to make it Ackley, whom they found at breakfast in a triplex Park Avenue apartment with its owner, a bejeweled society widow who was outraged at the interruption. Ackley was a tall, lean, handsome man with dark curly hair and piercing black eyes.

"Ackley?" echoed the lady furiously. "This gentleman is Lord Rogers, the big-game hunter, and his lordship has been entertaining me since the cocktail hour yesterday afternoon with his fascinating adventures in Kenya and Tanganyika—"

"Continuously, madam?" asked Inspector Queen politely.

"I ah—put him up for the night," said the lady, coloring. "We—he retired at two A.M. Will you please get out!"

"After you, your lordship," said the inspector; and the jewel thief shrugged and went along.

Ellery followed in troubled silence.

He was not to break that silence for a long time. For the three alibis remained unshaken, and Ackley, Chase, and Benson had to be released for lack of evidence.

"One of those alibis is rigged!" yelped the inspector. "But which one?"

The letters and the money failed to turn up.

Inspector Queen raged and fumed, but the case had to be written off. Ellery fumed, too, but for other reasons. Something about the circumstances of Burke's death was wrong, he felt in his bones, but what it was he simply could not diagnose. And Inspector Burke's body and effects were shipped back to England, and the cables from London suddenly stopped, and that seemed the end of it.

But it was not, and it broke out again in the oddest way. One night, weeks later, Inspector Queen came home bemoaning the deterioration of the new generation of police officers. They had all reverted to childhood, the inspector snorted at dinner, spending their spare time at headquarters playing games.

"Games?" said Ellery.

"Crime puzzles. They make 'em up and challenge one another to solve 'em. They've even got the chief inspector doing it! Though come to think of it," the inspector chuckled, "one he tossed at me today is pretty darn clever. Typical detective-story situation: Rich man with three no-good heirs who need money bad. He's bumped off, one of the three did it, and each claims an alibi for the time of the murder. One says he was in the Museum of Art looking at some eighteenth-century American paintings. The second says he was dialing his bookie's private phone number, Aqueduct four-two-three-two-oh, putting down a horse bet. The third says he was in a Flatbush bar talking to a French sailor named Socrates Papadapolis who was on his way to Indochina. Question: Which alibi was the sure-enough phony? Get it, son?"

"Sure," grinned Ellery; but then the grin faded, and his fork bonged against his plate. "The Burke case." He choked.

His father stared. "The Burke case? What about the Burke case?"

"I knew we were played for suckers, Dad, but till you threw me that puzzle just now, I didn't see how!"

"How?" repeated the inspector, bewildered.

"Burke didn't commit suicide—*he was murdered.* Take your crime puzzle," said Ellery swiftly. "The Museum of Art alibi and the Flatbush bar alibi might or might not have been false, and only an investigation would tell, but the phone-call-to-the-bookie alibi needs no investigation—it's false on the face of it. No one can dial an exchange like Aqueduct, which starts with the letters *AQ,* because every phone dial in the United States has one letter of the alphabet missing. *It has no letter Q.*

"And that told me what we'd missed in the Burke setup.

"Dad," cried Ellery, *"that note in Lester Burke's handwriting was a forgery.* If it was a forgery, Burke didn't write it. If Burke didn't write it, he didn't commit suicide—he was murdered. The devil sapped Burke, all right, and placed the unconscious man carefully in the armchair, shot him with his own gun, put Burke's prints on the gun and note, left the forged suicide note on the desk—the kind of note Burke might genuinely have written, a Shakespearean quotation—slipped out with the money and letters, and rejoined his alibi-ing confederates.

"But the fact that the note was a forgery identifies the killer. Ackley is a jewel thief and society impersonator. Chase is a cardsharp. Benson is a confidence man—but he's something else, too. One of his aliases is Phil the Penman—*a tag only a professional forger could have earned!"*

"Yes, but wait, wait," protested Inspector Queen. "But how do you *know* that suicide note was a fake?"

"Benson pulled a boner. Do you remember how he spelled the word 'honor'—spelled it twice—in the quotation?"

"Honor?" The inspector frowned. "H-o-n-o-r. What's wrong with that, Ellery?"

"Burke was an Englishman, Dad. Had he written that quotation, he'd have spelled 'honor' the way all Englishmen spell it . . . *h-o-n-o-u-r. It had no letter U!*"

Sea of Troubles

BY HENRY SLESAR

To attract attention on Rue de Montparnasse, to swivel the heads of lovers, aperitif-nursers, and bickering artists, requires something unique in performance or appearance. Owen Layton accomplished the feat with a rumpled English tweed suit, a gray-flecked beard in the style of U. S. Grant, and a pair of crutches that kept his monstrously bandaged foot off the Parisian sidewalks. But there was something else that distinguished him, a cheerfulness, a jaunty face and manner that belied the crutches and bandages and their implication of pain and suffering. He was 'le brave Americain' that morning, and he seemed to be enjoying the role.

He maneuvered the crutches skillfully as he swung into a seat at one of Patrick's outdoor tables, and the waiter moved swiftly to his side. With a laughing apology for his bad French, Owen asked for a Pernod and inquired after *"mon frère,* Monsieur Gerald," but the waiter only shrugged. "Never mind." Owen smiled. "He should be here any minute."

Robin Gerald Layton took longer than that, and brought with him the reason for his tardiness. It was a black-haired, sloe-eyed young woman with a swishing pony tail and a pouting mouth. The pout became more pronounced when Robin saw his brother, for he slapped her playfully and sent her on her way. Then he joined Owen at the table.

"Owen!" he said gleefully, pumping his arm with both hands. "How are you? When did you get here? Were you waiting long?"

Owen laughed, and pried loose the thick, paint-stained fingers from his sleeve. "Easy." He chuckled. "You want to put my arm in bandages, too?"

Robin spotted the shrouded foot for the first time and clucked in quick sympathy, but Owen shrugged off explanations. "Let me look at you," he said. "It's over a year since I saw you last; you look more Frenchy than ever." He grasped Robin's shoulders and studied the young, bearded face, a face not unlike his own, especially around the clear, smiling eyes. Robin Gerald (he had dropped the Layton) was six years his brother's junior, and five years of pleasant expatriation had kept him even younger looking.

"You look different yourself." Robin beamed. "That beard! A real beaver! And you used to kid *me* about my shrubbery!"

"Yes, it's pretty grim. I'm thinking of trimming it, as a matter of fact, more in your style. Here," Owen said, pushing his glass across the table. "Finish this Pernod for me. I shouldn't be drinking it, with my foot."

"Your foot?"

"Gout," Owen said ruefully. "You remember, I wrote you about it a few months ago. I had an attack just before sailing, and I probably would have gotten over it if I hadn't succumbed to those damn French chefs. From now on, I stick to the British line."

"A rich man's disease." Robin chuckled. "You shouldn't mind that, Owen."

"Yes," Owen said thoughtfully. "And neither should you, old boy. Remember where your money comes from."

Robin looked embarrassed. His sole income was contained in the American Express checks that bore Owen's name. Owen had sent him to Paris to "paint," and occasionally, when not preoccupied with wine and women, Robin did. As for Owen, he always had a legitimate excuse for his Paris trips. He came to do business with the wine-exporting company his wife owned.

"And how is Harriet?" Robin said. "Still the same?"

"Yes, still the same amazing Harriet. Some women would have been content to let their inheritance lie snugly in the arms of some trust officer. But not Harriet. No, indeed."

"But she must have changed some," Robin said. "That beard! If she let you grow that, she's not the same Harriet I remember!"

Owen smiled pensively and lifted his glass.

"No," he said. "She's not the same. And that's exactly why I grew this beard, and why I came abroad."

"But why? I don't understand."

"You will," Owen said. "Because you're going to help me."

"Help you do what?"

"Help me kill Harriet," Owen said. Then he took the Pernod from his brother and finished it with a lip-smack and a sigh, and inhaled deeply of the invigorating air of Paris.

Robin had moved into the Hotel Raspail since Owen's last visit, and his enormous studio room overlooked the eight-sided corner where Boulevard du Montparnasse met Boulevard Raspail. Robin must have found it an inspiring view as the parade of Parisian lovelies continued all day long. As for Robin's work, the results were evident. The studio was filled with canvases, almost all of them unspoiled by paint.

When Owen preceded Robin into the room, he did something that made his brother gasp. He dropped his crutches on the floor and walked unassisted to the daybed.

"Your foot," Robin said. "What about the gout?"

Owen laughed, and stretched out on the bed.

"The gout," he said, "is the cornerstone of my plan, old boy. Oh, it was genuine enough at first. I suffered the agonies of hell with those early attacks, but it's simply a matter of controlling my diet. However, I have already established a medical history of the disease, if questions arise later."

Robin sank into a sling chair, his face bewildered.

"I've never seen you like this, Owen. You're not making any sense at all. Those crutches, the beard, all this crazy talk about killing people—"

"It's not crazy at all. It's a beautifully rational scheme, and one you will be eager to see succeed. That is, if you enjoy the life you lead."

"Enjoy it? Of course I do!"

"It would be a pity to lose it all, wouldn't it? All this devotion to—art? And all the pretty women of Paris?"

"Has something happened between you and Harriet?"

Owen lit a cigarette.

"Nothing sudden," he said. "No head-on collision, at any rate. It's been a gradual affair, perhaps the inevitable result of the advancing years. You know I was considerably younger than Harriet when we married, and I believe the age difference excited her. But after ten years, the difference is suddenly not so great. Harriet is discovering that there are younger men in the world."

Robin swore, and went to the window.

"Are you cutting me off? Is that what you came to tell me?"

"Nothing of the kind," Owen said. "As long as my income can support it, you can continue to develop your 'talent.' The question is, how long will my income continue?"

"And that's why you want to kill her."

"But killing her very carefully, old boy, with due regard to the dangers involved. I might never have considered it at all if I hadn't arrived at this plan. So you see, even an attack of gout can have its beneficial side. I lay prostrated with pain for a month, while Harriet indulged herself with nondomestic pleasures—her current hobby is dancing lessons. You haven't seen anything until you've seen that woman doing a gross exercise they call the Twist. But in that month's time, I was given time to think. And I thought about something quite marvelous."

"What?"

"A unique phenomenon of the modern age." Owen smiled. "The magnificent paradox of transatlantic travel."

"Travel?"

"Of course. Now you know me, Robin, I'm a great champion of sea travel. For me, an ocean voyage is a tranquilizer, a remedy for every ill. But a ship makes its journey in five days; a jetliner takes only a few hours."

"But you hate planes. You've never been on a plane in your life."

"Planes terrify me. I've never tried to conceal the fact. Yet for sheer speed, old boy, you must admit they have the edge."

"I still don't understand! What does it all have to do with killing Harriet?"

"Everything," Owen Layton said. "For you and I, dear brother, are going to put that transatlantic paradox to use. We're going to prove that the difference between a ship and a plane is a lovely way to commit murder."

The *S.S. Empire,* flagship of the British Line, wasn't the largest vessel anchored at Le Havre, but on Saturday morning it was the busiest. In the bustling excitement that preceded its departure for New York, the progress of the two bearded men on A Deck seemed painfully slow. One of them, grunting with every swing of his crutches, held the other's arm as they threaded their way through the chattering, scurrying, celebrating crowd of passengers, visitors, and crewmen.

Finally, they made their way into Stateroom G, and Owen stripped off his green plaid topcoat and Homburg, and collapsed on the bunk with unsimulated fatigue. It took the sight of Robin's blanched face to make him smile again.

"Relax." He chuckled. "Everything will be fine. Let's take care of the passports first, and then we can call the steward."

Robin locked the stateroom door before taking the passport from his coat pocket. Owen produced his own, and set about the delicate task of removing the small photographs from both books. He squeezed glue from a tiny tube and replaced them, one bearded face substituted for the other one.

"All right," he said. "Now let's ring for the steward."

The man who answered the call delighted Owen at once. He was an aged cockney with a thin crest of white hair, the mouth of a pixie, and the squinty eyes of a myopic.

"Yes, sir, everything all right, Mr. Layton?"

"Everything's fine," Owen said. "You're Mr. Pawkins?"

"Yes, sir, that's me, sir," the steward said.

"Come here, Mr. Pawkins," Owen said, hoisting himself to sitting position with the aid of one crutch. "I'm afraid I'm going to be something of a burden to you on this voyage, and I'd better make things clear right now."

"Oh *no,* sir," Pawkins said, shaking his head vigorously. "You couldn't burden *me,* sir, not the likes of me. Service is me middle name, sir, you can count on that."

"You see?" Owen grinned at his brother. "That's why I like the British Line: dreadful food but lovely people. Mr. Pawkins—"

"Yes, sir?"

"As you can see, I'm something of an invalid."

The steward clucked. "Oh, my, sir. Your poor foot, eh?"

"Yes, my poor foot. As a result, I'm going to be forced to take all my meals in here, so you'll have to arrange matters with the dining steward. I trust that can be done?"

"Oh yes, sir, don't you worry none about that."

"Nor will I be spending any time on deck. Don't tell me about your magnificent stabilizers, I know all about them. The least bit of roll is extremely painful to me, so I'll be in the stateroom until we reach port."

"Tut!" Pawkins said. "What a pity, sir."

"It's all right." Owen smiled. "I've got a great deal of business to take care of between here and New York. I'll have enough paper-work to keep me busy. So if you'll just bring me my meals and keep me from being disturbed, you'll be doing your job handsomely. All right?"

Pawkins snapped two fingers against his cap.

"Right you are, sir!"

Owen grinned, and waved a parting salute as the steward went nimbly out of the stateroom.

"Whew!" Robin said. "We were lucky. He's a cooperative old geezer."

"Don't be so sure," Owen said warningly. "He's a mite too friendly. If he tries to make conversation, ignore him. Make him knock before he enters, so you'll have time to get to the bunk and bury yourself in papers."

"Right."

"You might even pretend to be asleep sometimes, face to the wall, that sort of thing. Never let him get a solid look at you, Robin, that's essential."

"I know, I know," Robin said testily. "You've told me that a thousand times."

"I can't repeat it often enough. You've got to be a *prisoner* in this stateroom, understand?"

"It won't be any fun."

"No," Owen said. "Nor would it be any fun to fill gas tanks in Hoboken. Not as much fun as living on the Left Bank, with those pony-tailed women of yours—"

"I said I would do it, Owen! Stop nagging me!"

Owen smiled. "I'm doing all the hard work. Including that plane trip tonight." He shuddered. "For me, that's the worst part of all. How high do those bloody things fly?"

"Thirty thousand feet, I think."

"Preposterous." He reached down and began to undo the bandage on his right foot. "All right," he said. "Let's get started. They'll be putting visitors ashore in ten minutes."

Ten minutes later, his crutches left behind him, his bandages now neatly wrapped around Robin's right foot, with Robin's gray tweed topcoat belted around him, and Robin's flop-brimmed hat on his head, Owen Layton left Stateroom G. He strolled casually across A deck to the stairs and the visitor's gangplank, and left the *S.S. Empire* to its business.

He brought only one suitcase to the air terminal at Orly Field. The immigration man looked at his passport with only a cursory glance at the photograph, and handed it back with a brisk, "Thank you, Mr. Gerald." The customs officer was gracious, and the ticket agent couldn't have been more courteous. But when Owen saw the Air France jetliner standing on the tarmac, saw the immensity of its wingspread and the relatively small size of its jet engines, his knees weakened and his face turned the color of the gray flecks of his beard.

A loudspeaker in the terminal informed the passengers of Flight Five that their liner was ready to be boarded. Owen knew it was the worst moment he had to face; not even his image of Harriet's murder was as terrible as this. But he forced himself into a leaden walk in the direction of the ramp.

His memory of the flight was imperfect. He recalled five minutes of sheer terror during the steep takeoff, eight hours of alternative fright, numbness, and drowsiness, and an agonizing half hour following the captain's announcement of their approach into Idlewild.

Then he was down, and safe, and ready for the most important part of his plan.

It was midnight in New York when he claimed his baggage and climbed into a taxi. He gave his destination as Grand Central Station.

In the railroad terminal, he deposited his luggage in a public locker, and took still another taxi to the street where he and Harriet had spent the last four years of their marriage. The brownstone was an unimposing building from the exterior, but Harriet's money had scooped out the interior of it and transformed the structure into a duplex of cunningly modern design.

It was after two A.M. before Owen used the key that admitted him, when the streets were empty and the shades of the opposite buildings were drawn against the night.

He went quietly up the stairs to the bedroom, and found it empty.

Harriet wasn't home.

Owen registered no surprise. It was Saturday night. Presumably, he was in Paris, and Harriet had already demonstrated her willingness to enjoy evenings on the town without his company. But while it was no surprise, there was chagrin. Harriet was making the moment easier for him; she was proving the justice of his actions with her behavior.

He stretched out on the bed, and waited in darkness.

An hour later, the front door opened, and he tiptoed to the bedroom doorway to watch for Harriet's entrance.

She wasn't alone. There was a shadow following her, tall, lean, and with exaggerated broad shoulders. He couldn't hear their voices until they were inside, and couldn't define Harriet's company until she flicked on the hallway light.

"Oh, my feet!" Harriet was laughing. "Douglas, you're a brute, you know that?"

Douglas was a mustachioed brute, with long sideburns. Owen, frowning into the shadows, guessed that he was one of Harriet's dancing instructors, on extracurricular duty.

The man encircled Harriet's waist with both arms.

"Don't," she said carelessly, primping in front of a mirror. The man dug his chin into her neck and she giggled. "Did I tell you that I heard from my husband?" she said.

He pulled her into an embrace.

"He cabled yesterday," she said. "He's coming back on the *Empire* on the twelfth."

"Maybe she'll sink," the man said, and Harriet laughed.

"That's just what I'm doing, sinking. I'm awfully tired, Douglas; be a good boy and go home."

"I'd rather be a bad boy and stay here."

She moved away from him, and went to the door.

"Call me tomorrow," she said.

When he was gone, Harriet came up the stairs. Owen flattened himself against the bedroom wall and allowed her to enter the room. Then, with a melodramatic flair that pleased him, he flicked on the lights.

"Owen!" she screamed.

He killed her with a modern Gres vase purchased, appropriately enough, in Paris.

Now there was a distasteful part, distasteful for a man of fastidious bent. He would require five days of anonymity, and he had previously decided that it would best be found in that region of the city where the lower depths were at their lowest.

It was painful to discard his British suit in a trash can, but he did. And then, wearing only a pair of rumpled slacks and a heavy wool sports shirt, his hair and beard dirtied and disheveled, he made his way to the Bowery. His first act was to join a shambling, silent line of vagrants outside a Clothing Relief agency, and he emerged with a costume that was superior to any he might have invented—a moth-eaten sweater of mottled blue color, a double-breasted jacket with a shredded lining and a thousand unironable creases and a felt hat with a stained brim. He left the relief center, bought a bottle of sauterne for ninety-eight cents, and rented a bed in a hotel called Lamb's for fifty cents a night.

He hated it, but there was one satisfaction. There would be no surprise recognition here, no danger of running into old friends or acquaintances. Or, he thought with amusement of some of the people he had known, was there?

At noon on Monday, in a steam-filled diner where the coffee tasted like antiseptic, he picked up a damp, mudstained newspaper from the dirty tiled floor. There was an item on the second page that gave him an appetite, even for the diner's foul-tasting bill of fare.

WOMAN FOUND MURDERED
IN EAST SIDE
BROWNSTONE
Dancing teacher held as suspect

It was an aspect of the situation that hadn't occurred to him, either in the planning or the execution. But he found it very much to his liking.

The *S.S. Empire* docked the morning of the twelfth. An hour before it anchored, Owen made a short visit to Grand Central Station. He removed his luggage from the locker, and in the terminal washroom he shaved and changed into clean clothes. Then he rented an automobile in his brother's name, and drove it down to Pier 16.

The passengers began to trickle out of the customs shed. He knew Robin would be among the last to appear.

Finally, he did, wearing Owen's green-plaid topcoat with the collar pulled around his throat, with Owen's Homburg hanging low over his eyes. He handled Owen's crutches awkwardly, but he was a convincing cripple nevertheless.

Owen went to help him, full of solicitude. But he made his greeting from between clenched teeth.

"The steward?" he said tightly. "Did you see him before you left the ship?"

"No," Robin grunted. "I managed to avoid him. And I didn't tip him either, just like you said."

"Good!"

Owen helped him into the waiting auto. "Make it fast!" he snapped. "Get the bandages off, and let me have that coat and hat."

They made the switch as before. When Owen stepped out of the car, he was dressed in the Homburg and green plaid topcoat, and the bandages were back where they had originated. The crutches seemed like old friends as he hobbled back to the entrance of the pier.

There was a ship's petty officer emerging from the passenger's exit. Owen grinned as he came toward him, simultaneously greeting him.

"Pardon me!" he said jovially. "Can you tell me when the rest of the crew members will be coming off?"

"Crew members? Well, some won't be getting off at all, of course. Whom did you want?"

Owen smiled. "It's rather embarrassing. There's a steward I meant to see before I left my stateroom. He was very kind to me."

"What's his name?"

"Pawkins. An old fellow, extremely nice."

The officer chuckled. "Ah yes, I know him. Well, tell you what, seeing that it's Pawkins. You come back with me to the purser's office, I'll see if we can get Pawkins up there. And you can remember him properly."

"Thank you," Owen said. "Thank you very much."

Pawkins was more than pleased. He looked at the two fifty dollar bills with moist eyes, and shook Owen's hands vigorously.

"I'm most grateful," he said. "Most grateful, sir. And I hope you'll be back with us soon again."

"I will be," Owen said. "You can be sure of that."

He gave Robin the car that had been rented in his name, and instructed him to take an apartment in the Village and lie low. Then he took a taxi to his home. He expected to find company there on his arrival, and he wasn't disappointed.

"Mr. Layton?" the police detective said. "I'm afraid we have some bad news for you. . . ."

The shock of Harriet Layton's death kept Owen confined to his home for a week. Understandably, he discouraged visits from his friends, and accepted their written and telephoned condolences with a gravity befitting the situation. When the press interviewed him concerning the murder, and asked cruel questions about the handsome dance instructor who was facing indictment by the grand jury, he was restrained in his replies. He had no reason to suspect his wife of infidelity; he didn't know the man called Douglas Farr; he was sure there was no scandal, and if Farr had been responsible for his wife's death, he was equally certain that the man had acted impulsively. His performance earned him good notices. The newspapers portrayed him as the bereaved husband. returning in innocence from a business trip abroad to find his home and his happiness destroyed. If there was another implication, in their mention of the large fortune that would be his upon probation of Harriet's will, it was unimportant in the light of the simple, uncomplicated facts of the matter:

When Harriet Layton died, her husband was in mid-Atlantic. And a dance instructor, whose moral scruples were both a public and police record, had been the last man to see her alive. A lover's quarrel? So the tabloids speculated. But Owen offered no theories. With admirable dignity, he awaited the outcome of both the criminal and probate courts, in full confidence that human and fiscal justice would reign.

On a Friday evening, two weeks after his return from abroad, Owen sat alone in the downstairs living room, patiently depleting the best of Harriet's brandy stock.

The house was quiet, quiet in a way that was enjoyable and gratifying. When the stillness was shattered by the ringing of the telephone, Owen was annoyed. But he picked up the receiver, and heard the voice of a strange woman.

"Owen? It's Sheila."

"I beg your pardon?"

"It's *Sheila*. God, I feel terrible not calling you before this, but I just found out what happened, honestly. I read it in the papers, the whole awful thing. You must be in a *state*."

"Are you sure you're calling the correct number? This is Owen Layton speaking." Who was Sheila?

"Well, of course it is!" The voice was exasperated. Then it adopted an oddly hostile tone. "Listen, what are you trying to do? Is there somebody there with you?"

"No."

"Then why the big act? Listen, I told you not to try any of that shipboard romance stuff on me. I won't stand for it."

"Shipboard romance?"

"Listen, Owen, I want to see you right away. We have to talk about things."

Owen covered the mouthpiece with his hand, and stared incredulously at the instrument. Then he had a sudden and terrible notion.

"Did you say Sheila? From—the *Empire?"*

"Of course from the *Empire!* Listen, don't tell me that you're *that* mixed up! I know it must have been a shock and all that, but from the way you talked about your wife, she didn't mean a fig to you. So cut it out!"

Owen swore a mighty oath, silently. It included the name of Robin.

"I don't have much time," Sheila said. "I want to see you tonight."

"No," he said quickly. "No, that's impossible. I can't see you."

"Listen, if you think you can try a brush-off—"

"I didn't say that! I said I can't see you tonight. I—I'm having visitors, important people, business."

"Tomorrow then. Early."

"It's impossible!"

"Look, Owen, you don't get rid of me that easily. Not after that week on the ship. Do you understand me?"

"I tell you it can't be done! I'm going away, leaving town. I don't know when I'm coming back—"

"Now *listen!"*

He dropped the receiver as if it were burning his hand. It fell back into the cradle and rocked to a halt.

Owen swore again, aloud.

Then he dialed Robin's number.

"You idiot!" he screamed into the mouthpiece. "You damned fool idiot!"

"Owen?"

"Yes, Owen!" he roared. "Do you know who I just heard from? Sheila! Does the name mean anything to you?"

There was no reply, except for a vague sound that might have been Robin swallowing hard.

"Well? Who is Sheila?"

"Owen, listen to me—"

"You were supposed to be a *prisoner* in that stateroom, weren't you? You were never supposed to leave! How many other women did you take up with? I suppose you went to the lounge and played bridge with the passengers? Or maybe you sat at the captain's table?"

"I swear it wasn't like that! I did everything you said, Owen, I swear I did. The steward never even saw my face, not even once—"

"And what about Sheila? What did she see?"

"She was the only one, Owen, honestly. I was going crazy alone in that damn room. I just went for a little stroll on deck, at night—"

"Just a little stroll! And that's how you picked up Sheila, was it, just strolling?"

"Owen, I swear to you—"

"You did plenty of swearing, all right. From the way that woman talked, you must have sworn to anything. She's demanding to see me. She's read about Harriet's death, and now she wants some of the gravy. Do you know what that means?"

"Gosh, Owen, I never thought—"

"Do you know what it means? If she comes up here, I'm cooked! Roasted! Fried! One look at me and she'll know I wasn't on that ship! You think it'll take her long to put two and two together?"

Robin made a bleating sound of misery.

"Couldn't you put her off? If you put her off long enough—"

"And just how do I do that? After you've been so charming?"

"Couldn't you go away for a while?"

Owen juggled the receiver like a club. Then he said:

"Maybe you're right. Maybe it's the only answer for now. If I went back to Paris, to finish up my 'business' . . ."

"I'm sorry, Owen."

"You're sorry!" he snarled, and slammed the receiver down again.

There was one more call he had to make, to the ticket office of the British Lines.

There had been no staterooms available on the *S.S. Empire.* For the first time in his shipboard travels, Owen was forced to accept accommodations on B Deck. But it was an indignity he was ready to accept in order to make the sailing on Saturday.

This time, the steward who showed him to his cabin was a gruff, uncommunicative gentleman who made no promises of devoted service. Owen himself had few requests to make. The week before he had discarded both bandages and crutches, declaring his gout healed.

His cabin was small, with poor ventilation and crowded furnishings, and the weather forecasts for the crossing were generally unpleasant. There were ominous storm signals in the ship's barometer. It wasn't going to be a tranquilizing voyage, that was for sure. But it was escape.

The ship sailed at four that afternoon. At five, there was a knock on Owen's door.

"Come in!" he said.

The door opened, and the woman in the neat blue and white suit paused in the doorway and looked at him with parted lips. Her hair was severely styled, and her blandly attractive face was denied prettiness by too forceful a mouth and chin.

"I'm sorry," she said. "I thought this was Mr. Layton's cabin."

"Yes, I'm Mr. Layton. What can I do for you?"

Her eyebrows met. "You're not Owen Layton."

"Yes, that's right."

She laughed uncertainly. "But you couldn't be. I mean—Mr. Layton's a much younger man. I'm sure there's some mistake—"

"Would you mind telling me what you want?"

She stepped into the room, with cautious movements.

"I saw your name on the passenger list. But the Owen Layton I mean—well, he's about your height, and he has a beard like yours, but—well, he's in the wine business. Are you in the wine business?"

The room's ventilation seemed worse than ever, and Owen, sitting at the cramped dressing table, found breathing difficult. He looked at the woman with wide, horrified eyes.

"Who are you?" he said hoarsely.

"My name is Sheila Ross," the woman said, her lips tightening. "I'm the ship's social director."

"The social director?" Owen said. "You work on the ship?"

"That's right. And what I want to know is—who the hell are *you?*"

Then she turned, and clicked her heels hard as she went back to the door.

"Never mind," she said grimly. "I'm going to find out who you are. You see if I don't!"

The door slammed after her. Above decks, the *Empire*'s whistle hooted into the skies, warning the seas ahead that it was on its way, troubled waters or not.

The Unlocked Room

BY JOHN F. SUTER

The Carbon case is one which is seldom discussed in Uniontown, Pennsylvania. It was a case with overtones of antique lore harking back to the ancient Egyptians and beyond. A man died where he should not have died, and because of that, the affair was to become known to the principals as The Case of the Unlocked Room. Colonel Perrivale, who has been involved in more than one peculiar murder, has nothing to say about this one, although he was present from the time the body was found until the sticky moment when the murderer was unmasked.

It was the sort of case that would shake the calm of even a policeman. . . .

Patrolman George Witmer had just come off duty. Still wearing his uniform, he was on his way home, with one stop to make on the way. Jon Dickens Carbon, the internationally famous detective-story writer, had promised to buy a ticket to the Policeman's Ball, and Witmer had been asked to deliver it.

Witmer eyed the sky uneasily, hoping to complete the ticket transaction and get home without wasting time. The gathering dusk was deepened by an evil, spreading blackness in the western sky. An unhealthy stillness in the air and an occasional fitful flicker on the horizon threatened the approach, in early June, of the summer's first thunderstorm. The effect was as though someone were lifting, briefly, the cover of an entrance to the Pit.

Witmer brought his car to a smooth stop directly across the street from the old brick three-story that was the Carbon house. It was one of a row of stone-stepped mansions with large back yards, and its ancient, lack-luster red bricks badly needed repointing. Even the incongruous television antenna leaned at a gallowslike angle.

As Witmer climbed from his car and started across the street, he glanced upward. He could not be sure, but he thought he saw, momentarily, a figure looking at him from an upstairs window. The thing looked *wet*. . . .

He crossed an undulating brick sidewalk and started up the three worn stone steps to the front door. Two crouching stone lions cast baleful eyes at him, and he was startled to observe that an irregular, damp trail crossed the top step, as though a giant slug had crawled over it.

He was about to ring when the door opened and a girl started out. She stopped short when she saw him.

"This response is almost unbelievable," she gasped. "Uncle Harry must have just hung up. No matter. He's upstairs. I'd better show you."

Witmer was stunned. He started to say, "It's not your Uncle Harry—" but no words came. If any had, they would have been concentrated in a single, explosive "Wow!"

Cynthia Diamond, at twenty-three, was aware of the reaction which a combination of deep-copper hair, sea-green eyes, flawless creamy complexion, and a whistle-at figure customarily produced in men.

She was the Goddess-Made-Mortal, the Living Dream, the Show Stopper. At any other time, she would have basked in the radiance of Witmer's reaction, but just now her attention was on other things.

Dazed, Witmer followed her into a shadowy hallway, barely noticing an elegantly furnished living room on his right and a glowing dining room at the rear of the hall. He trailed his guide's long, shapely, silk-clad legs up a high staircase at the left of the hall.

"Uncle Harry has already called Doctor Hauer," Cynthia was saying, "so you won't have to do that. I'm afraid that it's no good, just the same. It looks so *final.*"

Witmer shook himself, realizing that none of this made sense. Jon Dickens Carbon was reputed to be an eccentric, and bedroom interviews were not unheard-of, but to buy a ticket—? The policeman paused at the head of the staircase, where the landing gave into a hall obviously leading to a group of bedrooms and baths.

"Stop a bit," he said. "It's Mr. Carbon I want to see."

Cynthia's green eyes clouded. "You mean that Uncle Harry didn't make that clear? Or perhaps your captain or lieutenant or whatever-he-is didn't pass it on? Uncle Jon *is* the one. Up here is where he is."

A firm voice with Muscles in it cut in. "I suspect that the young man is somewhat confused, since I had not yet called the police when you brought him in, Cyn."

They turned. Witmer saw a man reminiscent of Charles Atlas in tweeds regarding him from a spot beside a telephone on a wall bracket. This new person had wavy, light-brown hair and a beautiful tan.

"Uncle Harry!" said Cynthia. She looked doubtfully at Witmer. "Then you really don't know—?"

"I dropped by to see Mr. Jon Dickens Carbon," Witmer said cautiously. "It sounds as though you have something else on your mind."

"Haven't we, though!" Cynthia's voice was ragged. "We can let you see Uncle Jon, but looking is all you'll be able to do."

"Steady." The muscular man crossed quickly to the girl's side and gripped her shoulders. "After all, Cyn, Doctor Hauer hasn't had a look at him yet."

"But it's so *horrible.*" She shuddered. "He's in there like—that—and we daren't try to help him."

Witmer cleared his throat. "If this is police business, maybe one of you could show me what it is."

Cynthia reached with long fingers and grasped his sleeve, nearly causing him to forget that he was expected to behave like a policeman. She led him along the hall toward the rear of the house until they came to the last door. A strong odor of floor varnish came from the room.

"In there," she said, indicating the open door. "But mind the floor." She gave a half-hysterical laugh.

At first glance, Witmer saw only an empty bedroom, its oaken floor gleaming with wet varnish. It was only when he looked to his right that he saw it: the body of a middle-sized man lying in a crumpled heap in the corner.

Witmer had seen Carbon's photograph a few times—a slim-faced man with eyes full of sly humor—but he would never have recognized him in this rag doll with the contorted countenance. Even from eight feet away, Witmer could see the marks on Carbon's neck that signaled strangulation. It was not a pretty sight.

Then the short hairs on Witmer's neck lifted. He had noticed the varnish bucket standing beside the body on the uncoated segment of floor where Carbon lay. He had observed that a wide brush, sticky with varnish, was clutched in Carbon's outflung right hand. Sardonically, it had struck him that the man had painted himself into a corner . . . *a corner completely surrounded by still-wet varnish unmarred by a single footprint.*

Witmer turned quickly on his heel and faced the girl and the man. "Is this some kind of hoax?"

Cynthia was biting her lip to keep back hysteria. "I—I swear that's the way I found him ten minutes ago when I went to ask him a question."

"But this is—"

"Impossible?"

The elephantine wheeze sounded loudly in the hall as the bedroom door at the far end—from the room overlooking the street—opened and a huge figure lumbered into view. It was an awesome sight: a gleaming bald head, a handlebar mustache, an array of chins, and a ballooning figure. A walking stick was clutched firmly in each hand, and a third was crooked over the left arm.

"Impossible, would you say?" said this personage with a ferocious scowl. "Burn me, young feller, I'd not blame you. But, lookee here—have you considered that window, hey?"

Witmer swung around and stared at the room again. Opposite the door was a window overlooking the garden in the back yard. The sash was up, to allow the room to air, and Witmer could plainly see that the roof of the back porch gave easy access to the room.

"Why, yes— No. Stop a bit. You're trying to confuse me, sir. There are no footprints leading to that window, and it's too far to jump from the corner to the window sill."

The large man was now opposite the telephone, which protruded from the wall on a sort of lazy-tongs arrangement. He brushed the phone back with one of his sticks and advanced.

"Confuse you? Hmff, ha. I realize that what you say is true, yet— You must think about this, young feller. That's why I just finished a shower. I had to think, and I think best in the bath. Yet, if I were to say to Harry, here, *go soak your head,* he'd get his dander up."

"I think," said Witmer firmly, "that I had better call in and report this."

He stepped forward and found the tip of a cane resting against his chest.

"Now, lookee here, son," said the huge man. "Let's you and me work this out together, hey? Don't you think that it would be more to your credit than letting some cocksure detective lieutenant hog it all? Besides," he said, beaming and twinkling, "I'll include you in my mee-moirs."

"You haven't told me who you are, sir. Or who these other people are, either, if you'll forgive me."

The large man drew himself up. "Son, the dolly, here, the luscious wench, is Cynthia Diamond, Carbon's niece by his sister, Jane. Gargantua there is Harry Cole, his half brother. As for me, I'm G.P., the Old Man—Colonel Goliath Perrivale, an old friend of Jonny's from across the Atlantic."

Witmer acknowledged the introductions and introduced himself. Staring at G.P., he said, "Colonel Perrivale? Of the British Army?"

Colonel Perrivale's chins waggled as he chuckled. "Army? Oh, my hat! It's a *Kentucky* colonel. Honorary, of course, in memory of the time I bested Louisville's William Tecumseh Lee in a julep-swiggin' contest— Harrump! That has nothing to do with this, unfortunately."

"Your occupation, Colonel?"

"Retired. But occasionally I help the police to orient their brains, as it were. It hasn't been too long since I was involved in that Grimm's fairy tale business. Maybe you heard of it."

Seeing that Witmer was about to question the others, Colonel Perrivale rumbled on. "The little gel is quite a scientist, son. Works for the Appalachian Atomics Laboratory. Hairbreadth Harry, here, runs a glorified gymnasium which he calls a Reducing School. To give him credit, he does get results. Reduces their pocketbooks, too."

Impassive, Witmer noted this information. "Anybody else around when this happened?"

Cynthia spoke up, "But we don't know when it happened, do we?"

G.P. assumed a wise look.

Harry Cole cleared his throat. "That hardly matters. There have been only the three of us—and Jon, of course—since late afternoon. Wait a bit. There was Annie."

"Annie?"

"Our cleaning woman," said Cynthia. "But Annie was surely gone. She worked in a fearful rush. She even left her window-wiping squeegee lying in the hall earlier, instead of putting it away. And when I let Officer Witmer in, I saw that she had only mopped the front steps with a lick and a promise. She's not strong enough—"

Uncle Harry set his square jaw. "She ought to be riding her broom, instead of pushing it. She's strong enough to manhandle all this furniture by herself. She's not as frail as she looks."

Meticulously, Witmer asked for, and got, Annie's full name and address. "Now," he started to say. A violent peal of the doorbell cut him off.

Cynthia ran to answer it and returned with a small, neatly dressed man with a black spade beard and a doctor's bag. She introduced him as Dr. Hauer. The doctor wasted no time in small talk, but insisted on being taken to the room where Carbon lay.

As soon as he observed the situation from the bedroom door, he turned to them, his dark eyes glittering. "This," he snapped, "is intolerable. Someone get a board—old newspapers—anything."

"Go ahead," suggested Uncle Harry. "Don't mind the floor."

"It's not the floor that I care about," said the doctor peevishly. "It's my shoes."

Cynthia hurriedly vanished and returned with an armful of old newspapers. Partially unfolding them, the doctor laid them down ahead of him, making a path to the body.

Colonel Perrivale huffed up to the bedroom door. He now selected his third cane, performed some manipulations, and ended up flourishing a shooting seat. With unswerving aplomb he drove the point into the hall floor; then to Witmer's amazement he settled his bulk on the seat of the stick with ease, although Witmer could not have told you how this was accomplished.

G.P. pointed to the glistening floor with the ferrule of his right-hand cane. "The ancient Egyptians knew all about varnish," he wheezed, "but the lore goes all the way back to the Cro-Magnons in their murky caves. And men have been painting themselves into corners ever since. Varnish! I don't like this."

Dr. Hauer was examining the body with some incredulity. He looked around at Colonel Perrivale with anger and bafflement.

"Who is trying to pull my leg?"

Colonel Perrivale's shabby brows rose. "Pull your leg? Solons of Sparta! He was strangled, wasn't he?"

"Of course he was," snapped the doctor. "And he's dead, if anyone had any doubts. What I want to know is the reason for this jiggery-pokery." He stared at Colonel Perrivale, then his face cleared. "I should have known. You're that expert on 'locked room' cases. You attract them, as a lightning conductor attracts electricity. Well, let's see if someone *else* can't—"

He stopped and began to peer at every inch of space from floor to ceiling in the corner. G.P. watched him keenly.

"You want to see if someone else can't solve this?" the colonel asked genially. "Go ahead. I assume that you're looking for a hook that one might string a rope on. Mister X kills Jonny, slings his body on a rope, and slides it across to that corner without touching the floor. He dumps the body, twitches the rope, and presto, an impossible crime! But it won't work."

"I see there is no hook," admitted Dr. Hauer.

"No. But you missed the critical point, Doctor. O Bacchus! Where is the trail in the varnish that the loose rope would have to leave as it was pulled out of the room?"

"That's all very interesting," remarked the doctor impatiently, "but it's not what I had in mind."

"No?"

"No! Why couldn't the killer simply have put the body into the corner and varnished the floor all around it, using another brush and another can of varnish?"

Colonel Perrivale blinked and cleared his throat. He was about to speak when Harry Cole cut in.

"Because there wasn't time for that." As they all turned to him, he went on. "Have you any idea how long that would take? That floor is covered completely. It should require at least an hour. And I talked to Jon while he worked, only about twenty minutes before Cyn found him. He was varnishing then."

"You seem determined to misunderstand me," said Dr. Hauer testily. "I didn't suppose that the whole room was unvarnished when the body was put there. What if Carbon had it all done except a narrow strip from corner to door, a strip for Carbon to come out on? *A strip which the killer could coat in just a few minutes?*"

Colonel Perrivale stared at the doctor with respect. "You know, that's a very shrewd observation. Burn me, it is. But I'm sure that it won't do, either. How long do you think it would take to coat that narrow strip, Doctor?"

The doctor contemplated the body and the floor. "Five to ten minutes."

"Even working at top speed?"

Dr. Hauer began to look uncertain. "Well—hang it, yes. The brush would have to be refilled several times."

Witmer spoke up. "With everyone's permission, we could make a test." As their attention turned to him, he went on, "If it's all right with Miss Diamond and Mr. Cole, I can varnish a strip of hall equal to the probable area Dr. Hauer means. I'll work as fast as I can." He glanced at Colonel Perrivale. "Then I want an explanation."

G.P. merely watched him with ferocious benevolence, withholding comment as Cynthia and Uncle Harry distractedly agreed to the experiment. As Uncle Harry rolled up the hall runner, Witmer carefully removed his coat and asked Dr. Hauer to hand him the bucket and brush.

"Now, if someone will time me . . ." he said, dipping the brush and working it against the side of the can to make sure that it had not stiffened.

As the doctor noted the time, Witmer filled his brush and began to varnish the floor, swiftly, but covering every inch. At the end of several minutes he stood up and looked at Dr. Hauer inquiringly.

"A little over seven minutes," said the doctor.

"And that's what tears it, son," said the colonel. "Because I went to the door of that room and spoke to Jonny no more than five minutes before our Miss Diamond screamed. I wanted to ask him where to find a fresh bar of soap. I did not," he said, fixing a scowl on his face, "notice how much of the floor was covered, I'm sorry to say."

"You're right, I'm afraid," said Uncle Harry. "I heard your voices."

"But who would want to kill Uncle Jon, anyway?" asked Cynthia brokenly.

Colonel Perrivale regarded her closely. "You sure you want that question answered, dolly? True, Jonny was a solid citizen, even if he did get mixed up about electromagnets and guns and the difference between benzene and benzine. He never really offended anyone. But he had money, and both you and Hercules, there, could use some, couldn't you?"

"Take care," growled Uncle Harry.

"It would be useless to deny it," said Colonel Perrivale, unperturbed. "I happen to know that when Jonny's father—your stepfather, Harry, and your grandfather, gel—died, he left the bulk of the money to Jonny, with small portions to each of you. Further, Jonny was asked to administer your inheritances, and I'm sure that he hasn't handed it out fast enough to suit you. Finally, I suspect that all the money comes to you two on Jonny's death."

"I don't *need* the money," gasped Cynthia, deathly pale. "I have a job that pays me well."

"You said, yourself, that my business is successful," gritted Harry Cole.

Colonel Perrivale struck the floor with a cane. "Yes, I said that. But, Lord love a duck! How much of what you take in are you putting into the bank, eh?"

The three of them seemed frozen there, glaring at each other, then Cynthia stepped to Witmer's side and laid a hand on his arm.

"You don't believe these accusations, do you?"

Colonel Perrivale's thick eyebrows rose. "Accusations? I was only reciting facts and suggesting motives."

"What about your own motive?" asked Witmer quietly.

As a thunderous scowl gathered on Colonel Perrivale's face, Dr.

Hauer laughed. "Bull's-eye! You *are* a suspect, you know, G.P."

Colonel Perrivale's face relaxed into shrewdness.

"So I am. Fairly put, son. Well—assuming that I *had* done Jonny in—which I'm not admitting—it would have been because he outright used my ideas, without ever paying me a cent for them. Oh, he let me appear in his stories, and I always got the credit for solving the case—which I'd outlined to him in the first place. Paper credit. 'Take the cash and let the credit go' is not a bad motto, I say."

"Now," he said, struggling to his feet, "let me show you how our friend, Harry, could have done this little job."

"Blast you," raged Harry. "I've had enough of your lies!"

He lunged forward, aiming a fast right at Colonel Perrivale's head. The colonel raised one of his canes with deceptive speed and whacked the oncoming fist across the knuckles. At the same time he reversed his other cane and drove its head into the pit of Harry's stomach. Cole collapsed, gasping and wringing his right hand.

"As I was saying," said G.P., "I'll demonstrate how it *could* have been done. First, Jonny Carbon has a reputation for painting himself into a corner. Let's suppose that, this time, he forgets to coat that corner and paints himself out of the door. He meets Harry in the hall. They have words, and Harry does him in. What next? Looking into the room, Harry sees the dry corner and remembers Jonny's habit. He's a strong man, and Jonny's only average weight, so what does Harry do? He picks Jonny up and chucks him across the wet floor, right where we found him."

He looked at Witmer, his eyes twinkling. "Well?"

Witmer stepped to the door of the bedroom and pointed. "What about the varnish can?"

G.P. gave a fat chuckle. "Good. Oh, very good. No, Harry could have pitched the body over there, but he couldn't have heaved the bucket without spilling some of the varnish."

He drew himself up. "D'you want to hear how it was really done, son?"

"Just a minute," said Witmer.

He turned and made a quick, but thorough, run-through of the bath and the remaining bedrooms. He came back looking satisfied. In his hand was a large paper bag, which bulged oddly.

"Forgive the interruption. Go ahead, Colonel."

"We must realize," rumbled G.P., "that Jonny was killed where we found him."

Witmer nodded. "I agree."

Colonel Perrivale paused and looked at him quizzically. "Hmff. Well. He was killed in that corner, and he was strangled. By some freak with long arms? No. By someone who weighs so little that he won't mar sticky varnish? Not even the ancient Egyptians could do that. Are there any lassos or bull-whips around the house, for long-distance strangling? No. You didn't find any just now, did you?"

"No."

Colonel Perrivale struck the floor with a cane. "No long-range implements? Stop a bit. *There is one*. Son, go back there and take that telephone off the bracket."

Witmer obeyed.

"Now, lift that folding contraption off the wall and bring it here."

Witmer brought the expandable bracket and handed it to Colonel Perrivale. The colonel grasped one end like a pair of tongs.

"Unusually long beggar," he commented, then pressed. The bracket expanded into a series of connected diamonds and shot far down the hall. Witmer now noticed that the far end seemed to have a pair of half-circular clamps, which were closing.

"Know what this is?" Colonel Perrivale asked. "A lazy-tongs. You can make it do almost anything your hands can do." He manipulated it, picking up a small vase from a table and replacing it. "You could even strangle from a distance, if you knew how to use it."

He stopped and lowered his huge head. His mustache quivered. "And one of us does know how to use it. Why? Because they have these things all over the place in an atomics laboratory. They call 'em servo-mechanisms. Isn't that so, *Miss Cynthia?"*

Cynthia stepped backward, her knees buckling. Witmer grasped her by the arm. She tried to speak, but could not.

"She supposed that nobody would think of it when it held the telephone," said Colonel Perrivale softly. "I used to use one of these things when I was a mere nipper, to knock off plug hats, and I recognized it in short order. Of course—" he shrugged—"she killed him just before she screamed for the rest of us."

Witmer beckoned to Dr. Hauer. "Look after her, would you, Doctor?"

"So," said G.P., beaming, "you can wrap it up as your own case, son. I make you a present of it."

"Thank you, sir," said Witmer, "but I can't do it."

"Eh?" said Colonel Perrivale. "But you must. I'm—"

"The Old Man? Yes. And do you know what I do in my spare time? I'm an odd-jobs painter."

He gestured toward the unlocked room. "This murderer didn't need any lazy-tongs, or servo-mechanism, or whatever you call it. *The varnish was unmarked because a strip of the floor was still unvarnished from the corner to the door when Carbon was strangled.* The murderer simply coated the floor behind him as he went out."

Colonel Perrivale glowered. "But the time it would take—you, yourself, proved that there wasn't time to do that."

"That's right," Witmer agreed, "if a *brush* were used. However, look at this." He opened the bag and took out a rubber-bladed, T-shaped object with a short, hollow, metal handle. "This is Annie's squeegee which she uses on windows, I imagine."

Before G.P. could protest, Witmer reached over and twitched one of the canes from his surprised fingers. Quickly he rammed the point of the stick into the hollow handle of the squeegee.

"All our murderer needed to do," the policeman said, "was to pour a puddle of varnish on the floor and wipe it back along the uncoated strip with this rubber blade. He didn't even have to stoop. I could do it in a minute or two, at most. Then there'd be plenty of time."

He held up the squeegee. "This is clean—all except the place where the blade and handle meet. There's a trace of varnish there. And there's other proof, I'd lay odds."

He looked steadily at Colonel Perrivale. "Your bath was a waste of time. Soap, alone, won't remove varnish. And I found the squeegee in your closet."

He reached out and grasped Colonel Perrivale's hand, turning it over. "Here on your hand is the final evidence. You've already told us your motive. Colonel, unless he wears gloves, the painter doesn't live who can handle paint without getting his hands smeared."

Murder Delayed

BY JOSEPHINE BELL

One late October evening, with a heavy mist of rain falling in the crowded streets and flowing on the water-logged pavements, a man limped into the casualty department of a hospital in Wigan. His dirty check jacket and threadbare jeans were soaking wet. His long uncombed hair was plastered to his forehead. His face was ashen gray and twisted with pain.

A nurse, seeing that face and his general condition, took charge of him at once. He was indeed on the point of collapse and submitted dumbly to her guidance as she helped him at once to a couch in the examining room and hurried out again to find Sister.

The written formalities were hurried through, the surgical officer on duty was sidetracked to the case. He found a large abscess at the upper part of the right thigh in front. It was a large purplish-red swelling, the skin stretched tight and glistening over it. When he attempted to feel its extent and depth the wretched victim gave a hoarse scream, while beads of cold sweat stood out on his gray cheeks.

"All right, old chap," the young casualty surgeon said gently. "You must have had a pretty ghastly time walking about with this thing. How long have you been cooking it?"

"Three weeks," the man muttered, in a marked London accent.

The doctor and nurse exchanged surprised glances. They were accustomed to Lancastrian voices; cockney was seldom heard in Wigan. Had the silly chump walked all the way up here, and if so, why?

"It's an abscess," the doctor said, looking again at the patient. "Any sores on your feet or legs?"

He began a close inspection, finding nothing to suggest a source of infection that could have produced this thing, except a small red healed spot low down on the right buttock.

"What was this?" he asked, slightly puzzled by its appearance.

"Boil," said the man.

The doctor hesitated, not quite satisfied. As he had his patient half rolled over and did not want to move him more than he need, he began to prod up the spine. At the level of the third lumbar vertebra the man winced and gave a faint groan. The doctor turned him gently on his back again and stood up.

"I'll have to admit you," he said. "This abscess has got to be dealt with, but more important still we've got to get at the cause of it. It could be disease in the spine."

The man looked frankly incredulous.

"Abscess in me leg from me spine!" he exclaimed weakly. "You're kidding!"

But he was in no condition for argument and besides, the casualty officer had turned away and was making the necessary arrangements to admit him.

Before long he was lying in an isolation cubicle at the end of a surgical ward, drowsily staring at the ceiling, freed at last from the gnawing pain that had swelled and grown to a throbbing hell in the last three days before it drove him finally to this place. He wasn't quite clear what they'd done to him. Drawn the muck out by hypodermic, they'd said. Must have been a hell of a big needle, but he hadn't felt a thing after the first little prick. X-ray his spine tomorrow. Well, it was up to them. They knew their job. He hoped.

He drowsed off and presently, as the drug he had been given took effect, his sleep grew deeper and he did not wake up until the middle of the next morning, when a clanking and shuffling brought him back to daylight, with white-clothed figures moving round him and apparatus being pushed about his bed.

He was still too sleepy to take in what was happening. In fact, all that day he rested, semiconscious, taking food and pills as they were offered, asking no questions, content to lie there, feeling no pain as long as he did not move his right leg about.

On the following day he felt himself again. Whatever they had done to him they'd made a job of it. There was still a whacking great bandage on his thigh and he was not allowed to sit up on his own, but he felt rested and restored. Next thing was find a job of some sort for the time being. Till the heat went off.

A man whose face he did not recall seeing before came into the cubicle and congratulated him on his improved condition.

"I'm O.K.," he answered. "Hundred percent."

"Well, not quite," answered the other, "but Mr. Saunders, who is the surgeon in charge of you, will be along at the end of the morning to tell you how he proposes treating you."

When the young man had gone the patient lay back for a while, considering. Then, very cautiously and not without an occasional twinge of pain, he unhooked the notes from the bottom of his bed and studied them carefully. The name he had given was Ray Brown —he must remember that. No fixed address—just London. There was a description of the abscess, but the medical terms meant nothing to him and in any case his powers of reading were limited. There was a temperature chart and this too meant very little, except that a line on it, connecting a lot of little dots, had been high up to begin with and was now waving about over a red line drawn lower down across the paper.

He hooked the notes in place again and waited for the visit of this character—what was it— Saw something. Young fellow had a la-di-da voice— Difficult to make him out.

Mr. Saunders arrived late in the morning. In quick succession he delivered a series of shocks that momentarily stunned his hopeful patient.

"This abscess of yours comes from an injury to one of the bones of your spine," he said, after a few curt preliminaries. "Not a disease, such as TB, which we were afraid of at first. The cause of the injury is a bullet, which is still wedged in the bone. When were you shot and who did it?"

Ray Brown stared up at him, speechless.

"You were in some sort of scrap, I suppose," went on the relentless Mr. Saunders. "Why didn't you or your pals get medical aid at once? Scared?"

Ray found his tongue at that.

"I didn't ask for no abuse from you, mister," he said thickly. "Think I'm a ruddy kid? Believe fairy tales? Bullet, my arse!"

"Very probably," said Mr. Saunders briskly. He was not attracted by the sullen unshaved face on the pillow. "The point of entry is that small scar on your backside you say was caused by a boil. It is a bullet wound, not a boil. An abscess forming at a diseased or injured point in the lumbar spine tracts down the lines of the muscles and can come to the surface at the front of the thigh. We used to have that sort of thing from TB spines in the days before modern treatment of TB. Your x-ray picture shows a bullet quite distinctly. How did it get there?"

"If you want to know, in the war," said Ray sulkily. He had been thinking hard while Mr. Saunders spoke his piece. This would fix him.

"How old are you?" the surgeon asked at once.

If Ray had known the answer to this question he would have blurted it out and been confounded. But he did not. No one had ever told him, neither his foster parents, who disliked him, nor his schoolteachers, who went no further than to rub in that he was backward for his age. So he said the first number he thought of, without considering war dates or anything else.

"Forty-five," he growled.

Mr. Saunders did not believe him, but he did not say so. What he said was, "We shall have to operate to remove the bullet. The infection comes from it and it would be very dangerous to leave it where it is."

"Anything you say, guv," answered Ray. He had his own answer to that one. His jacket and jeans, dried and pressed, his shirt, washed and ironed, had been put in the locker at his bedside, since he had no relatives to take them home. That evening he got up, not without considerable and unexpected pain, dressed and left the hospital. He signed a paper to say that he took his own discharge. He refused to be persuaded by the nurses, the ward Sister, the house surgeon or the registrar, to change his mind. Mr. Saunders, on the telephone, said, "More fool he. Scared of his gangster friends, I suppose. Pity we haven't got the bullet. Can't very well go to the police without."

A month later a man known to his landlady as Bert Smith was admitted to St. Edmund's Hospital in South London. The woman had called the police when she found him delirious in his bed one morning. They had called the ambulance.

The man was found to have an open abscess in his right thigh and general blood poisoning. He was grossly emaciated, partly from persistent fever, partly, the doctors suspected, from simple starvation. He had only been in his lodgings two days. He had no money and no clothes except the ones in which he had arrived there, an old checked jacket and worn jeans.

A rapid examination produced two results. The pus from the wound did not suggest tuberculosis, though the site and chronic state of it did so. Also on probing a hard object was felt, which on being extracted proved to be a bullet from a .38 revolver.

Drainage of the wound, transfusion, and antibiotics were all applied but without success. Bert Smith died twelve hours after admission.

News of the bullet sent a mild wave of excitement through the hospital and most of the consultant staff, as well as the resident doctors and the students gathered at the postmortem. Among them was David Wintringham, who arrived just as the pathologist, after tracing the abscess back to the spine, was demonstrating the effect of the bullet upon the bone.

David stared at the injured vertebra. A sloping area of bone had crumbled away. The infection had evidently persisted for a number of weeks. As the pathologist traced the point of entry and subsequent course of the bullet, David remembered a newspaper paragraph. At the end of the afternoon he drove to Scotland Yard to find Chief Superintendent Mitchell.

"Did I read, Steve, about two months ago, about a gang fight in the East End which ended in the leader of one lot being knifed and killed in the hall of a dubious club, while a lad belonging to the other faction, who had done the stabbing, escaped by running upstairs and climbing out across the roof?"

"That's right. Joe Coroni was stabbed, though he had a gun lying beside him, empty, and firing had been heard. We traced the lad—don't know his real name even now—witnesses won't say a word—we traced him up the stairs of the club by a few blood marks on the banisters, a window ledge, and the roof tiles. Got away through the house next door. Coroni's blood, of course."

"No," said David. "The lad's own blood. On his hand because he'd clapped it over the wound. Coroni lay on the hall floor, dying, and fired his last shot up the stairs and it hit his killer in the seat."

"It'd have dropped him, surely? Anyway we found no bullet marks on the stairs."

"You wouldn't. It didn't drop him, or not for more than a few seconds. Perhaps he had a wallet in his jeans' pocket and that had a stopping effect. His muscles were hard, too, with the effort he was making. If he hadn't been stooped forward as he ran, the bullet would have gone through his abdomen and killed him. As it was, it cut through the flesh only and lodged against his spine."

Mitchell got to his feet.

"Where is he now?" he asked quickly.

"Dead." David explained the case. "Too scared to get advice, I suppose. Or too scared to take it. When I saw at the postmortem that the gun must have been fired at him from below while he was in a slightly stooping position and that the bone had had time to erode and drop off the bullet, I remembered this case I'd read in the papers."

"You don't miss much, do you?" said the superintendent, smiling.

"Boy of about eighteen," said David. "Called himself Bert Smith. You'd better come along and have a look at him. You may know him. I thought you'd like to wind up the case."

"So I would," said Mitchell. "But it's only just beginning. We nearly grabbed this lad at Wigan when he was in hospital there, calling himself Ray Brown. But he left. You see, it wasn't Coroni that shot him. It was his bodyguard, O'Brien. The gun was beside the body, but *we* know Coroni was scared of guns and only used the knife. Perhaps, now, the witnesses will talk. Because O'Brien isn't popular and he won't be coming out at the end of nine years to get his own back on them."

The Hoofs of Satan

BY EDWARD D. HOCH

The village of North Bradshire is much the same as a thousand others that dot the English countryside. It lies at the edge of a great forest, on one of the main highways from London to the coast, a relic of the Middle Ages that somehow survived to the twentieth century.

If the traveler is curious enough, he can find the history of the village engraved on a bronze plaque in the town square. But time and the weather have made the few short paragraphs almost unreadable. It really didn't matter, anyway, because everyone knew of the famous battle that had made the name of North Bradshire famous in the pages of history. The fact that the battle had been fought nearly a thousand years earlier did not bother the present citizens in the least. For North Bradshire was a town that lived in the past.

It was not until the late winter of 1954 that another event occurred to bring public attention to the village. And, as before, this second event brought death, as well as fame, to North Bradshire. . . .

It was a cold morning in early March, and the four inches of snow from the previous day remained on the ground, covering the fields with an unbroken white coat. Unbroken, that is, except for the single line of odd tracks that ran from the woods to the side door of a nearby house, and then back to the woods again. The milkman, making his usual morning rounds, was the first to notice the tracks in the snow.

He told others about them, and the word spread swiftly, as it does in places like North Bradshire. By noon of that day, half of England knew about the tracks in the snow.

That was why, on the afternoon express to North Bradshire, two men sat in a coach discussing the odd occurrence.

One was Chief Inspector Ashly of New Scotland Yard, a short, almost tiny man who nevertheless had the deep thundering voice of a much bigger man. "My voice never fails to amaze people," he was saying. "It is, perhaps, my greatest asset." He paused a moment and studied the big man with the placid face in the seat opposite him.

"What did you say your name was?" the chief inspector asked.

"I didn't." He exhaled a thick cloud of blue tobacco smoke, which hung suspended in the air between them. "But the name is Simon Ark. I, also, am on my way to North Bradshire."

"About these tracks in the snow?"

The man called Simon Ark nodded. He was a heavy, well-built person, who might have been extremely handsome twenty years ago. But now his flabby face and wrinkled brow gave him the appearance of a man much older than he actually was.

The train rumbled on through the white-covered fields, and occasionally through a patch of woods where the thick branches had protected the grounds from the snow.

Simon Ark shifted his gaze from the beauties of the English countryside and asked, "Since when do prints in the snow bring chief inspectors from Scotland Yard to investigate?"

Inspector Ashly frowned. "The circumstances involved are most peculiar. Of course, since the news of these latest tracks interested you also, I imagine you are well aware of the legend."

Simon Ark nodded. "Although I would not exactly call it a legend. Even though it happened a hundred years ago, the story is certainly true. The people of Devonshire and several other villages awoke one morning to find strange cloven hoofprints in the fresh snow. The tracks were single, and in a perfectly straight line, about eight inches apart, as if made by some one-legged animal running across the snow. But they were the tracks of no known creature. The tracks led across fields, over fences and rivers, and even over the roofs of houses. The townspeople followed the trail with dogs; but when they reached the woods nearby, the dogs commenced to howl and refused to go further. The legend grew that the strange foot or hoofprints had been made by the devil himself. In later years, similar prints were discovered in the snow at other places in the area, but no satisfactory explanation was ever arrived at."

The inspector looked at Simon Ark with new admiration. "I see you've made quite a study of the matter."

"I have made a study of all the strange and unexplained happenings during the past several centuries. I find it a fascinating hobby."

"Might I inquire as to what your real occupation is?"

Simon Ark's thick lips twisted into what might have been a smile. "I fear, my dear Inspector, that you wouldn't believe me if I told you."

They rode in silence for some time after that, until Simon Ark said, "You still haven't told me why the police are interested in this matter."

The inspector shrugged. "As you remarked, sir, you wouldn't believe me if I told you."

The train roared through a tunnel, then into the afternoon light once more. Ahead, stretching out along both sides of the tracks, they could see the groups of tiny shops and houses that made up the village of North Bradshire. "This is it," Inspector Ashly remarked, as he rose from his seat. . . .

This was indeed it. Inspector Ashly was met at the station by a portly, middle-aged man who was revealed to be the mayor of North Bradshire.

Mayor Beverson was a very excited man. "Tracks in the snow, Inspector. I saw them myself; this isn't like the other times."

Inspector Ashly grunted doubtfully. "Mayor Beverson, I must warn you that we believe this to be another publicity stunt dreamed up by yourself to keep North Bradshire on the front pages of the newspapers." He half turned to Simon Ark, who had followed him off the train. "We expect a great many tourists to come over this summer for the Festival of Britain. The mayor, here, apparently is attempting to attract visitors to his town by using any number of quaint devices."

Mayor Beverson had grown gradually pale with anger as the inspector spoke. Now, when he replied, his words tumbled over each other, making his whole speech almost incoherent. "This is not a publicity stunt of any kind, Inspector. I will admit that the other events of the past week were planned, but I knew nothing of this. And I certainly did not ask anyone to send you up here. In fact, what are you . . . ?"

Inspector Ashly held up a thick hand to silence the mayor. "All right, all right! Take us to see these tracks of yours."

The mayor shrugged, and turning, led the way down the winding white road. Behind him, Inspector Ashly, Simon Ark, and a score of the townspeople followed.

They passed the usual English country houses, lining the quiet road like silent sentries. Finally they halted before an old house that was small in comparison to the others. A tall, blond man of uncertain age came out to greet them, and the curious townspeople pressed closer.

The mayor cleared his throat, as if about to give a speech. "This is Mr. Roland Summers. The . . . tracks are on his property."

Roland Summers held out a muscular hand to greet Inspector Ashly, but the Scotland Yard man ignored it. "Summers? Summers? That name is familiar."

The tall man smiled slightly. "I was on the stage for some time, in the ballet; you might have seen me."

Ashly snorted. "I doubt it. Let's see these tracks of yours."

Roland Summers led the small group around to the side of the house. There were no breaks in the virgin snow. It stretched as far as the eye could see; a white vastness that seemed to reflect the awful whiteness of the winter sky.

Then they saw it.

From the woods a quarter of a mile away, there stretched a single line of indentations in the snow. They were almost round, and ran in a single line, each print being about eight inches from the previous one. They might have been the hoofprints of some one-legged beast.

Simon Ark's eyes followed the prints across the snow from the woods to the house, and then back into the woods again.

Inspector Ashly grunted and bent over, studying the prints. "They're all practically identical; there must be some animal . . ."

"Some animal with one leg?" Simon Ark asked.

"Those are not the tracks of any animal I have ever seen," Mayor Beverson insisted.

"Mr. Summers," the inspector turned to the tall man, "did you hear any unusual noises during the night?"

"None, Inspector. But then, I'm a very sound sleeper."

Ashly grunted. "This . . . thing . . . apparently came right up to your back door. Was anything taken?"

"No, Inspector, the door was locked from the inside. Whatever it was couldn't have gotten in."

Ashly turned back to the mayor. "I suggest you call all zoos within fifty miles of here and find out if any animals have escaped."

As Mayor Beverson moved off to carry out the assignment, Simon Ark spoke from the edge of the group. "Inspector, it might be advisable to get some dogs on the trail of this thing. It may be in the woods nearby."

The man from Scotland Yard seemed puzzled for a moment; then his face cleared. "Oh, yes. According to the legend, the dogs always stopped at the edge of the woods. All right, we can try it if you find some dogs."

Ten minutes later, Simon Ark had obtained four large hunting dogs, and they were ready to start. Mayor Beverson returned with the news that no animals had escaped from nearby zoos, and the news failed to surprise anyone. None of them really believed that the tracks in the snow had been made by something as simple as an animal. Or at least none of them wanted to believe it, for as much as they dreaded the other alternative, the thought of it was somehow fascinating.

But the expedition was postponed for a few moments by the arrival of a strikingly beautiful woman.

Diana Hunt was one of those women who was always unpopular with members of her own sex, while at the same time having a great attraction for the opposite sex. She was dressed in riding clothes, and her jet-black hair hung halfway down her back. But it was her eyes that Simon Ark noticed first. They seemed almost to be separate living pools, completely detached from the remainder of her masklike face.

Simon Ark bowed slightly when she was introduced to him. "I have seen you on the screen many times, Miss Hunt." Until her marriage two years ago to a wealthy manufacturer, Diana Hunt had been one of England's most glamorous motion picture stars. Now, as the wife of a socially prominent businessman, she had settled down to a quiet life in the country.

Diana Hunt flashed one of her famous smiles. "The name is now Mrs. Mark Eagen. I have retired from the films."

"Where is your husband this morning, Mrs. Eagen?" Mayor Beverson inquired.

The smile vanished for an instant, then reappeared. "He's gone to London on business, he should return later in the day."

"I suggest we get on the trail of this thing at once," Inspector Ashly said. "It's already got a twelve-hour start on us."

The others agreed, and the small band started out, led by the dogs. Simon Ark brought up the rear with Mrs. Eagen and Roland Summers.

"Really, Diana," Summers was saying, "you should go back to the house; there's no telling what we may find out here."

Diana frowned. "They must expect to find something, or else why send a Scotland Yard man?" She hurried ahead to join the others.

Simon Ark watched her long legs kicking up snow as she ran. "What is her husband's business, Mr. Summers?"

Roland Summers hesitated. "Why, I believe Mark Eagen is in the chemical industry. He owns a small but profitable plant that manufactures dry ice and other chemical refrigerants."

"Dry ice?" Simon Ark repeated with interest.

"Yes. He often takes long trips about the country on business. I'm afraid his wife finds it very lonely here. He rarely takes her with him."

"I'm sure that a beautiful woman like Mrs. Eagen would never be too lonely," Simon Ark replied.

Summers grunted. He was watching the group ahead with keen interest now. They were almost to the point where the odd tracks disappeared into the woods.

Once into the densely wooded area, the hoofprints became harder to follow. Little snow had fallen here, and the ground, for the most part, was covered with damp leaves.

They had gone about fifty yards into the woods when suddenly the four hunting dogs stopped dead in their tracks and began to howl.

Simon Ark glanced quickly around and saw the expression of terror and disbelief of their faces.

Inspector Ashly pulled a handkerchief from his pocket and wiped the sweat from his forehead.

The four dogs continued their mournful howling. . . .

Gradually, like some evil demon slipping over them, night came to the quiet English countryside, giving the snow a darker hue that seemed somehow in keeping with events of the day. The people had returned to their homes, but in everyone's mind was the same thought. Would the thing come again tonight . . . ?

Simon Ark and Inspector Ashly sat facing each other across one of the ancient oak tables in the local pub. They had consumed a few beers and a little time, while waiting for darkness.

"I still can't understand why the dogs acted that way this afternoon," Ashly said.

"I fear that there is something of great evil hiding in those woods," Simon Ark remarked.

"Don't tell me you believe this legend about the devil coming to the village!"

Simon Ark's face grew serious, and deep furrows appeared in his brow. "I believe that Satan did visit North Bradshire last night."

"What?"

"And he's still here, out in those woods, waiting. . . ." Simon Ark rose and walked toward the door. "Please excuse me, Inspector, but I have a few calls to make."

He continued down the lonely street, his dim eyes seemingly intent upon the glistening snowflakes that now and then drifted down from the black void above. Ahead, he caught a glimpse of Mayor Beverson hurrying across the street on some mission of his own.

Simon Ark paused for a moment in the town square, and tried to read the bronze plaque that rested there, but the single street light served only to cast dim shadows over it. After a time, he gave it up and moved on.

His first stop was the small home of Roland Summers. He rang the bell twice and waited, but no one came. After a few minutes' wait, he tried the knob and found the door unlocked.

Inside, a single light burned in the study, and another came from a stairway that apparently led to the basement. From there came the regular sounds of an ax hitting wood. Simon Ark descended the treacherous steps and found Summers swinging the ax at a decaying tree trunk which lay in a damp spot on the floor.

"Oh! It's you, Ark. Sorry I didn't hear the bell; I was busy chopping up some firewood."

"You seem to have enough of it there. That trunk must weigh over a hundred pounds."

Summers grunted and took a few more swings with the ax. "It's all damp and decayed. I'm afraid it won't be any good for firewood after all." He tossed the ax down in disgust and smiled slightly. "Well, enough of that. Let's go upstairs and have a drink, Mr. Ark."

Simon Ark followed him upstairs and accepted a partly filled glass of Scotch and water.

"Just what is your capacity in this investigation, Mr. Ark? Are you with Scotland Yard also?" Summers downed his drink.

"Oh, heavens, no! I'm just what you might call an interested party."

Roland Summers grunted. "I suppose it's the factory on the other side of the woods that makes this whole thing so important, eh?"

"Factory? What factory?" Simon Ark's eyebrows went up with interest.

"Oh, I thought everyone knew about the factory. It's some kind of a supersecret defense plant, probably making atomic bombs or something."

"So that's why Scotland Yard takes such an interest in the area."

Summers nodded. "Every time something happens up here, we're immediately investigated by the Yard, Army Intelligence, and several other government agencies."

Simon Ark lit a cigarette and appeared to study a faded painting on the opposite wall. "The inspector mentioned something about Mayor Beverson's attempts to get publicity for the town."

The other man laughed. "Yes, he's trying to attract tourists for the big festival this summer. But this doesn't look to me like one of his stunts."

"To tell you the truth," Simon Ark commented, "this doesn't look like much of anything to me."

Summers answered with a questioning stare.

"I've made quite a study of the odd appearances of tracks at Devonshire and other cities during the last century," the heavy man began. "These things in your back yard, while admittedly not the prints of any known animal, certainly bear little resemblance to drawings of the Devonshire tracks. And I'm at somewhat of a loss to understand why the comparison was ever made. I came up here to investigate what I believed to be a supernatural occurrence, and I find instead a publicity-seeking mayor, a spy-hunting inspector, and an ex-movie queen." He took another puff on his cigarette and then ground it out in the ashtray. "Which reminds me, I have another stop to make tonight. If you'll excuse me, Mr. Summers . . ."

"Certainly. Glad you dropped in. How long do you expect to remain in town?"

Simon Ark's lips curled in what might have been a thin smile. "I hope to finish my business tonight."

Outside, it was snowing harder now, at times all but obscuring vision. In another hour, the mysterious tracks would disappear forever.

It took him a few moments to discover in which house Mr. and Mrs. Mark Eagen lived. When he found it, he was not surprised. It was apparently the largest house in town, with arches, gables, and pillars stretching into the sky in a sort of quiet mockery of the staid English architecture that dominated the rest of the town.

He rang the bell and waited. Presently the door was opened by Mrs. Eagen herself, looking more like the old Diana Hunt than ever.

"Come in, Mr. . . . ?"

"Ark. Simon Ark. I'd like to talk to you."

She wore a simple green dress that seemed to add to her beauty in some unexplainable way. Simon followed her into the living room, where she poured two drinks in silence. "I saw you with the inspector this morning," she said finally. "Are you a detective?"

He moved his great bulk in the narrow confines of the chair and took a sip of the drink she'd offered him. "Not exactly. I really came over here to speak to your husband, Mrs. Eagen; has he returned?"

"No," she answered simply. They sat in silence for another few moments before she continued, "Well, I might as well tell someone. The whole town will know in another day or two."

Simon Ark sat very still and waited.

"The truth is, Mr. Ark, that my husband has left me. He departed during the night without a word."

"Did you have a quarrel?"

"Yes. He . . . he had some foolish idea about me seeing too much of our neighbor, Roland Summers. Of course he's always been jealous, ever since he married me."

Simon Ark nodded. "I can understand his concern. You have no idea where he has gone?"

"None whatever. For a time, I thought he would return; but now I fear he is gone for good."

"Could I see a picture of your husband, please?"

She rose and walked to the fireplace. The framed photograph she returned with showed her in a wedding gown, accompanied by a small, pleasant-looking man who appeared to be about forty years old.

"Thank you very much, Mrs. Eagen. I'll no doubt be talking to you again later."

And then he was out in the street again, where the snow was still falling.

He knew where he was going next, yet he was mildly surprised when his feet carried him around to the back of the line of houses, and he headed steadily toward the woods.

Once more the snow had covered everything, obscuring the tracks of the night before. He reached the edge of the woods and paused a second, listening.

But he heard nothing. . . .

Nothing . . .

The white curtain of snow in front of him, the black curtain of trees behind him . . .

He waited. . . .

Presently he moved on, carefully examining the ground at his feet. Somewhere a dog howled. . . .

He paused. . . .

And heard it. The soundless noise of hoofbeats in the snow . . .

It was coming again, as it had the night before, and as it might continue to. . . .

He waited. . . .

A dark shape formed against the white background. Closer . . .

But it was not a devil, only Inspector Ashly.

"Ark! What are you doing out here?"

"Solving your mystery for you, Inspector. I know what made those tracks. And the thing you want is here in the woods, now!"

"Satan?" The inspector was laughing.

"I told you there was a great evil in these woods, and I was right."

"Ark, if you're referring to the government's factory on the other side . . ."

"No, Inspector, this evil is much more ancient than atomic bombs."

"What, then?"

Simon Ark spoke grimly. "We need men, a lot of them. And some searchlights. We're going into the woods. Now! Tonight!"

"But why? What did you see in this village that I missed? How do you know it's in the woods now?"

Simon Ark said very quietly, "Because a man was chopping wood in his basement . . .

Roland Summers opened the door and greeted Simon Ark with a smile. "Well, back again!"

"Yes, Mr. Summers."

"What's all the activity in the woods? There seems to be a lot of men back there. And spotlights."

"That's right. They're digging." Simon Ark followed him into the small book-lined study.

"Digging? For what?"

"They're searching for the body of Mr. Mark Eagen, the man you murdered last night. . . ."

"The evil that came to North Bradshire last night was of a very ancient type—lust for another man's wife." Simon Ark spoke quietly, his eyes never leaving the pale face of Roland Summers.

"And the devil was here last night, Mr. Summers. But he wasn't out there making tracks in the snow. He was inside of you, when you killed Diana Hunt's husband."

"I . . . you're crazy."

"I don't suppose it was premeditated. He came to your house to tell you to keep away from his wife. There was a fight, and you killed him. Then you were faced with the problem that always confronts murderers: you had to get rid of the body. It couldn't be left in your house. You decided the best thing would be to bury it. But the ground was frozen; covered with snow, except in the woods where the trees protected the ground. So you decided to carry the body from your house to the woods and bury it."

Roland Summers sat frozen to the chair. His cigarette had almost burned down to his fingers.

"But that immediately presented a problem. A fresh snow had fallen, making the area you had to cross a spotless white carpet. In the morning, someone would be sure to notice the footprints leading from your house to the woods and back again. And if Diana Hunt became alarmed at her husband's absence, the police might have connected his disappearance with the footprints leading from your house to the woods. So you devised a way to make your tracks look like those of an animal."

"Those didn't look like any animal tracks." Summers' face had turned ashen now.

"No, but they might have passed an uninterested observer. They were better than footprints, anyway. Unfortunately for you, Mayor Beverson saw another opportunity to publicize his town; he called attention to the fact that they slightly resembled some mysterious tracks found in the area a hundred years ago. That was what really spoiled things for you; because sooner or later someone was sure to realize that the prints didn't necessarily start and end in the woods. They could just as well have started and returned to your house."

"And . . . and how do you suggest I was able to make almost round indentations like those in the snow?" He seemed almost afraid of the answer he knew would come.

Simon Ark said, "Very simple. They are the prints of the toes of ballet shoes or slippers. When you carried Mark Eagen into the woods, you walked on your toes. . . ."

The cigarette fell from Roland Summers' limp fingers.

"I know it sounds fantastic, even to carry a small man any distance while keeping on your toes, but a skilled ballet dancer like yourself must have much strength in his legs. And putting one foot directly ahead of the other when you walked would also be simple for you."

Roland Summers was staring at him with glassy eyes.

"Of course, the howling dogs this afternoon suggested that there was something, possibly a body, buried in those woods. And Mark Eagen was the only person who had disappeared last night. The prints, which were the only ones between the town and the woods, came from your house, which made you the logical suspect."

Simon Ark paused and listened to the renewed voice from the direction of the woods. Then he continued.

"And when I found you chopping up that old tree trunk in your basement, I was certain. It was obviously no good for firewood, and it had just as obviously been carried from the woods recently. Yet there were none of your footprints in the snow—only the odd cleverest part of your whole scheme. You carried a two-hundred-pound corpse into the woods, so you carried a two-hundred-pound tree stump out of the woods, thus making sure that the depth of the tracks in the snow was about the same, both coming and going. Otherwise, it would have been obvious that something had been carried into the woods."

Roland Summers continued to sit stiffly in the chair. . . .

Simon Ark was closing the door behind him when Inspector Ashly came up. "We dug up Eagen's body, Mr. Ark. It was where you said, near the spot where the dogs started howling. Is Summers inside?"

"Yes, he is. . . ."

"I suppose Eagen's wife was the cause of it all."

But Simon Ark did not reply. He was walking slowly through the snow to the road.

Inspector Ashly opened the door and went into Roland Summers' house. He found Summers in the study, still staring at the wall with glassy eyes. . . .

He was pulling a pair of handcuffs from his pocket when he suddenly realized that Roland Summers was dead. . . .

A heavy fog was obscuring London the next day, as Inspector Ashly sat in the office of his superior.

The man behind the desk shuffled some papers and said, "Summers apparently died of heart failure, as a result of some great shock. It all seems very odd, especially since he died while he was alone with this man, Simon Ark, who now seems to have vanished completely."

Ashly frowned and spoke very slowly, "It may sound fantastic, sir, but somehow I don't believe that Simon Ark belonged to our world. He came to North Bradshire because he believed he might find the devil there; instead he found only a murderer."

"What do you mean, he thought he would find the devil? Why should anyone go looking for the devil?"

Ashly rose and walked to the window, where he stood looking out at the gray mist that hung like a curtain over the city. "I don't exactly know, sir, but I found this on the table next to Roland Summers' body. Simon Ark must have left it there."

And he took a small wooden object from his pocket and held it out for his superior to see. It was shaped like the letter T, with a small circle on top, and it appeared to be very old.

"What is it, Ashly?"

"At the museum they told me it was an ansated cross, an early symbol of Egyptian Christians. . . ."

"Egyptian . . ."

"I know it seems fantastic, sir, but I believe Simon Ark is searching for Satan. I believe he has been searching for a long, long time. I wonder what will happen when they meet. . . ."

Something White in the Night

BY HERBERT BREAN

In that latitude, at that time of year, twilight falls swiftly.

The captain, working over a weekly report in the small prim parlor that had been the mayor's before the occupation, saw only shiny blackness when he occasionally looked up toward the window.

Occasionally, too, he laid down his pen and sipped lukewarm tea.

His orderly knocked, entered on being bidden, and closed the door carefully.

"Sir, it is the informer, Char. He has been dealing with Lieutenant Nubba, but says that it is important."

The captain looked through the orderly. He said, "I will ring."

When he was alone he went to a filing cabinet and drew out a thin dossier. It told him that before the occupation Char had been a minor official of the town, a bachelor and unpopular. Twice before he had come with information about the movements of the small Resistance group. Most of it had already been known to Nubba, yet Nubba had noted Char down as a man worth cultivating, and had paid him, once with food and once with occupation currency.

Returning to his desk the captain drained his tea and lit a cigarette.

There was no doubt in his mind that he should see Char, but he had no stomach for it. He did not like dealing with these people nor indeed with any men except his own kind. He was an ordnance officer whom the exigencies of the occupation had tossed helterskelter into commanding this small, cold mountain town with its small, cold population.

An inhuman people, these—insane!

They repeatedly risked being shot to chalk a word, FREEDOM, on buildings, to shout it from a window, even to mutter it in the presence of his troops. And they did not even understand what it meant. They did not appreciate that "freedom" really means freedom to work for the state, to follow joyously and unflinchingly the orders of the man above you, to give everything you are, and have, to advance the cause.

But even so! he thought. They might at least appreciate an opportunity to become part of a bigger and stronger country. Instead, they had fought their benefactors, openly at first, and now that their government had fallen, treacherously and viciously.

The captain crushed out his cigarette impatiently, straightened his tunic, and touched a buzzer.

Char, the informer, paused just inside the door. He was a slight, bony man with a big skull and watery eyes. The gap between his trousers and shoes revealed bare ankles.

"Before, I talked to the Sir Lieutenant," he began.

"I know. Sit down. Cigarette?"

Char took a cigarette eagerly and sat down nervously.

"I have come," he began, "because the Sir Lieutenant has been most kind. My children are in great need. . . ."

Char's voice died after every few words, like a wisp of smoke.

The captain, who knew that he lied about having children, also recognized that Char was starving. It pleased him.

"If you have anything of value you will be paid," he said.

Char did not seem to know how to proceed. "I—it is about the officers, Sir Captain."

The captain made a mask of his face. "What about the officers?"

Char looked down as though forced to speak of something indelicate.

"You have lost many."

"Well?" The mask was imperturbable.

But to keep it so wasn't easy. He had come here eighteen days before with five officers and a detachment of forty men. In the past week four of the officers had disappeared. They had left headquarters on missions or inspection trips and simply had not returned.

Morale was sickeningly low in the barracks; the men went out on patrol with set faces and fright-white eyes; there was nothing of the conquerors' pride in them. Only his own and Nubba's discipline held them together.

"I have learned what has happened to the officers," said Char. He added almost dreamily, "All five of them."

"Four!" snapped the captain.

"Five," said Char softly.

The captain's mask tore like chiffon. "Nubba—Nubba left last night for—"

"He did not get out of town," said Char.

There was a moment of silence.

"My countrymen," Char went on, "do not know what your coming means to our land. They do not perceive what annexation can do for them. They are only peasants, stupid enough to resent—"

"What has happened to my officers?"

The captain's fingernails cut his own palm.

"A trick, Sir Captain, a clever trick. It involves a flag. I can show you."

"Good! What is the trick?"

Char put both hands to his face as though in prayer, and coughed into them, and shuddered.

"First there is the matter of—of pay."

"What happened to my officers?" He did not recognize his own voice.

Char rocked unhappily. "My children, Sir Captain. You do not know how hungry they are."

Versed in the calculation of stresses and breaking points, the captain looked appraisingly at Char.

"The equivalent of twenty American dollars," he said.

"In advance?"

"Of course not in advance. When you have told me."

Char clearly wanted to argue and did not dare.

"It is not a matter of telling, but of showing," he said. "It is a symbol. The Freedom flag, my foolish countrymen call it. Only a few minutes from here. The captain can easily disguise himself like a villager—"

The captain snorted. "I will take twenty men," he said. "You will lead us."

"If you take any men at all," said Char, "their movements will be known throughout the village before they have marched six paces. But we could go together—"

The captain shook his head. He had no intention of venturing into the streets at night.

"But it would cost me *my* life to be seen with *you,* Sir Captain," said Char reproachfully, "and I will take the chance. Besides, the streets are patrolled."

As was his lifelong habit, the captain considered all sides of the problem. He wanted very much to deal these stubborn villagers a blow—and what it would do for his men's morale if, singlehanded, he destroyed the Resistance's most telling weapon!

And there was Nubba to be revenged. He'd been a pleasant fellow.

When duty presented itself, the captain was not one to flinch. He ordered civilian outer garments and, at the informer's suggestion, a pair of night glasses. While he waited for them, he drew a long automatic from his holster, inspected its magazine, and looked significantly at Char.

When they had slipped out the back door he kept Char in front of him, and kept his hand thrust through a slit in the cape, on the pistol's thick grip. They walked quietly along a dark, lifeless street for two blocks.

Char turned into an alleyway.

"Through here," he whispered over his shoulder. "Watch out for the rubble."

The captain recognized it as one of the places they had had to mine to blast out some of the last resisters.

A dozen paces and Char turned again into a narrow passageway between two buildings. Before entering it, the captain paused to listen and assure himself no one was following them.

But Char tiptoed to the end of the passage and looked out on another street.

"There, Sir Captain."

He flattened himself against the wall so the captain could stand beside him. "You see? On the dark house, across the way?"

The captain strained his eyes. "I see nothing. What is it?"

"The Freedom flag, they call it. A clever device. It has cost the lives of five of your men, Sir Captain. Use your glasses. Now you see it, eh?"

The captain braced himself to hold the glasses steady. Presently he glimpsed a gray flutter near the door of the house.

"Yes, I see it. What is it?"

"A flag, Sir Captain. The resisters whisper strange things about it so that your officers hear them. That is how they got your men to the house."

There was a motor's soft hum and a patrol car, turning slowly into the street, shone its headlights fully but momentarily on the house, the door, and a white rag fluttering from the doorknob.

"That's no flag," said the captain irritably. "It's only a white rag. It symbolizes nothing."

"That," said Char softly, "is the mistake all your people have made. The Freedom flag symbolizes everything."

And plunging his knife into the broad back presented to him, he twisted it hard.

Three Ex-Soldiers

BY JAMES MCKIMMEY

I had never gone to any regimental reunions in San Francisco, even though I lived nearby in Stockton. I had not been an enthusiastic member of the United States Army during World War II, for the usual reasons. But this latest announcement was for the first entire division reunion, to be held in the Gold Room of the Fairmont Hotel, ten dollars, wives welcome, fun guaranteed. The day before the reunion was to be held, Meg telephoned me at my office and said that she'd decided to drive the kids down to Fresno after school to spend the weekend with her mother. I couldn't get away from the office until late that night, so I had to say good-bye to her on the telephone.

The next morning, in an empty house, I decided, out of pure curiosity, to go. I wondered if Francis Pennyworth Shard, Jr., by some miracle, would decide to attend, coming all the way from New York. I decided that he would not. I could imagine him tearing that announcement into bits, making spitballs, and snapping them into a fireplace. Each would have Sergeant Albert Drummer wrapped inside.

I called San Francisco for a reservation. That afternoon I was in my car driving to the Bay Area. I checked out a room in the Fairmont and walked directly to the Gold Room. I wondered why the instant I stepped inside.

There were perhaps fifty men and women, and the gathering looked as though it were any civic-organization meeting of middle-aged people. I recognized no one among the separated groups ranged around the room.

I paid my ten dollars, got a drink, and moved into one circle. The conversation went around me for twenty minutes; then I saw a man come in who looked vaguely familiar.

He was wearing a brown sports jacket buttoned tightly over a beer paunch, an open-necked sports shirt, dark slacks, and scuffed loafers over white socks. He was a thick-shouldered man with a deeply lined face and gnarled large hands which he kept gripping and ungripping as though he were uncomfortable. I remembered a trim, slim-waisted, uniformed figure of nearly two decades ago. But I knew this was Sergeant Albert Drummer.

He was the last man I'd hoped to see here. But he was the only one I knew. I walked over and shook hands.

He looked at me with fading gray eyes, frowning. Then he grinned slowly, exposing a row of yellowed teeth, one of which was missing. "For Christ's sake—McCune!"

"Pfc. McCune." I smiled. "One-seven-one-one-six-six-six-eight."

"Goddamn. Your serial number?"

"Who could forget his serial number? How are you, Sergeant?"

"I'm all right. So you remember your serial number, and you hated the army, didn't you?"

"That's probably why I remember. Don't tell me you don't remember yours, Sergeant."

"Not offhand." He shrugged. "But don't call me sergeant. That was a long time ago. All right? I forget now. You were—?"

"Harold."

"Yeah," he said, nodding. "Well, you're looking good, Harold. How you been doing?"

There was something incongruous about his calling me Harold. But we were in the present now, and I was Harold and he was Al. "Pretty good, Al. How have you been doing? How's that lovely wife of yours?"

The one thing that had seemed human about Sergeant Al Drummer was his devotion to his wife. He'd carried her picture with him at all times, and the only time he ever relaxed with any of us was to talk about her and show us her picture. She had a soft, kindly look, not very pretty, but the kind of woman you could imagine devoting herself to kids and good cooking and a comfortable home.

"Delle's fine," he said. "She's back at our hotel right now. She had a little flu and couldn't come. I would've liked you to meet her. You married now, Harold?"

"Yes. Two kids, too. A boy and a girl."

He grinned again. "No kidding? That's good to hear."

I couldn't really believe that this was Sergeant Albert Drummer. He should, I thought, be about forty-six or forty-seven now, eight or nine years older than I. But he looked years older. "How about you, Al? I imagine you and Delle have about fifteen children by now."

"No." He shook his head slowly. "Didn't work out that way. Just me and Delle. She's a wonderful woman, Harold."

He started searching the room, frowning again.

"Outside of you," I said, "I don't know a soul in here."

"No. And I come all the way from Denver."

"Just for this reunion?" I asked, surprised.

"I got the notice it was for the whole division. I thought maybe it was going to be a big one, so everybody might show up. So me and Delle packed up and drove over. I thought—" He looked at me hopefully. "You wouldn't think maybe Shard was going to show, would you, Harold?"

Again I was surprised. I told him I could check that. I found the man who was in charge of reservations. Shard had not made one.

I went back to Al Drummer and told him that I was certain Shard wouldn't appear. He looked visibly disappointed. I couldn't understand that.

"Well, I'll tell you the truth, Harold," he said, "I don't feel too comfortable in a hotel like this. I seen some good bars on Market Street I'd feel a hell of a lot better in. You wouldn't want to go have a beer down there, would you?"

I was thinking about that time at Dix just before we'd gone overseas. I didn't want to go with him. But he had changed. And I was curious. I told him that would be fine. Twenty minutes later we were seated in a cheap Market Street bar where he seemed notably more comfortable.

"Harold," he said, "I've always been sorry about what happened at Dix."

He kept surprising me. I'd never expected him to make an apology for that, or even admit that it happened.

But it had happened, about three weeks after I'd been transferred into Headquarters Company and the care of Sergeant Al Drummer. . . .

I'd come from the college program the army temporarily ran. True to his type, Drummer was a college-man hater. There was only one other former college man in Drummer's command. That was Francis Pennyworth Shard, Jr., a tall, thin, intellectually inclined private who had attended Yale for two years before being drafted. Drummer knew that from Shard's records when Shard was transferred into the company two months ahead of me. He'd gotten on him immediately: extra KP, cancelled passes, doubled guard duty, the usual things. Because I gravitated toward Shard when I arrived, I was also into it.

At my first formation I listened to Drummer, standing before us like a steel statue, shout for twenty minutes about the way he was going to take a man's outfit into combat.

Guts, he said, were what counted in the end. The killer instinct was going to be a part of every one of us, including any goddamn college boys in the outfit. We weren't far from shipping out, and every day was going to be double-up to make something out of this group. We were going over there to kill or be killed. And it had better be kill.

He took another ten minutes to describe how he'd come from Wyoming, before he'd gotten into this man's army, and how he'd hunted there. He'd once tracked down an elk above Casper, going at it for two days, until he gut-shot it and tracked the blood on snow and then neck-shot it, never giving up until it was dead, because he had the killer instinct. Now, we were going to find that killer instinct too.

I glanced several times at Shard. Shard, quite an ugly young man, never moved. He just stood at attention, listening with a half smile on his mouth. When the diatribe was over, Drummer dismissed everyone for breakfast but Shard and me. We were ordered to do two miles of jogging before going to the mess hall. We had, he said, moved while at attention. I'd moved a little, all right, as had almost everyone else during that speech. But Shard had never shifted a muscle. He went the two miles without complaint.

Drummer put us on KP when we got back. I didn't get a chance to talk to Shard until that night. Then, in our corner of the barracks, I said, "What's he got against you, anyway?"

Shard lay flat on his back and smiled at the ceiling. "I went to Yale."

"He's on you just for that?"

"Yes. He's on you now, too."

"Why? I only had a semester at Cal before I was crazy enough to join this army. That's only a state university. I had a couple of semesters at Ball State. But the army sponsored that. I never went to Yale."

"That's all right. He's on you anyway. You're talking to me now. When he finds that out you're really finished. Do you want to leave me alone?"

"I don't take that kind of stuff from anybody. I'm getting myself transferred out of here."

"McCune, I'm rich. My father knows anybody who is anybody in this country. If he can't work a transfer out of here for me, you can't get an hour's pass out of the gate. This outfit's combat-ready and it's frozen. You're stuck and so am I."

"And what happened today is going to go on happening, and I'm supposed to take it?"

"That's right."

"I'll get the bastard."

"Sure. After I do."

"How?"

Shard turned on his side and looked at me directly. From a profile he'd appeared relaxed and calm. But when you saw his eyes this way, you saw a hate and fury so intense it was chilling. "Listen," he said softly, holding a thumb and forefinger a quarter of an inch apart, "he's got a brain this big. He's a stereotype, right out of a book. He's dangerous, and he's tough to get. It'll take time and thought. Because you don't know how a man like this thinks. He's like an animal. But I'm going to get him, McCune. I was reared in one of the finest sections of New York, and then I went to Groton. I went to Yale. I am wealthy in my own right. And if it weren't for the war I would jack this son-of-a-bitch down to the size of an ant in minutes. But there is a war. And so it's going to take time."

He rolled on his back again and picked up a copy of the Dialogues of Plato. He and I were on KP the next morning.

It was difficult, now, sitting in a San Francisco bar with former Sergeant Albert Drummer, to remember the entire intensity of feeling I'd had in those weeks before we finally shipped out of Fort Dix. But I could still remember that night Drummer had just apologized for. . . .

It had happened two nights before we moved to the staging area. It was late summer and we had been on the rifle range all day, where

Drummer, an expert shot, had worked us relentlessly under a blazing sun. It was Saturday and everyone was to receive his last pass out of Dix that evening.

Everyone did but Shard and me. When we got back to the barracks, Drummer told us we were on supply-room duty that night. I thought that his eyes looked peculiar. But anger blurred my own vision, so that I could barely see anything. Shard took it calmly.

Drummer acted as CQ that night and sent everyone off but Shard and me. Then he came into the supply room and instructed us to check every gas mask and small arm against the records. He talked with a slight slur, and I could smell liquor on his breath. He disappeared, and Shard and I went to work.

Two hours later he came back. This time he was obviously drunk. He explained that neither of us had what it took to face combat. He said that it was his duty, now, to make a final attempt to get us ready.

He removed a pint bottle from under his jacket and sat on the edge of a packing crate. He started us on push-ups and kept it up until my arms ached and breath seared my throat. Then he ran us in place. Legs quivering, I glanced at Shard. He had paled and his face was strained-looking, but he somehow managed to keep a faint smile on his mouth.

Then Drummer ordered us to pick up a rifle apiece and start lifting exercises. I did them, gritting my teeth, trying to see against the sweat pouring into my eyes. I could hear Shard's breath whistling thinly as he gasped for air.

Then Drummer got up, staggered across the room, and picked up a bayonet. He held it in one hand, spread his legs and said that now it was going to be hand-to-hand training. When I protested, he came at me.

He reeled across the room and took a vicious cut at my belly with that bayonet. I barely got out of his way. He crashed past me into a wall. He turned around, shaking his head stupidly, and looked at Shard with bleary eyes.

Then he slammed across the room at him. Shard tried numbly to get out of his way, but he was too slow. All that saved him was my swinging the butt of my rifle at Drummer. I ticked his hand, and the bayonet sailed out of his grasp.

But he got his hands around Shard's neck. Shard struggled uselessly, and I was ready to use the butt on Drummer's head, when he suddenly let go and slid to the floor where he passed out in a crumpled heap.

I stood over him, quivering with fury. "I'm going to smash his head."

"Let him be," Shard whispered.

We returned to the barracks, where Shard got into his bunk and lay silently. I tried to talk to him, but he wouldn't answer.

On Monday morning, without permission, I walked into the captain's office and told him exactly what had happened. The captain listened silently, then said:

"McCune, you're new in this outfit. Perhaps you don't understand certain things. We are going into combat shortly, and you don't replace a man like Sergeant Drummer. Now I'm going to try to understand why you would think up a ridiculous story like you just told me and then have the goddamn nerve to come in here without going through proper channels and take up my time with it. The only advice I can give you, McCune, is to get out of here and start trying to act like a man."

As soon as we sailed, Drummer sent Shard and me down to the galley, where we spent most of our crossing. We sat on wooden stools on a slick floor and peeled mountains of potatoes in that damp galley heat. Periodically Shard would get up and stagger to the head and throw up.

Two days out I still felt the fury caused by that night in the supply room. I told Shard, "The first shooting we get into, he gets it through the back of the head."

Shard laughed softly. "Don't be an ass, McCune."

Drummer frequently came down and looked at us, but we ignored him. The only time I saw him away from the galley was late one night when Shard and I got off duty. Shard had stumbled off to his berth. I'd gone up to the main deck for fresh air. Drummer came by and said, "Let's have a cigarette, McCune."

I gave him one, bitterly. I could see his eyes tighten in the light of the cupped flame. He said, "Shard's going to fold in combat, do you know that?"

A month after we landed in France, we packed into a train and rode to the German border. The night before we went into combat Shard and I stood on guard listening to the guns up ahead. I told him, "I wish I were on a boat going home."

Shard stood tensely and looked off through the night in the direction of those big guns. "I've been waiting for it."

We moved up the next morning and quickly found out what combat was about.

As a headquarters unit we were a mile behind the rifle companies. A mile, in a combat area, is a safety factor. After the first days, when we all jumped for basements like frightened rabbits every time one of the few remaining German fighters whined overhead, we realized that it was safer than we had expected. It became clear that most of the noise was coming from our own field artillery guns and antiaircraft units.

After a month of holding in the same positions, our rifle companies inched forward. We followed. Until then, the casualties had been light. But now the resistance stiffened. Evidence of it came late one winter afternoon when Shard and I, after a long stretch of guard duty which Sergeant Drummer had kept us on day and night, were sitting on the floor of a shot-up house where we slept, just back of the line. We were weary with little sleep and sat staring at nothing.

Drummer came in briskly, a shrewd look in his eyes. There was a clean, flashy look about him these days. He'd gotten hold of a tanker jacket, paratroop boots, and a .45 pistol.

He sat down on the edge of a table and carefully explained that a new job had opened up for someone who could assume responsibility.

Medics, he explained, had been dragging the bodies of our dead troops to a point just back of the line. They were piling up now. Somebody was needed to pick up those bodies and get them into a truck and cart them back for burial. It was really quite an opportunity for a good man.

Shard slowly drew a thumbnail down the length of his nose. "When do I start?"

"How about right now?" Drummer snapped.

I didn't see Shard often after that. Drummer increased my guard duty, so that I got only two or three hours sleep a night. Shard often slept back in Holland, where they buried the bodies. But I heard from the driver who'd gone up that first time with Shard.

He said that when they'd come up on the first body, Shard had climbed out, surveyed it calmly, then, with a strength none of us knew he had, picked it up and slung it into the back of the truck like a sack. He was grinning the whole time, the driver said.

On the other hand Sergeant Drummer appeared less happy than I'd seen him since we'd gone into combat. He hadn't expected this from Shard, I knew.

One noon I was getting some rare rest in our sleeping room. Drummer came in looking bitter and saying nothing. Then Shard walked in with a bounce. There was a truly cold, animal look in his eyes now. The other men in the company had begun referring to him as The Mortician.

"I figured," he said to me, "that you might want to pull on your spectator jacket and come join me today. It's tremendously interesting."

"For Christ's sake, Shard."

"What's the matter, college boy?" Drummer rasped. "No guts?"

I walked out with Shard. We went up the road and Shard said, "I've got a couple on the ground up here."

I had not, before that moment, seen a dead American soldier. They were lying on their stomachs, dressed exactly as I was, legs slightly sprawled. Fortunately, Shard had covered their heads with their steel helmets.

"My God, Shard. I'm going back. I'll take the sergeant anytime."

"I thought you were going to shoot him in the head."

"I may. Any day."

"I've got something better. Tell him I've invited him to join me tomorrow. We ought to get ten, maybe eleven, the way it's going."

When I saw Drummer, I told him. I watched his reaction with satisfaction. He paled, and I could see the anger going through him. "Are you going, Sergeant?" I asked him quietly.

"You're on guard all night," he snapped.

The next morning, when I came in, Drummer was drinking a steaming cup of coffee. I was bleary with lack of sleep, but I still felt an excitement wondering if he would accept Shard's challenge. He glared at me and said, "I'll be out with Shard all day. Get yourself an hour's sleep, then you're CQ today."

They came in late that afternoon. Drummer walked across the room and sat down weakly on the table. Shard looked freshly buoyant. I said, "How did he do, Shard?"

"Great, McCune."

I looked at Drummer in surprise. He said in a weary voice, "I got to hand it to Shard."

Shard grinned. "We've got a fine sergeant, McCune."

Drummer got up slowly and walked out.

I stared at Shard in disbelief. "What happened out there?"

"He's made out of steel, that's all. He had an arm come off in his hand and he laughed. I wouldn't have believed it."

"Neither would I," I said. "Absolutely neither would I."

The next morning Sergeant Drummer said to me, "I think I got something for you, McCune."

"I'm not taking Shard's place."

"He doesn't want to give up that job. I asked him this morning. They need someone back at division. Do you want it?"

"Do I want to become a civilian?"

I never saw Shard again, but I got reports that he carried out his job to the end of the war. I did see Drummer a couple of times, when he came back to division. But after that I didn't see nor hear about Sergeant Albert Drummer, until now, when we were sitting in a Market Street bar and Drummer was apologizing for that night at Dix.

"That's right, Harold. I was sorry about that."

"It was a long time ago, Al."

"Yes, but I wanted to tell you, because I don't even remember exactly what happened that night. I've done a little of that kind of drinking since, so I know how it goes." He shrugged. "I tried, Harold. Honest to God. See—before the army I never had much in my life. I wanted to be a good sergeant. I wanted all my men to look up to me and say there was a good sergeant. Oh, maybe I got on you and Shard a little too hard. But we're all human, ain't we, Harold?"

He looked at his beer glass and said: "I don't do so good with the whiskey sometimes, but I'm a little thirsty tonight." He ordered two more beers and a double shot of whiskey.

"Funny thing. I thought Shard was weak when I met him." He shook his head. "He wasn't."

He tossed off his whiskey and ordered another. He drank that and looked at me with shiny eyes.

"Listen, Harold, Shard told you, didn't he?"

"Told me?"

"That's all right, Harold. I know how it must have looked to you then." He shook his head sadly. "I was always like that. I went to a funeral when I was a little kid, and I saw the body in the casket. I keeled over. That was my mother. I had nightmares for weeks."

I watched him, frowning.

"It was like that the whole time I grew up," he said. "I'd see a cat or a dog dead on the highway, and I'd get sick. Couldn't sleep for days after."

"I remembered you talked a lot about hunting, Al," I said quietly.

"Yeah. That was a lie. I wanted to get you guys keyed up. Oh, I was a good shot. You know that. But I never used a gun to shoot anything alive."

He wagged his head and went on: "When I went out that day with Shard, I couldn't see any way out of it. And somehow he knew what was going to happen. We pulled up on that first one, and it's lying out there in the dirt, just a filled overcoat and legs stretched out and boots. And Shard says, Okay, you want to toss it in back, Sergeant?"

He spread his hands.

"What could I do, Harold? I got out and reached down and turned that body over. And there was just a half a face down there. All the rest shot away and bone and bloody—" He stared at me and blinked slowly. "I went down on my knees and started crying. I couldn't stop crying until Shard started kicking me. When we were coming back, I begged him not to tell anyone. I offered him money. He just laughed. When we got back he surprised me, saying what he did. But I knew as soon as I left, he was going to tell you the truth. He did, didn't he, Harold?"

I understood now exactly how it had been that day. "No. He didn't."

He turned from me and sat hunching his shoulders as though he were chilled. "He just kept that all for himself, didn't he?"

"Yes," I said. "I guess he did, Al."

Finally he signaled for another whiskey. He held the glass and looked at it, and I could see his hand trembling. He said:

"I was a pretty good sergeant, Harold, until Shard and me went out. That ruined it. So I been doing something about that since. When I got discharged I went out in the country and shot myself a squirrel, quick, so I didn't have time to think about it. Didn't go look at it after. Just left. Two days later went out and shot a rabbit. Went over and looked at it. Got sick. But I kept right on looking at it. I went out later and shot another squirrel. Looked at it and didn't get sick.

Touched it. Finally picked it up by the tail and slammed it into the ground. Got sick then. But I kept that up so I didn't get sick no more. I went out and shot me bigger things. I just kept it up, right through the years. Finally got me a real good hound, and him and me got goats and then one hell of a big elk. Shot him dead and skinned him. Didn't feel a thing. My dog, he loved that hunting. And I loved that dog. But he got old. And about a week before that reunion notice come in, I knew he was too old to go on. I took him out and shot him and looked at him and even if I loved him, I didn't feel much. I knew I wasn't like I used to be."

He turned and looked at me again.

"See? I thought maybe Shard would show up, Harold, and I wanted to tell him that." He downed his drink and grinned at me tightly. "Sure you don't want to switch from the beer and have a shot with me?"

I just wanted to get out of there. "Thanks, no, Al. I have to get an early start tomorrow."

We stood up and shook hands.

"It was good to see you again, Harold. If you ever bump into Shard, you tell him about me, won't you?"

"I'll do that, Al."

"I wish Delle could've met you. You'd have liked her, Harold."

"Please give her my best. And good luck, Al."

I slept overnight at the Fairmont. I was driving out of the city the next morning when I heard the news on the car radio. He'd killed her an hour after I left him. He'd gone back to their hotel and choked her with his hands.

I pulled off and sat with my hands tightly around the wheel. Then I drove to police headquarters to see what I could do. There was nothing. I saw him. He didn't recognize me. All that he said was, "They'll let me go to her funeral so I can see her, won't they?" I wasn't a criminal lawyer, and I couldn't help him that way. I found out that he would get a good public defender. The plea was obvious.

I drove home, blaming myself. I should have known something was seriously wrong from the moment he'd told me that he couldn't remember his serial number.

But by the time I'd got back to Stockton I was blaming Shard. He'd been too tough for Drummer. He'd been too tough for all of us.

I tried to look him up in the public library's New York telephone directories. He wasn't listed, but his parents were.

I bought a newspaper which carried the story. I mailed that and a short note to his parents, saying that I was an old Army friend. I asked them to forward the clipping to Shard, explaining that he would understand what it was all about.

I received an answer from his mother. She said that she didn't know what to do with my request since her son had been dead for seventeen years.

Shard had come home from the war worn out and with a cold. Complications had developed. He'd died six months later. She said she didn't recognize my name nor the name of the man written about in the newspaper story. Her son had never talked about anything concerning the war. But the story would have upset him, she was certain, because he had never been able to stand violence.

I wrote her that I was sorry about her son's death. I told her that the clipping was unimportant.

That was true. It was all over. I could think, of course, about what Shard's mother had written me and know, now, how much he had given to defeat Drummer. I could think about the years that Drummer had spent trying to defeat a dead man.

Yet none of it really mattered. They were poles apart, minute realities of a world's social conflict, and yet they were much alike. But they had destroyed each other, and I was simply caught in the middle. I could forget them now.

But I knew that I wouldn't.

United Nations Murder Case

BY LAWRENCE TREAT

The corpse was well dressed in a suit of foreign make, and it lay in a gully well below the wide veranda of the house. Now, at night, the dead, vacant eyes were open. If you looked at them from the proper angle, you could catch the cold glint of starlight. No one, however, did.

The house overlooked the Hudson River, at a point within sight of the George Washington Bridge. Inside, the ambassador was asleep. The mound of blankets on his side of the bed was higher than on hers, for the ambassador was a portly man, layered with fleshy substance. By contrast the blonde beside him was decorated with a mere hint and suggestion of it, just enough, say, to give chic to her figure. She had formerly been a model, and one of the elite.

She waited until his breathing came slow, deep, and even. Then she slipped out of bed, draped a robe over her slim shoulders, and tiptoed out of the room. She closed the door cautiously.

In the hallway she felt lost, and she shivered, although not from cold. The house was strange to her, she was scared of the dark corridor and panicky with the fear that she'd stumble over an unfamiliar object and wake him with the crash. She groped along the wall, feeling doors and wall brackets and then the console table. The turn in the hallway was just beyond.

She found the study at the end of the corridor and she entered and switched on a light. She closed the door gently and glanced at the desk. The original and two carbons of the report were lying there, in plain sight. Anyone, anyone at all, could sneak in and steal them. With a shock, Isabel realized that his carelessness made the murder senseless, unnecessary. Then it occurred to her that he'd been careless on purpose.

At the thought, she had misgivings. He'd been a master of international intrigue when she'd been learning to add and subtract. She was no match for him, she was a child compared to him, and she looked it, too. The sweep of her hair, combed straight back from her face, gave her glamour in the daytime, but here, with no make-up and with that soft, guileless look in her blue eyes, she was the picture of innocence.

"Vickie," she said to herself, "please don't blame me." Then she sat down and picked up the document.

On the second page she saw a passage that differed from the version she'd seen yesterday. She penciled it and went on, reading attentively and judging in terms of the politics of his country.

"It's a small nation," he'd remarked once, "and a sort of international plaything. Very few of its people have the advantage of an Oxford education like myself. Nevertheless they have rights."

He had told her that he had to perform a delicate balancing act and make endless compromises, else he might lose his job. There were two factions, he said, and they were bitterly opposed. He called one of them the democrats' party and the other one the cartel's party. When she had accused him of oversimplification, of omitting nationalistic trends and Communist intrigues, he had replied, "Perhaps. But it's preferable to overcomplication, which can lead to a state of stasis. And whatever I am, I'm not static."

"If you were," she'd said archly, "I wouldn't be here."

She frowned and marked another paragraph. The alteration was crucial and yet subtly hidden in a statistical summary. He could easily have missed its significance while under the stress and strain of his formal presentation.

She realized more clearly than ever that the pages in front of her were of enormous importance. Once read, they would be beyond recall. They would be recorded verbatim, and filed and accepted as a matter of course by the U.N. temporary committee, the specialized agency, and finally the assembly itself. The fate of his country would be decided by the contents of this document.

Feeling pleased with herself, she retyped three pages and inserted the vital statistics which she had memorized earlier in the day. The last paragraph she redrafted completely, using phrases that would come naturally to his lips. But the ideas, the policies laid down, were hers.

They were American in concept, and strongly anticartel.

When she had finished, she fitted the new sheets neatly into the three stacks, carbons and original. She took the old sheets to the bathroom, where she burnt them and flushed the ashes down the toilet. She felt that her work would sway nations and change the course of history. Cleopatra could not have done as well, for Cleopatra could not type.

Isabel returned to bed.

Lying next to the ambassador, she began to calm down. She thought of his massive, almost monumental honesty. She thought of the respect in which his fellow delegates held him. Then she let herself think of the man who lay dead in the gully below the house, with a bullet in his brain. She shivered.

Her shuddering woke the ambassador. "Cold?" he said.

"No," she murmured. "Nervous about tomorrow."

"Nothing to be nervous about," he rumbled. "These things are arranged in the delegates' lounge. Report's ready. I read it, they accept it. Tomorrow I'm what you Americans call the Big Shot."

She nestled closer to him. "Big Shot Vickie," she said.

He breathed with deep contentment. "Ah," he said. He was not a demonstrative man.

At dawn, the first spread of light revealed a trail of partly crushed grass in the steep slope behind the house. A handyman next door, emptying garbage, noticed the swath and investigated. He called the police, who swarmed, investigated, and converged on the ambassador's residence.

When he and Isabel came downstairs, arm in arm, a tall, pug-nosed police officer with a lopsided mouth and a crop of dark, stiff hair was waiting for them.

"I'm Lieutenant Greenwood, of the local precinct," he announced.

The ambassador nodded pleasantly. "You're an early riser. I suppose you have a purpose in being here?"

"Homicide. We found a body behind the house."

Isabel started to ask, "Was he—" but the ambassador's voice drowned her out. "Male or female?" he asked.

"Male. Apparently a foreigner. All identifying objects were removed from his person, and I'd like you to look at him."

"That would be idle," the ambassador said. "Even if I knew him, I'd deny it."

"What for?" the lieutenant asked sharply.

"Because I am my nation's chief representative in the United States, and with my position goes a patriotic obligation to involve myself in no scandal. I am consequently allergic to associating my name with crimes of violence."

"Who mentioned a crime of violence?" Greenwood demanded.

"My dear fellow, would you be setting traps for me if he had died gently?"

The lieutenant switched the subject. "You haven't lived here long, have you?"

"As a matter of fact we don't live here at all," the ambassador answered. "Just a borrowed house. It belongs to a friend of mine who recently received a foreign appointment and sold out. New owner doesn't receive title until next month, and the day before yesterday we took over the diggings, complete with servants. When the new owner comes, we go."

The lieutenant grunted, and his lips twisted into a vague, wet smile of disapproval. In a perverse way and because he scared her, Isabel liked him.

"Come and have breakfast with us," she said. "And be as gruesome as you want. I love it."

She led the way into the tiny breakfast room with the green table and two small, green benches. Paul, the butler, waited in silence, but Greenwood ignored him. Unsmiling, Greenwood picked up a folding chair, fumbled with its mechanism, and couldn't quite open it. When he finally sat down, it spread the last couple of inches and locked itself with a sharp click. He squirmed, and escaped damage.

"American gadgets," observed the ambassador, "are wonderful things, but they require an engineer to operate them. Or at least a chap with your Yankee know-how."

The lieutenant cleared his throat, as if to indicate that the remark was not funny. The butler, smiling discreetly, went out and then returned with an extra cup and saucer.

"I'd like to know where you were yesterday afternoon," Greenwood began, addressing Isabel.

"I went to a concert at Carnegie Hall," she answered promptly.

"Alone?"

"Oh, no. There were hundreds of people there."

"Anyone who knew you?"

Isabel trained her large, limpid blue eyes on his glittering dark ones. "Practically everybody."

"Who, for instance?"

She mentioned several people whom she had seen, and the lieutenant jotted the names down on a pad. Then he turned to the ambassador. "And you?" he said.

"What is the precise purpose of this?" asked the ambassador.

"The man whose body we found was shot. His suit, his shoes, his hat, his underwear—all came from your country."

"Yes?"

"We traced him to this house."

"How exciting!" Isabel exclaimed. "You mean a murder—here?"

The lieutenant glared, a hard, professional glare that nailed you down and dared you to squirm.

Isabel winked. Then, as if by prearranged signal, the ambassador went into action.

"I might remind you," he said, "that I'm a U.N. delegate. I have an important report to give at eleven o'clock this morning and it concerns the welfare of several million people. For just such a contingency as this, I have a contract granting me certain immunities. I'm due at the U.N. building this morning and I can give you—" he consulted his watch—"precisely ten minutes."

"Where were you yesterday afternoon?" the lieutenant asked.

"Upstairs working. And I was quite alone."

"Did you hear a shot?"

"My dear man, I wouldn't have heard a cannon go off."

"Were you expecting anyone?"

The ambassador sighed. "In my wretched business I'm always expecting people, but if anyone came yesterday they could have walked off with the house without my realizing it. However, I venture to make two suggestions: that you pursue your inquiries about me without publicity and through the proper channels, which are the offices of the U.N. Secretary-General. And, before you do so, note and consider the chair you're sitting in. It folds in a rather ingenious manner." He stood up ponderously. "Might save you a bit of work," he said. And, smacking his lips in pleasure, he lumbered out.

The lieutenant frowned. "U.N.," he muttered. "Diplomats. Chairs. Secretary-General. What the hell is this, anyhow?"

He got up and went to the telephone. Isabel heard him saying that a U.N. delegate was involved and asking how reporters should be handled, but she couldn't overhear the answer. Besides, she was worried, for the lieutenant was sitting in the gray Cogswell chair in which a man had been murdered. And, in her shapely bones, she knew that the lieutenant would find out.

She said good-bye to the ambassador upstairs.

"He's fun, isn't he?" she said, referring to the lieutenant.

"My dear, you have a perverted sense of humor." The ambassador studied her gravely. "And thank God for it," he added.

"Thank *you,* Victor," she amended, and curtsied low.

From her window, she watched him leave. He gave no suggestion of worry, no hint of whether he knew. But that, she told herself, was his strength and his greatness. He had played the game of international poker for so long, the habit of repression was so ingrained, that he maneuvered equally to conceal his innocence or his guilt.

Thoughtfully she entered the study. The three piles of papers were lying on his desk, exactly as she had left them last night. For a brief moment she wondered whether he had forgotten them, but she was certain he hadn't. His mind was too well organized, his thinking too precise. He could never have forgotten them.

Therefore he was guilty.

She changed her clothes rapidly and put on a cream-colored suède jacket. She came downstairs humming and went into the kitchen. The butler, Paul, wiping the silver, said, "They've asked us not to leave the house. We were at my cousin's yesterday afternoon. We can prove it, and we have, but the police don't care. We're practically under arrest. Ten years of service, and now this."

Katie, the cook, looked at Isabel as if it were Isabel's fault. "It wasn't like this before," Katie said pointedly. "We're respectable. We want to give notice."

"You may leave at the end of the month," said Isabel. "When we do."

Then she headed for the front door. A uniformed cop was standing guard.

"Lady," he said, "the lieutenant wants you to stay in."

"But I'm going out, and he has no right to stop me."

"He can do anything he wants. You want to get locked up as a material witness?"

"All alone?" she said. "Goodness, no!"

She removed her hat and sauntered into the living room. From the rear French doors that opened onto the veranda, she could see the lip of the ravine and a half-dozen police searching the slope, between there and the house. From where she stood, the trail made by dragging the body through the high grass showed unevenly, like a line drawn with a faulty pen. At one point, the police were taking pictures.

She looked for Lieutenant Greenwood, but she didn't see him. Presently he barged into the living room and, without glancing at her, walked straight to the telephone and picked it up.

She said, "Wouldn't you like permission to use it?"

He stopped dialing. "These calls go free."

"I didn't mean the money. I was just thinking of the courtesy. I'm used to it, you know."

He stared at her and his eyes dropped to her gold ankle bracelet. "Nuts," he said, and resumed his dialing.

She bit her lips and glanced at the gray Cogswell chair. She seemed still to see a dead man sitting there, with two suitcases next to him and a dispatch case chained to his wrist. Blood had dripped slowly from the wound in his head.

She turned swiftly and left the living room. Upstairs, she lifted the extension phone. The lieutenant was saying, "There was only one reporter and I told him it was just a tramp. The lab men are working and—" He broke off. "Somebody's listening in on the extension, Inspector."

There was a long pause. Isabel said, "It's my extension."

"I'll call you back, Inspector," said Greenwood. A minute or so later, a cop came to the door of her room and asked her to lay off.

She obeyed, but she found a spot on the stairs where she could overhear most of what the lieutenant said. He was speaking to the inspector again, and then he called the U.N. and tried to get through to the Secretary-General. Later, she heard him listening to reports, mentioning Paul and Katie and describing them and saying over and over, "Yeah, I know. They had the afternoon off and they went to see this cousin, they didn't get back here till eight o'clock, long after he was dead. The cousin backs them up, every detail. And that leaves our two friends, this diplomatic big shot and his one-girl harem."

Isabel smiled happily for the first time all day. She wanted to thank the lieutenant, but she thought better of it. Still, it *was* a nice compliment.

At eleven o'clock the police experts found traces of blood in the living room. Isabel heard talk of the benzidine test and of blood groupings. She went as far as the entrance to the living room, but she didn't go in. The chair was covered with a dark blue blanket.

She tried to reason out the ambassador's behavior. He had not taken the courier's documents with him. And, although she supposed he was delivering his report orally and without notes, relying on his prodigious memory, the question she kept asking was *what* was he remembering?

To her, the situation was clear. A courier had arrived yesterday with new instructions, which undoubtedly favored the cartel. The ambassador sympathized with the people's party, but he could hardly register their views in the face of contrary instructions and in the presence of the courier who had brought them. Therefore—get rid of him and pretend the instructions had never arrived. Then submit to the U.N. the report that the ambassador had previously drawn up, and his object would be accomplished.

Isabel began weeping with uncontrolled wretchedness, because her husband was a murderer and because he'd be caught. They were twin tragedies, and they overwhelmed her.

Shortly after lunch, she saw the lieutenant climb the stairs to the attic. He came down with two cowhide bags. Then he was on the phone again, raging at someone and saying he was the lieutenant and he didn't want any personal assistant, he wanted the Secretary-General and this was a homicide and did they know what the word meant or didn't they.

After that, Greenwood had another long talk with the inspector, and again Isabel heard the same thing. U.N. or not, the lieutenant kept saying, he had enough evidence to make somebody fry, and was this New York or did it belong to the U.N. now? Then he calmed down and said sure, he'd get a warrant, and if that would make everybody happy, why hadn't they told him in the first place?

He was gone for an hour and then he came back and went into the study. An assistant D.A. arrived and Isabel could hear the lieutenant saying that the report was written on two different typewriters and he could prove it.

She saw now that she had only drawn the net tighter and provided one more piece of evidence against the ambassador. She'd sought to be clever, loyal, resourceful. From the moment she'd returned from the concert yesterday and found the body in the living room, she'd thought only of her husband. She'd been petrified, dazed, and the gruesomeness of that corpse would haunt her forever. Nevertheless, she'd forced herself to approach it and pick up the briefcase. It was chained to the dead wrist, she couldn't open it.

She'd assumed she was alone in the house, for the ambassador's hearing was acute. No matter how deeply he was absorbed in his work, he heard every sound. The shot would have brought him running.

She'd stood there, scared, shocked, uncertain. Then, afraid she'd keel over and faint, she'd rushed out of the room, banged the door shut, and fled the house. She'd wandered aimlessly and tried to decide what to do, but she couldn't make up her mind until she knew where the ambassador had been at the time of the shooting.

After she'd managed to calm down, she returned to the house for the second time. To her surprise, the body was gone and the ambassador was sitting downstairs. His shoes were scuffed and there were two small, brown seed burrs clinging to his trousers. He said she was late and that there was barely time to dress for the dinner that the South American delegates were giving. They had at no time mentioned to each other the existence of the dead man.

Now, worried by the events of the day and fearing the worst, she went to the bedroom and waited anxiously for the ambassador.

Around six she saw a U.N. car drive up to the house. A uniformed chauffeur opened the door and the ambassador got out. He was carrying a cowhide dispatch case. The chain that had fastened it to the courier's wrist was missing, but she could have identified the case anywhere.

She flew downstairs and she was at the entrance when the ambassador walked in. He said, "Hello, Isabel," and she said, "Hello, darling. Did it come off all right?"

He smiled contentedly. "Oh, quite. No trouble at all."

"We won?"

"Naturally."

"And who are we?"

"We," he said, "are what we always were. The stanch adherents of our convictions."

Then the lieutenant appeared. "Hello," the ambassador said. "You still here? Crime still flourishing?"

"That's up to you," Greenwood answered. "I want to ask you a few questions. The Secretary-General—" he twisted his lips and pronounced the title with sarcasm— "said it was okay."

"Well, come along, then. You too, Isabel. You won't want to miss this."

The lieutenant gave her a sour look, but he acquiesced.

The ambassador led the way to the living room. He had removed his coat, but he still had the dispatch case under his arm. He sat down on the couch and said, "Well, found out anything?"

"Quite a bit," said the lieutenant. He leaned back in the blanketed chair and took a paper from his pocket. "This means I can make an arrest. It has the name of the person who killed André Madise."

"So you've found out the victim's name, have you? Although that shouldn't have been difficult."

"It was a cinch," said the lieutenant, "even if you held out on us this morning. Madise got to the airport early yesterday afternoon. He was carrying two bags and he had a dispatch case chained to his wrist. The chain made a mark and we have photographs of it. He had confidential papers to deliver personally to you. I guess you got them all right."

"Let's not guess. Let's confine ourselves to facts."

"Facts," the lieutenant said. He took a number of papers from his pocket and consulted them.

"Madise took a taxi from the airport to here, driven by George Pisano. It was a six-buck ride and he paid in new currency, with a dollar tip. He walked into this house at four o'clock and was shot in the chair I'm sitting in right now." He looked for an effect and didn't get it. "I ripped the seat off the chair and sent it down to the lab. It's got Madise's blood on it. And you were here at four, you admitted it."

"Upstairs, working," said the ambassador.

"The body was dragged across the room and pushed out of that French door and dumped off the veranda. Then it was hauled down the hill and left in the gully, where a man by the name of Oscar Smith spotted it this morning. We found Madise's two suitcases upstairs in the attic. The dispatch case is in your lap right now. And the stuff that was in it was lying on your desk, only there were some changes made on it that had the identifying characteristics of your own typewriter. That explains your motive, too. You switched documents and didn't want the courier to give you away. So I got a warrant for your arrest. For homicide."

The ambassador shrugged. "If you believe I killed Madise in order to substitute a document, you have to know what document he brought with him. Otherwise he might prove to be my friend and political ally, whose backing I needed. Do you know his political affiliations? Or mine?"

"International politics don't interest me," the lieutenant said. "I'm a cop."

"You're doing yourself a disservice."

"Listen, I know you got a big fight on back home, the National Socalist party and the Social Nationalist party, and they knock each other off like a bunch of Brooklyn hoodlums. But to me, a killer's a killer, and I lock 'em all up."

"Commendable zeal, but are you using your great powers of intelligence?"

"About this warrant—"

"Certainly, but let us return to logic first."

"I never left it, mister."

"Good. Then isn't it obvious that the only people who could have been waiting here for the courier were myself, my wife, and the two servants?"

"She was at a concert, and Paul and Katie were with this cousin. I never saw alibis that checked out so good."

"In my country, we have a saying that only the guilty have good alibis. For the man—or woman—is poor indeed who hasn't a friend ready to commit perjury for him. So, for the moment let us forget alibis and consider the character and reputation of the servants."

"They been working here for ten years," the lieutenant said. "A good, church-going couple with money in the bank. Are you telling me that, after being respectable all their lives, somebody can come along and pay them to commit homicide?"

"You make my point nicely, and now let's consider me for a moment. You have a warrant with a name written on it. How do you know I'm that person? Simply because I walked down the stairs this morning, looking as if I lived here?"

"With your harem," Isabel added.

Greenwood gave her a wry look, and she reacted with a sunny

smile. Greenwood said to the ambassador, "Do you deny your identity?"

"Lieutenant, I'm trying to help you avoid a serious blunder. How do you know I'm that man? Have you made sure of the point?"

"I'll bet my gun and shield on it."

"I'm not interested in acquiring them, but I have an important request to make before you serve your warrant. Would you be good enough to call Paul, the butler, and ask him to fetch the Christmas ornaments?"

"Huh?" said Greenwood. "What do you want that stuff for, in April?"

"I don't. But if he doesn't know where they are, after ten years, it proves he's an impostor, doesn't it? I believe the possibility is well worth investigating. Don't you?"

For answer, the lieutenant left the room.

After the arrest, he explained. "I located the real Paul and Katie. They said they got a wire Friday morning telling them you weren't coming and not to stay on in the house. When I showed this pair in the kitchen that I had another Paul and Katie who knew every detail of this place, they cracked. They killed Madise and substituted papers that would change the whole nature of your report. They had you down for the fall guy, too. But how did you figure they were phonies?"

"The folding chair," said the ambassador. "I mentioned it this morning. Would a real butler watch a guest struggle with the mechanism of one of those idiotic folding things and not even offer to help? Impossible, my friend."

Greenwood broke into his lopsided grin. "You spotted it all right," he said. "But why didn't you come out with it this morning?"

The ambassador looked shocked. "What!" he exclaimed. "Spoil Isabel's fun?"

The lieutenant blinked, then gave up, and left.

Isabel said, "Vickie, I think you're a humbug. I bet you saw Paul come back here yesterday afternoon, when according to his alibi he was miles away. You didn't deduce anything at all."

"Perhaps," the ambassador admitted. "But if I'd said so this morning, my report would have been suspect, or at the very least buried under the headlines of a murder story. Whereas this way I gained a day's time and forced the police department to learn something about the U.N."

"Big Shot?" she said, smiling.

"Quite. Big Shot Victor. And I have a piece of advice for you, my dear. You see, the wisdom of my country is preserved in traditional proverbs, and one of them says, 'At night a woman's place is in her husband's bed, and not at the typewriter.' "

"We have a proverb, too," she said. " 'To the victor belong the spoils.' "

He gave her a look of appreciation. "Nothing spoilt about you. . . ."

Fear and Trembling's

BY MICHAEL GILBERT

"You can book straight through to Heidelberg," said Mr. Leonard Caversham, "but it's a long and tiring journey, and I'd suggest that you break it at Cologne. You can go on next morning."

"I've never been to Germany before," said the man. "Matter of fact, I dropped quite a few bombs on it during the war."

"It might perhaps be wiser not to mention that when you get there," said Mr. Caversham with a smile.

"Could you book me a room in a hotel at Cologne?"

"Certainly. It will take a couple of days to arrange. If you come back at the end of the week, I should have the tickets and reservations all ready for you."

"And if I am going to stop the night at Cologne, I suppose I ought to notify the hotel in Heidelberg that I shall be a day late."

"We could do that for you, too," said Mr. Caversham.

Before he had come to work at Trembling's Tours, Mr. Caversham sometimes wondered why anyone should employ someone else to do a simple job like booking a ticket or making a reservation. Now he was beginning to understand that such a simple assignment could be stretched to include quite a number of other services. He had spent the previous afternoon telephoning four different hotels in Amsterdam in one of which a lady was certain she had left her jewel case. (It was found later in the bottom of her husband's suitcase.)

As the ex-bomber pilot departed, Roger Roche came through from the back office. He looked dusty, disorganized, and depressed. In the last two respects, as Mr. Caversham knew, appearances were deceptive. Roger had shown himself, in the short time he had been with Trembling's Tours, a competent and irrepressibly cheerful courier.

"What a crowd," he said, running his stubby fingers through his mop of light hair. "What a bleeding marvelous collection."

"Were they worse than the last lot, Roger?"

"Compared with this crowd, the last lot were a school treat. We had a dipsomaniac, a kleptomaniac, five ordinary maniacs, and two old women who never stopped quarreling. What bothered 'em most was who sat next to the window. 'On my right,' I said, 'you will hobserve the magnificent Tyrolean panner-rammer of the Salzkammergut.' 'I *told* you it was going to be extra-special today, Gertrude. I can't think why I let you have the window. We'll change at lunchtime.' 'You had it all yesterday.' '*Yesterday* was just forests.' "

Mr. Caversham laughed. He noticed that when Roger was reporting his own remarks he lapsed into exaggerated cockney, while the observations of his passengers were reproduced in accurate suburbanese.

"You get well tipped for your pains," he said. "The last lot were mad about you."

"Ah! There was a girl on the last lot—and when I say a girl, I mean a girl. Nothing in this bunch under ninety."

The bell sounded behind the counter.

"I'm wanted," said Mr. Caversham. "You'll have to hold the fort."

"I was going to have lunch."

"It'll only be five minutes."

Mr. Caversham went through the door behind the counter and along the passage. He was of average height, thick, and he moved with deliberation.

The room at the end of the passage was still known as the Founder's Room, having belonged to Mr. Walcott Trembling, who had organized and accompanied tours at a time when a visit to the Continent was an adventure, when a tourist expected to be swindled from the moment he arrived at Calais, and a careful family carried its drinking water with it.

Arthur Trembling, his great-grandson, rarely found time to visit the Continent himself, being, as he told his friends, "snowed under" with the work of the agency, the largest in Southampton, and still one of the best-known in the country.

Mr. Caversham looked at him inquiringly.

Mr. Trembling said, "I believe you've got a car here, haven't you?"

"Yes," said Mr. Caversham. He drove into Southampton every day from the furnished cottage he had rented on the fringes of the New Forest.

"I wouldn't bother you, but my car's tied up at the garage. I wondered if you could run a parcel round to my brother Henry's shop."

"No trouble at all," said Mr. Caversham. "The only thing is that it'll leave the front office empty. Mr. Snow is away this week, and Mr. Belton's having lunch."

"Who's there now?"

"I left Roger holding the fort."

"He can go on holding it. It won't take you more than ten minutes."

"Right," said Mr. Caversham. "Where's the parcel?"

Mr. Trembling had the grace to look embarrassed.

"I'm afraid I assumed you'd say yes. The parcel's in the trunk of your car already. It's quite a big one."

"That's all right," said Mr. Caversham. He was placid and obliging—qualities which, in the few weeks he had been there, had already endeared him to his employer.

His ancient Standard was in the corner of the yard, outside the garage (in which, when they were not speeding down the motorways of Europe, the Trembling forty-seater touring coaches were housed). Mr. Caversham glanced into the trunk compartment of his car. In it was a large square parcel, wrapped in brown paper and well corded. It would, he guessed, be books. Henry Trembling, Arthur's brother, was a secondhand bookseller.

Mr. Caversham drove slowly and carefully. He was not sorry to be out of the office. His course took him along the quays, outside the ramparts of the old town, and into the modern area of shops clustered round the railway station. Henry, a stouter, whiter, more paunchy version of his brother, helped him take out the parcel. It was surprisingly heavy—but books always weigh a lot. Henry pressed a pound note into Mr. Caversham's hand.

"For your trouble and your petrol," he said. It seemed generous payment for a quarter-mile run, but Mr. Caversham said nothing. As he drove back to the office he whistled softly between his teeth.

Strangely enough, he was thinking of Lucilla.

Lucilla was something of a mystery in the office. She was Arthur Trembling's secretary. She had been there longer than any other member of the staff—which was not saying a great deal, for Trembling's paid their employees badly and parted with them rapidly. But it made Lucilla all the more inexplicable, for she was not only competent, she was positively beautiful.

The only theory which made sense to the other employees of Trembling's was that she was Arthur's mistress. "Though what she can see in him," as Roger said to Mr. Caversham, "beats me. I should have said he had as much sex in him as a flat soda-water bottle." Mr. Caversham had agreed. He agreed with almost everybody.

When he got back, he found Lucilla in the front office, dealing with a lady who wished to take four children and a Labrador to Ireland. He thought she looked worried and, for a girl of her remarkable poise, a little off-balance.

When she had dealt with the customer, she came across to him.

"I suppose Roger wouldn't wait any longer for his lunch," said Mr. Caversham.

"The poor boy, yes. He was hungry. Where have you been?"

"Running errands for the boss," said Mr. Caversham. He was an observant man, and now that Lucilla was close to him he could read the signs quite clearly—the tightening round the mouth, the strained look in her eyes; he could even see the tiny beads of perspiration on her attractive, outward-curving upper lip.

"What's up?" he said.

"I can't talk now," she said. "I've got to go back—to him. Can you get out for half an hour at teatime?"

"Should be all right," said Mr. Caversham. "Four o'clock. Belton can carry things for half an hour. We'll go to the Orange Room."

Lucilla nodded, and disappeared. Mr. Caversham reflected that it was girls who were cool and collected most of the time who really went to pieces when trouble came. And trouble was coming. Of that he had been certain since the previous day when he had heard Lucilla screaming at Arthur Trembling in his office.

The Orange Room was one of those tea shops which shut out the sunlight with heavy curtains, and only partially dispel the gloom with economy-size electric bulbs. A table in the far corner was as safe a place for the confessional as could have been devised.

Lucilla said, "He's a beast—a vile beast. And speaking for myself, I've stood it long enough. For over a year he's been stringing me along, promising to marry me. First he was ill. Then his mother was ill. His mother! I ask you. What's she got to do with whether he gets married or not?"

Mr. Caversham grunted sympathetically. It was all he felt that was expected of him.

"If he thinks he's going to get off scot-free, he can think again," said Lucilla. "He's up to something, something criminal, and I'm going to put the police on to him."

Mr. Caversham leaned forward with heightened interest and said, "Now what makes you think that?"

"It's something to do with the tours. Every time a tour comes back, there's a big parcel in his office. It's something he pays the tour drivers to bring back for him."

"All of them?"

"I don't expect all of them. Maybe there're some he can't bribe. But Roger's one of them. There's a secret compartment in each of the coaches."

"Did Roger tell you that?"

"No. Basil told me."

Mr. Caversham remembered Basil—a black-haired boy, with buck-teeth, who had been very fond of Lucilla.

"What is it? Watches? Drugs? Perfume?"

"Basil doesn't know. It was just a big, heavy parcel. But I'm going to find out this evening. He's leaving early—there's a Rotarian meeting."

"The parcel isn't in his office now. I took it down to his brother's bookshop."

"Yes, but he took something out of it first. I came in when he was packing it up again. And if it's something valuable, it'll be in his private safe."

"To which," said Mr. Caversham, with a ghost of a smile, "you have, no doubt, a duplicate key."

"No, I haven't. But I know where he keeps his key. It's in a stupid little so-called secret drawer in the desk. I found out about it months ago."

"Few things remain hidden from an observant woman," said Mr. Caversham. "Are you asking me to help you?"

"That's just what I am asking."

"I agree. Two heads are better than one. What I suggest is this, I'll go down this evening and keep an eye on the bookshop. You have a look in the safe. I shouldn't take anything—just look. We'll meet later and add up what we've got. If it's enough to put old Trembling away, we'll let the police have it."

"Could we talk out at your place?"

"It's a bit off the beaten track."

"All the better. I've got a car."

"Eight o'clock, then," said Mr. Caversham. "Nip back now. We don't want to be seen together."

He gave her two minutes' start, paid the bill, and walked back thoughtfully. Possibly he was wondering how Lucilla knew where he lived. He could not recollect that he had ever told her.

At twenty past five Arthur Trembling walked through the front office, scattering a general "Good night" as he went. Mr. Caversham thought that he, too, looked preoccupied. Evidently his Rotarian speech was weighing on his mind.

Mr. Caversham helped Mr. Belton to close down the front office, got out his car, and drove it toward the station, parking it in the yard. The last bit, he thought, would be better done on foot. He had noticed a sidewalk café nearly opposite the bookshop. He took a seat in the bow window, ordered plaice and chips, opened an evening paper, and settled down to watch.

In the first half hour one old lady and one schoolboy entered the bookshop. Neither stayed more than three minutes. Shortly after six Henry Trembling emerged, put the shutters up, padlocked an iron arm into place across the door, and departed.

"And that," said Mr. Caversham, "would appear to be that." Nevertheless, he remained where he was. His interest had shifted to the office building next to the bookshop. This was a building with an entrance opening on the street, inside which he could see a board, with names on it, and a staircase which no doubt served the several offices in the building.

Mr. Caversham noted a number of men and women coming out. He also noted quite a few middle-aged and elderly men going in—a fact which seemed a little odd at that time of night. But what was odder still—none of them seemed to reappear.

Mr. Caversham scribbled a rough tally on the edge of his paper. "White hair, horn-rims, 6:18." "Fat, red carnation, 6:35." "Tall, thin, checked ulster, 6:50." By half past seven he had a list of eleven people, and had exhausted the patience of his waitress. He paid his bill and left. As he came out of the café, a twelfth man was disappearing into the office building.

Farther down the street, on the other side, a red-faced man was sitting at the wheel of an old gray Buick. There was nothing odd about him except that Mr. Caversham, who missed little, had noticed him there when he went into the café nearly two hours earlier.

He walked back to his car and drove home.

The furnished cottage he had rented lay at the end of a short straight lane, rutted and dusty in summer, barely passable in winter. Some people might have found it lonely, but Mr. Caversham was fond of solitude. Now, in late spring, the trees were in full leaf, and the approach to the cottage was a tunnel of shadow.

He touched on his headlights as he swung in off the main road, and braked just in time. The smart two-seater Fiat was parked in the middle of the drive, and not more than two yards in.

"Women!" said Mr. Caversham. He got out and approached the car cautiously. Lucilla was in the passenger seat. She did not turn her head as he came up. Mr. Caversham opened the door on the driver's side. The opening of the door operated the interior light, which came on and showed him Lucilla more clearly.

She was dead, and had been dead, he guessed, for some time. Her face was already livid. She had been strangled, and the cord which had strangled her was still round her neck, cut so deep into the flesh that only the ends could be seen, dangling at the front like a parody of a necktie.

Mr. Caversham got out of the car and closed the door softly. He stood in the drive, balanced squarely on his legs, his thick body bent forward, his arms hanging loosely. His head turned slowly, left and right. He looked like a Western gunfighter at the moment of the draw.

Abruptly he swung round, returned to his own car, jumped in, backed it out into the road, and drove it a couple of hundred yards before turning through an open field gate and running in under the trees. He had switched off all the lights before he started. Now he locked the car, and ambled back, at a gentle trot, by the way he had come. At the corner of the lane he stopped again, to look and listen. Dusk was giving way to dark. Nothing disturbed the stillness of the evening.

Mr. Caversham allowed a slow minute to elapse. Then he walked up to the car, opened the door, and climbed in without a second glance at the dead girl. The ignition key, as he had noted, was still in the lock. The engine, which was still warm, started at first touch. He backed the car out into the road. From the direction of Southampton a car was coming, fast. He could see the headlights as it roared over the humpback bridge beside Shotton.

Mr. Caversham grinned to himself unpleasantly, swung the little car away from Southampton, and drove off.

Half a mile down the road he turned into a drive and got out. It took him five minutes to shift the body into the back seat and then cover it with a rug. After that he switched on his sidelights and took to the road again. He drove quickly and surely, handling the strange car as though he had been driving it for months. A fast circuit of Southampton's sprawling suburbs brought him into the town again from the west. A few minutes later he was examining the road signs in a large development, which seemed to have been laid out by a naval architect.

Beyond Hawke Road and Frobisher Drive he found Howe Crescent. Number 17 was a pleasant, detached house, with a neat garden and a separate entrance to a fair-sized garage. Mr. Caversham drove straight in. The owners were, as he well knew, in Venice. He had himself sold them their tickets a fortnight before, and had helped them make arrangements for the boarding-out of their cat.

A bus ride and a few minutes' walk brought Mr. Caversham back to the place where he had left his own car. He climbed in and drove it sedately toward Southampton. As he entered the car park of the cinema he looked at his watch. It was just over three quarters of an hour since he had found Lucilla. He seemed to have covered a lot of ground.

It was a cowboy film, and Mr. Caversham settled back to enjoy it.

The film finished at eleven o'clock and ten minutes later he was turning into the lane which led to his cottage. A police car was parked in front of his gate.

"Can I help you?" said Mr. Caversham. "Perhaps you have lost your way."

"Is your name Caversham? We'd like a word with you."

"Come in," said Mr. Caversham. He opened the front door, which was not locked, turned on the lights, and led the way in. The last time he had seen the red-faced man he had been seated behind the wheel of an old gray Buick, on the opposite side of the road to Henry Trembling's bookshop.

The man said, "I'm Detective Sergeant Lowther of the Southampton Police. This is Detective Sergeant Pratt."

"Good evening," said Mr. Caversham. He managed to add a question mark at the end of it.

"We've come out here because we had a message that a girl's body had been found in a car."

"And had it?"

Sergeant Lowther looked at Mr. Caversham. It was not exactly a look of hostility, nor was it friendly. It was the sort of look that a boxer might give an opponent as he stepped into the ring.

He said, "Neither the body nor the car was here when we arrived."

"And had it been here?"

"According to a boy who came past the end of the road at half-past seven, there was a car here. A Fiat. He happened to notice the number, too."

"Boys often do notice these things. I expect you'll be able to trace it."

"We have traced it. It belongs to a Miss Lucilla Davies." The sergeant paused. Mr. Caversham said nothing. "We contacted her lodging. She hasn't been home."

"The night," said Mr. Caversham, "is still young."

"Look—" said the sergeant, "I said—Lucilla Davies. Do you mean to say you don't know her?"

"Of course I know her. She works in the same place that I do. On a rather superior level. She is Mr. Trembling's secretary."

"Then why didn't you say so before?"

"Why should I?"

"Look," said the sergeant, "do you mind telling us where you've been?"

"I've been to the cinema. The Rialto. The film was called *Two-finger Knave.* And just in case you think I'm not being entirely truthful, I should mention that the film broke down after the third reel, and we had to wait five minutes while it was being mended. The manager came on the stage and apologized."

"Look—" said the sergeant.

"And now, would you very much mind going away and letting me get to bed. If you will, I'll consider forgiving you for entering my house, without a warrant, in my absence."

"Entering—?"

"Well," said Mr. Caversham, "I'm quite certain I didn't make that muddy mark on the linoleum there. You can see it quite clearly. It looks to me like a boot, not a shoe."

"Look—" said the sergeant.

"However, you did at least have the delicacy not to search my bedroom."

Sergeant Lowther's face got a shade redder than before. "Assuming," he said, "for the sake of argument, but not admitting it—assuming that we had a look in here, just to see if you were at home, how would you know that we didn't go upstairs as well?"

"I don't think you could have." Mr. Caversham whistled softly, and the great dog rose from the pool of shadow at the top of the stairs and came padding down, his tail acock, his amber eyes gleaming.

"Well, I'm damned," said Sergeant Lowther. "Has he been lying there all the time?"

"All the time," said Mr. Caversham. "And when you're gone, I expect he'll tell me all about you. I understand a lot of what he says —and he understands everything that I say."

The dog's mouth half opened in a derisory smile, revealing white teeth.

"He's our man all right," said Sergeant Lowther to Inspector Hamish next morning. "I didn't like his attitude—not one little bit."

"That dog of his," said Sergeant Pratt. "Fair gives me the creeps to think he was lying there all the time, watching us, and never made a sound."

Inspector Hamish was tall, bald, and cynical, with the tired, empty cynicism of a life devoted to police duties.

"Have you checked at the cinema?"

"Yes, and there was a break in the film—just like he said."

"Then what makes you think he didn't go to the cinema?"

"He was too damned cool. Too ready with all the answers."

"You ask me," said Sergeant Pratt, "I wouldn't be surprised if you found he'd got a record."

"Do you think he's mixed up with Trembling's little game?"

"Could easily be. He was hanging round watching the bookshop last night, like I told you."

The telephone rang. Inspector Hamish answered it. His expression changed not at all. At the end he said, "All right, thank you." And to Sergeant Lowther, "We're going out to seventeen Howe Crescent. The car's there. The girl's in the back."

At about this time Mr. Caversham and Roger were opening up the front office at Trembling's. Roger seemed to be suffering from a hangover. Mr. Caversham appeared to be normal.

"It was some party," said Roger. "One of the old buffers who was on the first tour organized it. A reunion—can you imagine it?"

"I can," said Mr. Caversham with a slight shudder.

"The idea was, we had a bottle of booze from each of the countries we'd visited. All nine of them. We finished them, too. And that girl I was telling you about—the one on the first tour—"

The bell behind Mr. Caversham's desk rang.

"What does *he* want?" said Roger. "He's never been in before ten o'clock since I've been here."

The bell rang again. Mr. Caversham sighed, put down the three-color triptych advertising an economy tour in the Costa Brava, and made his way along the passage.

Mr. Trembling was sitting behind his desk. His face was half hidden by his hand. When he spoke his voice was under careful control.

"Have you any idea where Miss Davies is?"

"Hasn't she got here yet?"

"No," said Mr. Trembling. "I telephoned her house. The lady there was most upset. Lucilla hadn't been back all night. They've just telephoned the police."

"How *very* worrying," said Mr. Caversham. "But I expect she'll turn up. Mr. Foster was saying how sorry the Rotarians were to miss your speech last night."

For a moment it seemed that Mr. Trembling hadn't heard. Then he raised his head slowly, and Mr. Caversham saw his face. If he had not known what he did, he might have felt sorry for him.

"Yes," said Mr. Trembling. "I was sorry to disappoint them. I felt unwell at the last moment. A touch of gastric trouble."

"You ought to have gone straight home. Not come back to the office," said Mr. Caversham severely. "There's only one place when your stomach's upset. In bed, with a hot water bottle."

What was left of the color in it had drained out of Mr. Trembling's face. The pouches under his eyes were livid. Mr. Caversham thought, for a moment, that he might be going to faint, and took half a step forward.

"What do you mean?" It was a croak, barely audible.

In his most reasonable voice Mr. Caversham said, "I left my wallet in my desk and had to come back for it. I happened to see your car in the yard and a light on in the office. Are you sure you're all right?"

"Yes," said Mr. Trembling, with an effort. "I'm all right. That'll be all."

It won't be all, Mr. Caversham thought to himself, as he walked back. Not by a long chalk, it won't. You set a trap for her, didn't you? Let her see where you kept the key. Let her see you take something out of that parcel and put it in the safe. Let her know you were going to be away at a Rotarian meeting. Came back and caught her. She must have told you she was meeting me. Perhaps she did it in an attempt to save her own life. So when you'd finished, when she was no longer your secretary, no longer anything but a lump of dead flesh, you put her in her own car and drove her out to my place. Not very friendly. Then, I suppose, you rang up the police. Lucky you didn't do it ten minutes earlier. *I* should have been in trouble.

By this time Mr. Caversham was back in the shop. Mr. Belton was talking to a girl with a pony tail about day trips to Boulogne, and a sour old man was waiting in front of Mr. Caversham's desk with a complaint about British Railways. Mr. Caversham dealt with him dexterously enough, but his mind was not entirely on his work.

Most of it was on the clock.

The police, he knew, worked to a fairly rigid pattern. Fingerprinting and photography came first, then the pathologist. Then the immediate inquiries. These would be at Lucilla's lodgings. How long would all that take? A couple of hours perhaps. Then they would come to the place where she worked. Then things would really start to happen. No doubt about that.

"Where's that Roger?" said Belton.

"He was here earlier this morning," said Mr. Caversham. "I expect he's somewhere about."

"He's not meant to be gadding about. He's meant to be helping me," said Mr. Belton. "I don't know what's come over this place, lately. No organization."

It was nearly twelve o'clock before Roger reappeared. He was apologetic, but impertinent. Nor did he explain where he had been. Mr. Caversham said, "Now that you are here, I'll go out and get lunch, if no one has any objections."

No one had any objections. Mr. Caversham hurried into the public house down the street and ordered sandwiches. He was back within twenty-five minutes, and found a worried Mr. Belton alone.

"I'm glad you've got back so quickly," he said.

"What's up?"

"I wish I knew. Mr. Trembling isn't answering his telephone. And Roger seems to have disappeared."

A prickle of apprehension touched the back of Mr. Caversham's neck.

"Which way?"

"What are you talking about?"

"I asked you," said Mr. Caversham in a new and very urgent voice, "which way Roger went. Did he go out of the front door into the street?"

"No. He went out down the passage. Into the back yard, I should guess. What's happening? What is it all about, Mr. Caversham? What's going on, for God's sake?"

People had sometimes accused Mr. Caversham of being hard to the point of insensitivity. He did, however, appreciate that he was dealing with a badly frightened man, and at that moment, when there was so much to be done, he paused to comfort him.

"There's nothing here which need bother you," he said. "I promise you that. Indeed, I should say that right now you were the only person in this whole outfit who had nothing to worry about. Just keep the customers happy."

He disappeared through the door behind the counter, leaving Mr. Belton staring after him.

The door of the Founder's Room was closed, but not locked. Mr. Caversham opened it, without knocking, and looked inside. Arthur Trembling was seated in his tall chair behind his desk. He looked quite natural until you went close and saw the small neat hole which the bullet had made under the left ear, and the rather larger, jagged hole which it had made coming out of the right-hand side of the head.

Mr. Caversham sat on the corner of the desk and dialed a number. A gruff voice answered at once.

"Southampton Police," said Mr. Caversham calmly. "I'm speaking from the offices of Trembling's Tours. Yes, Trembling's. In Fawcet Street. Mr. Trembling has been shot. About ten minutes ago."

The voice at the other end tried to say something, but Mr. Caversham overrode it.

"The man responsible for the killing is using the name of Roger Roche. He's thirty, looks much younger, has untidy, light hair, and is lodging at forty-five Alma Crescent. Have you got that?"

"Who's that speaking?"

"Never mind me. Have you got that information? Because you'll have to act on it at once. Send someone to his lodgings, have the trains watched and the roads blocked."

"What did you say your name was?"

"I didn't," said Mr. Caversham, "but I told you what to do to catch this murderer, and if you don't do it quickly, you're going to be sorry."

He rang off and cast an eye round the office. There was no sign of any disturbance. A neat, cold, professional killing. If Mr. Belton had heard nothing, the gun must have been a silenced automatic.

The key was in the safe. Using a pencil, Mr. Caversham turned it, then carefully swung the safe door open. On the bottom shelf was a quarto-sized volume, in a plain gray binding, with no title.

He carried it to the desk and opened it. There was a blatant Teutonic crudity about the photographs inside which made even such an unimpressionable man as Mr. Caversham wrinkle his nose. He was still examining the book when a police car drew up in the yard, and Sergeant Lowther burst into the room.

"Ah," he said. "I might have known you'd be in on this one too. What's that you've got there? Yes, I see. *Very* pretty. Now, Mr. Caversham, perhaps you'll do some explaining."

"Not to you," said Mr. Caversham. He had heard another car draw up in the yard. A few seconds later Inspector Hamish came through the door. He looked coldly at Mr. Caversham.

"Have you picked him up yet?" asked Mr. Caversham.

"I got some garbled message," said the inspector, "about a man called Roger Roche. I thought I'd come and find out what it was all about before sounding a general alarm."

Mr. Caversham got to his feet. "Do you mean to say," he said, and there was a cold ferocity in his voice which made even the inspector stare, "that you have wasted ten whole minutes? If that's right, you're going to have something to answer for."

"Look here—"

"Would you ask the sergeant to leave the room, please."

Inspector Hamish hesitated, then said, "One minute, Sergeant—"

By the time he turned back, Mr. Caversham had taken something from his pocket. The inspector looked at it and said in quite a different tone of voice, "Well, Mr. Calder, if I'd only known—"

"That'll be the epitaph of the British Empire," said Mr. Calder. "Will you please, please get the wheels turning."

"Yes, of course. I'd better use the telephone."

An hour later Mr. Calder and Inspector Hamish were sitting in the Founder's Room. The photographers and fingerprint men had come and gone. The pathologist had taken charge of the body; and a police cordon, thrown round Southampton a good deal too late, had failed to catch Roger Roche.

"We'll pick him up," said the inspector.

"I doubt it," said Mr. Calder. "People like that aren't picked up easily. He'll be in France by this evening and God knows where by tomorrow."

"If someone had only told me—"

"There were faults on both sides," Mr. Calder admitted. "I expect I should have told you last night. There didn't seem any hurry at the time and I didn't know about Roger, then."

"If you wouldn't mind explaining," said the inspector, "in words of one syllable. I am only a simple policeman, you know."

"Let's begin at the beginning then," said Mr. Calder. "You knew that Trembling was smuggling in pornographic books for his brother to sell?"

"Yes. We're on to that now. There's a side entrance into his shop, from the ground-floor office next door. The cash customers used to go in that way after the shop was shut, and out by a back entrance into the mews. You'd be surprised if I told you the names of some of his customers."

"I doubt it," said Mr. Calder. "However, it wasn't an easy secret to keep. Too many couriers were involved. Soviet Intelligence got on to it. They put in an agent—Lucilla Davies—to nurse it along. She blackmailed Trembling. He could go on bringing in his dirty books, as long as he agreed to take out letters—and other things as well—for them. Trembling's became the main south coast post office for the Russians."

"Neat," said the inspector.

"Then our side got to hear about it, too. And sent me down. What happened was that Trembling got tired of being blackmailed into treason, and decided to remove Lucilla. I don't bame him for that, but I do blame him for leaving her in my front drive. I thought that was unnecessary. And very cramping for me. So I shifted her. However, I did ring up and tell you where to find her next morning."

"That was you, too, was it?"

"That was me. I thought if we played it properly, we'd be bound to provoke a countermove from the other side. They don't like their agents being bumped off. I guessed they'd send one of their best men down here—what I didn't realize was that he was *already* here. Roger fooled me completely."

"There's a moral to it somewhere, no doubt," said the inspector.

"The moral," said Mr. Calder, "is that if the various Intelligence Departments and M.I.5. and the Special Branch and ninety-six different police forces didn't all try to work independently of each other, but cooperated for a change, we might get better results."

"You'd better put that in your report," said Inspector Hamish. "Not that anyone'll take any notice."

"I'll put it in," said Mr. Calder. "But it won't do a blind bit of good."

These Good Children

BY GLADYS CLUFF

Eight-year-old Dotty Thompson opened the children's charades as Elaine, and the guests at the Pension Schwarz—all except Dotty's father and mother—settled back in their three rows of high-backed, red velvet seated chairs to wait politely for the program to be over: then Fraülein Elspeth would pass deliciously strong black coffee topped with whipped cream—*schlag,* she called it—and rich little seed-sprinkled cookies; for this was a party, a double farewell to the Thompson family, who were leaving for home the next morning, and a young vacationing teacher of mathematics from San Francisco, who happened to be returning on the same ship.

But Mr. Thompson had exclaimed aloud—and hastily subsided, red-faced, without explanation: how could you say your own child looked as if she belonged in a stained-glass window? A martyred saint, or sainted martyr! Martyred by what, for Pete's sake? As if there weren't enough saints around here now. America got along all right, didn't she, without dead saints and bishops everywhere you stepped: she had Teddy Roosevelt, what more did you want? (Mr. Thompson had been homesick from the day he sailed.) Good old America could take care of herself. And so, incidentally, could his daughter Dotty, who was no seventh daughter of a seventh daughter, but the considerably spoiled only child of J. L. Thompson, Hardware, Newbank, Ohio.

In that queerly dignified costume, though, and looking, through the frame of those big sliding doors, so *apart* from him in his regular blue serge suit, Dotty suddenly suggested—a Shining Messenger! He saw the idiotic words in heavy Old English lettering, as a picture title; he actually heard them—and scrubbed them from his mind in shocked embarrassment. That's what came of this foreign travel, rooting around in crazy old-world relics and superstitions. High time they were getting home.

"Sie ist wie eine Blume!" chanted Grossmutter Schwarz, and her daughter, who ran the pension, appreciated even more gratefully this angelic little girl who cast such a Pied Piper spell over less well-behaved children. So did the gaunt choirmaster from the village who gave Dotty singing lessons—free, by invitation!—in his Class of Mixed Children, and whom Mrs. Thompson had invited today because she guiltily suspected he could use the cookies and *schlag*. Dotty herself had also invited two village boys from the class, Franz because he spoke some English, and Adolf to help paint costumes.

"Schöne!" breathed all the ladies each time Dotty appeared—in every number; Dotty knew her showmanship. Square little Erica Schwarz, for instance, could hardly have floated down the river to Camelot on that ten-inch bench. Dotty had cast her as one of the buildings that marched by on the bank; she waved a flag that said RATHAUS in large German lettering, and both she and her family swelled solid with pride. True, in one of the more juvenile numbers Adolf broke all the ladies' hearts as Strewel Peter, child-victim of a horrifying avalanche of Just Desserts. And Franz had stolen the stage as the Hansel and Gretel witch. But next had come Joan of Arc on

her horse, and since the horse was no actor at all but only the old Shalott-to-Camelot ferry, Dotty as Joan led the field again.

And justly.

No one smiled even when the Maid stood on the wrong side and swung a reckless left leg over her mount, and four Angel Voices unveiled themselves from kitchen stools. For no one saw anything but Joan's face. Not Dotty's. Joan's.

It was white, lit from within; it would have burned your finger if you had touched it. It was literal absolute Dedication.

Transubstantiation. So that's what they mean, thought her mother, who did not believe in transubstantiation.

Nobody made a sound.

Then the doors slid back together, but the other children's mothers were still glancing uneasily from each other to Mrs. Thompson and away again when Franz announced that the final tableau would be Saint George and the Dragon, and it would take a minute to get the dragon ready.

"And you are to be this terrible dragon, no?" said his singing teacher, who had heard little else for days.

"Not any more," regretted Franz with surprising lack of bitterness. "All of a sudden this morning Dotty decided I couldn't be that after all." He grinned. "But I got to be the witch!" He banged the doors together.

"What's the matter, dear?" asked Mr. Thompson. His wife was looking strained. "Headache?"

No, just worried about Dotty again, she said, and muttered something that sounded to him like "possessed."—"That terrific intensity, John. It isn't healthy, it isn't *normal.* Oh, you never *will* understand. It's dangerous!"

"Shucks. That's the dramatic temperament, you've got it yourself—my cabbage."

Mrs. Thompson sighed. "It was those my-cabbage Frenchmen started her off. From the minute she set foot in Notre Dame Cathedral, she *was* Joan of Arc. I hoped that in this gentle fairy-tale

Austria she'd get unexalted and be something simple and *gemütlich,* like Snow White. But last night I heard her talking in her sleep, and when I woke her up she said she'd been "listening to her Voices!"

"A nightmare," diagnosed Mr. Thompson. "I told you, when she took that third piece of cherry strudel last night— Goodness, Dotty's healthy *enough.* Strong as a little horse."

"John, the child hasn't eaten a bite all day, I couldn't *make* her. And do you know why not? She says the Voices told her not to!"

"Probably the mothers of all those calves. If *I* have to eat veal just once more—!"

"Oh—! Didn't you see her *face?* Everybody in this room is uncomfortable."

"Say, you're the one seeing things! Gosh, sweetheart, you *are* upset!" He turned to Madame Michot on his left. "Headache," he explained, indicating his wife, and the guests forgot their self-consciousness in warm solicitudes and the virtues of Bromo-Seltzer. When the doors reopened on Saint George and the Dragon they gave wholehearted applause.

The dragon writhed stunningly in poison green, obviously the upstairs hall rug rolled into a cocoon; a fringed leather pillowcase made the head; the tail was masterly. The small boy inside this monster, little Adolf, had been happily surprised at this last-minute switch in casting, from scene painter to dragon, until in dress rehearsal his heretofore gentle friend Dotty had set her foot hard on his neck with a cry of triumph not to be borne from a girl; quiet little Adolf threw such a fit of temper that Dotty had to make him three feet more tail to swish and flourish before he would tolerate the indignity.

So the dragon outclassed Saint George at first. It roared and slashed around with its tail wonderfully, but in the end Saint George again got his foot on its neck and cried in a high, heartbreaking voice, "For God and Merrie England!"

The audience clapped and blew their noses, and this being the final number, Franz left the doors wide for friends and parents to come up and congratulate the actors. But Saint George still held his pose, head high and rigid, his heel grinding into the dragon; when the dragon tried to get up and take its bows, it couldn't. It squirmed so furiously that all the children and Mr. Thompson cheered.

As Saint George—Dotty—with white, stiff mouth tried to keep her foot in tableau position, Mrs. Thompson stared curiously at her determined, unmoving face; the child would bite right through her lip if she didn't relax. Even after the applause was all over, Dotty stood there, in character.

"Look, John!" said Mrs. Thompson under her breath. "His arms are fastened *inside* that rug. He can't even see to guard himself. If that's his neck she's stepping on, she'll hurt him." Her eyes, translating Dotty's tense face, narrowed. "I think she *wants* to hurt him. Stop her, John!"

"Of course she does, it's a fight." He leaned forward happily. "Hold 'em, Varsity!"

Abruptly Mrs. Thompson stood up.

"That *is* his neck!" she exclaimed.

Grossmutter Schwarz stumbled to her feet, too, and pointed with croaks of alarm to the frantically kicking dragon.

"Dotty!" commanded Mr. Thompson.

Dotty stood rigid, unhearing.

Mr. Thompson hurdled to the stage. But he tripped on the dragon's long tail. That hard-pressed animal gave one outraged roar, and with a final desperate heave, succeeded in rolling over and upsetting Saint George.

Sheepishly Mr. Thompson dusted himself off. "What you get for butting in," he muttered, and felt his bruised kneecap, and glowered at his wife. "But kids play so hard. They don't seem able to draw any line between a fairy tale and the Revolutionary War."

Everyone groaned agreement, except Mrs. Thompson. But this went unnoticed until she cried suddenly, "John! *Stop* her!"

Then they all saw what was happening.

Dotty had fallen, or hurled herself, on top of the dragon, and where her heel had ground, her hands now squeezed tightly, the thumbs bent back with pressing. Neither she nor the dragon moved.

Madame Michot screamed, everybody rushed forward, and Mr. Thompson jerked Dotty away, resisting wildly. Even when he had her off the floor in his arms, her hands continued tautly to encircle the dragon's neck, so that its head lifted too. In twenty seconds—Dotty was still screaming, "Let me go!"—they had the boy free and out of his costume. But he did not move.

Authoritatively Grossmutter Schwarz took over. Very gently she lifted his head and turned it, while Mrs. Thompson looked fearfully from the child's face to the old woman's. Then Grossmutter Schwarz laid the small head back, smoothing the dark hair from the brow, and in answer to the terror in Mrs. Thompson's eyes, she nodded reassuringly. "Watch."

The boy's chest shuddered, rose in a stuttering sigh, and he coughed.

"Gut," pronounced Grossmutter Schwarz. But she turned to stare at Dotty, crying passionately in her father's arms. *"Warum?"* she asked, bewildered. "Why?"

Mr. Thompson took his hand away from his child's mouth.

"You spoiled it!" she screamed. "The Voices told me to *kill* the dragon!"

"Dotty," ordered her mother, "stop talking like that. Little girls don't—"

"You didn't *let* me!" Dotty sobbed. "I *could* have done what they said! Joan of Arc did, I could have, too!" Her voice rose high in hysteria. "The dragon got away! I'm *afraid* of the dragon!"

Mrs. Thompson comforted the stunned little boy while her husband strove to quiet Dotty. "There there, darling," he soothed her. "My goodness, it wasn't a *real* dragon!" He laughed with his old bluster again, now that everything was all right. "Look, honey—it's only little Adolf!"

But Dotty cried and cried, until she was sick.

Her father welcomed this anticlimax with pure relief, and tweaked his wife's ear. "You see, my cabbage?" he boasted kindly. "Cherry strudel all the time!"

Halfway up the stairs Dotty was asleep in his arms, exhausted.

With their door closed and Dotty in bed, Mrs. Thompson burst into tears. "I'm glad we're going *home,*" she said violently. "I don't know why we ever came."

"Because Dotty wanted to, that's why. Some trumped-up reason about a friend of a friend of a friend. That child winds you right around her little finger."

"She could wind the Statue of Liberty around her finger. John—I'm *afraid* to cross Dotty. Oh, yes, I know, she's healthy. But in some *other* way she's too—vulnerable."

They stood looking at the still-flushed face of the heavily sleeping little girl.

"Just the same," announced Mr. Thompson, as head of a family that needed some heading, "Miss Dotty has got to come down off her high horse. Beginning now. She got crossed all right today, in the very nick of time."

"And it made her sick."

"Well, whatever made her sick, she got over it."

"I'm not so sure," said Mrs. Thompson uneasily. "I don't like the way she looks. Or breathes. Do we *have* to go tomorrow?"

"Yes, we do," said Mr. Thompson fervently.

All the way to Paris Dotty was train-sick, and the first night at sea, very suddenly and unaccountably, she ran up an alarmingly high fever. The doctors on board couldn't find a thing wrong with the child, but she died that night.

The young teacher did what he could for the stricken parents, but he felt it to be useless: what they said was true, their lives were over with the death of their only child. Mr. Thompson thought, for a little while, that Mrs. Thompson had encouraged Dotty into living so wholly in an unreal, exalted world that she came not to know the difference between it and reality, and couldn't take it when she found out. Mrs. Thompson thought, for a little while, that Mr. Thompson had never understood Dotty, and his violence had snapped something vital in her: like wakening a sleepwalker too abruptly, which everyone knew could be fatal. And to start out on an ocean voyage with a child still in shock—they should both have known better than that.

The young teacher knew nothing, of course, of their private thoughts, but he did know that whatever these might be, and whether true or false, they would merge, given time, into the single too simple fact that Dotty was dead, what matter whose fault?

But *he* had a year's class work to organize in two weeks' time, and he liked his subject. The sad but brief little Thompson drama would fade comfortably from his mind; after all it was not his drama. As a matter of fact he never saw the Thompsons again.

He hadn't thought of them now, he would have guessed, in a quarter of a century.

But over the disturbing years since those pleasant, early nineteen hundreds, even a mathematics teacher had to wonder about many things. The clean-ruled line between the beliefs and the disbeliefs of the middle-aged professor listening to Mr. Kaltenborn's doomful voice announcing the abandonment of Czechoslovakia already had become a jagged graph of crevasses and stalagmites.

And then one of those sharp new up-slants in his recognition of the possible occurred with such a jolt that the wild tilt of it would stay with him the rest of his life.

As he turned off the radio, suddenly he saw, complete, unfaded, that last day at the Pension Schwarz.

And reason tilted. For the time fitted. And Bavaria; a village in the Salzkammergut. And how could you be mistaken about a name like that? That boy's name *was* Schicklgruber. Adolf Schicklgruber.

The Queen's Jewel

BY JAMES HOLDING

When she found the contorted body of Duke, her dog, lying half concealed in the long grass on the hillside behind her hotel, Jane Farquhar knew that the American was more interested in the jewel than he was in her—and would kill to get it.

She stared at the stiffening body of the big dog. In Duke's convulsed posture and the rictus of pain that had bared his teeth, she could plainly see the cause of his death. Poison.

She felt first shock, then grief, and finally, stronger than these, she felt anger—a searing sense of outrage that focused on the American and blotted out in an instant any tender womanly feelings she may have entertained for him before. Perhaps he *was* her only living relative, as he said, the final leaf on the last twig of the American branch of her family. But standing over her murdered mastiff, it was very clear to her that Arthur Campbell wanted the jewel from her and nothing else.

He had arrived from Hluhluwe driving a rented Plymouth sedan in which (he said) he had been taking a leisurely trip about Southern Africa, visiting the diamond mines, gold fields, and game reserves. As a fitting climax to his vacation trip, he had planned (he said) a few days' visit at the Upland Hotel in Swaziland, of which small inn he knew his last surviving relative, Jane Farquhar, was sole owner and proprietress.

Jane had made him welcome, of course. He was a pleasant, handsome man who soon let Jane see that he was not unaware of her back-country charm and her generously feminine figure. He was a tall rangy fellow with pale eyes the color of weathered thatch and a marvelously modulated baritone voice that compensated for his faintly raffish manner.

Jane assigned him the largest and airiest of the half dozen rondavel huts that made up the hotel's "cottage" quarters. It was only one cottage removed from the one to which she herself retired each night in an attempt to escape momentarily the pressing demands of guests and staff, most of whom were housed in the main building of the inn.

"Well, Jane," he said that first night after dinner, "it's wonderful to meet you. Mother used to tell me you were the last of the Farquhars and that I ought to look you up sometime. So here I am!"

Jane smiled. "I'm glad to meet you, too, Arthur," she said. "Think of it! I have a cousin! How did your mother know about me?"

"She was a nut on genealogy," the American said reminiscently. "Had all the dope on our relatives back for hundreds of years. And that's pretty far back, for Americans."

"How was she related to the Farquhars?"

"She *was* a Farquhar until she married my father. She was the last one left in America. We're about forty-second cousins, eight times removed, I'd say at a guess. But cousins, all the same."

"How nice," Jane said.

"You bet." His gaze was approving. "Mother said that back about eighteen twenty, the Farquhar family split up. There were three brothers, the way she got it. The youngest one went to America, the oldest one emigrated to South Africa, and the middle one stayed in Scotland. You're the last of the African branch, I'm the last of the American branch, and the Scottish branch died out a hundred years ago."

She said, "That's about the way father explained it to me. Except he didn't know that any of the American branch survived. You've no idea how glad I am to have a relative, Arthur. Even a forty-second cousin."

His beautiful baritone reached out to her caressingly. "My dear Jane," he said softly, "you're not a bit gladder than I am." He lit a cigarette and went on in his casual, gossipy way, "Mother was a great one for family history, all right. But she had one queer bee buzzing around in her bonnet all the same."

Jane could feel it coming. She felt the premonitory whisper of uneasiness that invariably preceded mention of the jewel by anyone outside the family. But then, she told herself with quick relief, the American wasn't an outsider. He was a member of the family. In fact, he was all the family she had left.

She said, "What do you mean?"

"Something about a wonderful heirloom in your branch of the family, Jane. Mother said your father had it, since he was the oldest son of the oldest son and the last of the line. Mother called it the Queen's Jewel, but she didn't know much about it, I guess, except that you'd have inherited it, now that your father's gone."

Jane was silent. She found herself liking this man very much. Already his presence had removed some of the weight of loneliness she carried about with her. She said slowly, "We *do* have an heirloom, Arthur."

The American's pale eyes narrowed a little. "Tell me about it, Jane."

Jane took a deep breath and patted the broad head of Duke, who was curled up at her feet, his chin upon her toe. "Well," she began, "it belonged to Mary, Queen of Scots. It was given her on her wedding day by her first husband, Francis, the Dauphin of France."

The American said, "Mary, Queen of Scots! Even *our* history books mention her." He wrinkled his forehead at her in a manner she considered quite droll. "What does this jewel look like?"

"It's quite beautiful, really. It's on a great heavy chain of gold. A pendant, I suppose you'd call it. It's formed of one large—very large—ruby, set about with a circle of diamonds. Thirty-three diamonds, none of them less than four carats."

She paused and looked at her cousin. He seemed impressed.

"There's a wide band of gold about the ruby, in which the diamonds are set. The diamonds are blue-white and all flawless, but the central ruby is a little out of the round and is not an absolutely flawless gem, I've been told."

The American stubbed out his cigarette. "It sounds fabulous," he said in his mellifluous voice. "If it belonged to Mary Stuart, how did the Farquhar family get hold of it?"

"We didn't steal it, if that's what you mean," Jane said, laughing. "It was given us as a gift. Mary was held prisoner by Queen Elizabeth in Fotheringhay Castle in England before her execution, you know. And while she was there, she was waited on by a page boy named Lionel Farquhar, sent from Scotland to serve Mary by Mary's son, King James the Sixth. Now do you see the Farquhar connection?"

"Sure," said Campbell. "Mary gave the kid the jewel, eh?"

"Exactly. As she was being led to the scaffold, she lifted the jewel from about her neck and put the chain over Lionel's head, telling him to keep the jewel in remembrance of his poor unfortunate queen, or words to that effect."

The American asked abruptly, "What's the jewel worth, Jane?"

"Worth? It's been in our family for nearly four hundred years. It's worth a great deal to me, of course."

"I mean, how much in dollars and cents?" Campbell grimaced humorously. "The Farquhars are Scotch, after all, Cousin. Surely some of them have had the jewel appraised?"

Jane, her spirits considerably dampened by his question, said shortly, "The last appraisal placed its value at thirty thousand pounds."

"Whee!" he said. "Thirty thousand pounds! That's better than eighty thousand skins, my dear African heiress! Do you realize that?"

"We never think of the jewel in those terms," she said gently.

"Why not? What's wrong with money? I hope you're going to let me see this fabulous jewel of yours before I go home?"

She shook her head. "I'm sorry, Arthur. I don't keep the jewel here, of course. It's in a bank, in England."

Campbell hesitated, then he said, "Too bad. I'd like to see a hunk of jewelry worth that kind of sugar."

Later, he had walked with her and Duke to her rondavel hut, wished her a warm good night as she unlocked her door, and sought repose in his own hut some yards away.

Two nights later, having finished the hotel chores, she left the hotel, bone-tired, for her rondavel. It was well after midnight. As she manipulated the keys to open her door, she suddenly realized that Duke, her protective shadow, was not with her . . . and that she hadn't seen him since dinner. She called softly for him several times, gave the low whistle that usually produced him instantly, and felt a thin wedge of worry work into her mind when he did not appear.

She secured a flashlight from her cottage and began to search the hotel grounds for him. And before long she found him. Dead.

Her anger kept tears from her eyes. She snapped off her flashlight and entered the hotel through the kitchen entrance at the back. She roused the Swazi waiter who had served the American at dinner. A few words with him made Campbell's guilt quite clear. For the waiter had seen Campbell carry away from the table with him, concealed in a paper napkin, a large chunk of the beef that had been on his own plate. Where he had obtained strychnine with which to load his lump of meat she couldn't guess. But she was sure he had.

She considered calling the police, three hours away in Mbabane.

And she thought of telling her Swazi waiter what had happened to Duke and asking his help in dealing with Campbell. But she was deterred from doing either, not only by her shame that the man who could commit such an atrocity was her cousin, but also by the bitter anger in her that made Duke's death a peculiarly personal matter between the American and her. So she returned to her cottage.

When she got there, the American was leaning negligently against the doorpost of her hut, slapping at mosquitoes. "Anything wrong, Cousin?" he asked.

She went by him into the hut, switching on the light. He followed her in.

"I can't find Duke," she said.

He threw her an odd look. Then he closed the hut door and leaned against it. Behind his back, she heard the bolt slide into its socket. "Look, Jane," he said, "may I sit down? I want to talk to you."

"Is that why you locked the door?"

He had the grace to flush. "I want to see the Queen's Jewel," he said simply.

"Why?"

"To photograph it. I'm a free-lance photographer. I could sell an illlustrated article on your heirloom."

"I told you the jewel was in England."

"Oh, come on now, Cousin," he rallied her. "We're both adults, you know. Why would you keep a family heirloom in England where you'd never get a glimpse of it? Maybe your daddy told you before he died to hand that kind of jazz to strange men, but I'm your cousin, Jane. Your only cousin. You can level with me."

She sat down on the edge of her bed.

He said, "I'm smart enough to know that you wouldn't keep a man-eating watchdog at your heels and have three separate Yale locks on this cottage door here, if you had the famous jewel of Mary Stuart safe in a vault in London. *I* think it's right here, in this virginal little bedroom, my dear Cousin. Am I right?"

"And if you are?"

"You'll let me see it."

"No."

He drew in his breath. "Jane," he said, "I'm not fooling. I want to see the jewel. Now."

"Look for it yourself, then. You've nothing to be afraid of since you murdered Duke."

"So you found him," he said, pushing himself away from the door and walking toward her. "O.K. So he's dead. And I've got all night to make you cough up the jewel."

"It's in the top drawer of that chest," she said in a dull voice. "In a blue velvet case."

His face lighted up. "That's better, Cousin," he said, crossing to the chest. "Much better." He unstrapped the blue velvet case he found in the drawer and opened it out to expose the Queen's Jewel to the anemic electric light in the hut. His fingers were shaking.

Jane said, "Now will you please get out of my room?"

Campbell took from his pocket a jeweler's glass, screwed it into an eye socket, and examined the Queen's Jewel carefully under the hanging light bulb. When he removed the magnifying glass and looked across at Jane, he was furious.

"This is a fake," he said tightly. "A copy." It was astonishing to her that he didn't raise his voice, yet managed to inject such vitriol into it. She sighed. He must indeed be a confirmed jewel thief, she thought with wry inconsequence, if he went everywhere equipped with a jeweler's glass.

She stood up in one swift motion. The feel of the cool metal key and its identification tag that lay against her bosom under her blouse gave her courage. She said, "Get out, Arthur. Or I'll call my Swazis to come and tear you to pieces." She darted to the door. She grasped the handle in one hand, the bolt in the other. She opened her mouth to scream.

Something struck her with great force at the base of the skull. She knew an instant of surprise that he had really resorted to violence. Then, sinking into fire-shot darkness, she thought fuzzily, My word, he carries a cosh, too.

When she regained consciousness, it was still dark. Before she opened her eyes, a jolting motion told her she was in a moving vehicle. This puzzled her momentarily; then her brain cleared. Of course. Her own Land Rover. Or the American's rented Plymouth. She opened her eyes a slit. It was her car. She felt a weak thrust of satisfaction. But principally, she felt sick.

She was slumped like a sack of yams in the front seat of the car, her head lolling back against the cushion. The American was driving. The thick choking smell of dust was in her nostrils, the airborne mud the natives called the Red Dust of Gollel, brushed up from the unpaved road by the Land Rover's passing.

She became conscious that the front of her blouse was not only in disarray but slightly torn at the neck. The key, which had hung from a thin chain around her neck, was gone. She lifted her aching head and put up a hand to order her blouse and bra.

The American, without turning, said, "So you're with us again, are you, darling?" He seemed in high spirits.

Jane asked the time-honored question timidly, "Where am I?" Her voice was hoarse.

"In your own car, dear Cousin, driving to Mbabane. To be there in the morning when the bank opens. So you can use the lock box key I found around your neck to get me the Queen's Jewel. That's where you are, dear."

She was silent.

"Nothing to say," he asked mockingly, "after that juvenile attempt to con me with a copy of the jewel? How stupid do you think I am, anyway?"

"You hit me," she said.

"I apologize. But I couldn't have you yelling for help, could I? No offense meant, honey." He lit a cigarette, driving with one masterful hand around a perilous ungraded curve above a six hundred foot drop.

Jane said, "Don't call me honey. Why did you take my car instead of your own?"

He turned his eyes from the road to slant a sly glance at her. "I want you to be driving your own car when we go to the bank in the morning," he said lightly. "So everything will look kosher."

She said, "The jewel is in London, Arthur."

He laughed aloud. "Sure. That's why you carry a safe deposit key in your bra. With an Mbabane bank label attached to it."

She fell silent. Was this American truly her cousin? Or merely a clever rascal who had somewhere picked up information about the jewel? She didn't know. Nor did she care any longer. She leaned forward, a hand to her head, and opened the glove compartment of the car. She took out a battered leather flask of brandy. Unscrewing the cap, she said in a weak, thready voice, "I need a drink. I feel faint." She tilted the flask against her lips. The American watched her with amusement.

"What is it?" he asked.

"Brandy. Van der Hum." She began to put the cap back on the flask.

"Wait a minute," the American said. "Give me a jolt of that before you put it away." He took the flask from her; she saw his Adam's apple bob three times as he took long swallows.

She reached over and removed the flask from his hand. "That's enough, you fool," she said harshly. "It's terribly strong."

"Whoo!" he said, smacking his lips. "You're not kidding, sister. Bitter, too."

She turned her head and watched him. A spasm crossed his face. He gripped the wheel very tightly. For several minutes, he drove steadily enough, saying nothing. Then he wiped a hand across his eyes. The car slowed down. He shook his head angrily.

Slowly he brought the car to a stop. He pulled on the emergency brake like a man working under water. The cloud of red dust they had raised drifted across the car. He muttered thickly, "Why, you double-crossing . . ." and fumbled in his jacket pocket.

Jane hit him on the temple, almost gently, using the leather brandy flask as a bludgeon.

He collapsed like a head-shot kudu.

When he opened his eyes it was full day and the sun already was hot on his forehead. He lay spread-eagled on the ground, arms and legs tied amateurishly but securely to stakes driven into the rocky soil. He seemed to be on a hilltop, for he could see the sky around him on all sides.

He groaned and licked his lips. He said, "Hey!" aloud, indignantly. Jane came into his field of view. "Did you do this?" he asked, jerking at his bound wrists and ankles.

"Of course," she said matter-of-factly. "With the help of two of my Swazis in the hotel. It's just down the hill, there." She pointed.

He gave her a calculating look. "That brandy was doped, I suppose?"

She nodded. "Sleeping pills dissolved in it. I always carry it."

Bewildered he said, "What the hell for?"

"For just such occasions as last night, Arthur. Before my father died, he worked out some simple safeguards to protect me and the jewel from people like you after his death. He knew a woman alone in Africa is very alone indeed."

"Safeguards?"

"Certainly. First, I had Duke. If anything happened to him, I had the three stout locks on my door. If you got past them, I had a reproduction of the jewel in my rondavel, good enough to fool anyone but an expert. An expert like you." Her tone was savage. But after a moment's pause, she went on more calmly. "If, by a remote chance, the deception of the fake jewel was detected, then I carried the lock box key with the bank's name on it around my neck . . . to point the way to Mbabane as the location of the genuine jewel. The bank guards at Mbabane would take care of anyone who presented that key at the vault. For there is no such vault number." She smiled at him. "And of course, I had the doped brandy."

"No pistol in your girdle?" asked Campbell sourly. "Well, Cousin, let me up now. You've had your joke. You turned out to be pretty cute, you know it?"

"Cute enough for the likes of you, Cousin Arthur," she replied evenly. "How do you feel?"

"Hot," he said. Sweat was beaded on his cheeks and upper lip.

Jane said, "It isn't the heat you need to worry about."

"What do you mean?"

She pointed up into the high sky. "Begin to think about that."

In lazy circles, two birds were sailing round and round, their wide wings motionless.

"Vultures," Jane said. "They'll gather here soon." She went off to one side and came back dragging something heavy. "Because I have this to attract them."

By straining his neck muscles, the American could see what it was: the dead body of Duke, the mastiff. Jane left it five yards from him.

"Jane," he said, his baritone not so resonant now. "Jane, you can't do this."

"Why not?" She wasn't smiling now. "You can test out the old theory that vultures won't touch anything that's still alive. I'm going to telephone the police now. They take a dim view of American gangsters who come to Swaziland to steal and kill. They should be here in about three hours."

"Don't leave me here, Jane." His eyes went past her to the blue. There were a dozen birds now, far up but circling downward.

"Only until the police arrive," said Jane. "I can't have you in my hotel, you know." Her voice went hard. "I advertise a very high-class clientele. And I fear you don't qualify."

She stooped and patted the stiff body of the dog. "Good-bye,

Duke," she murmured softly. Then, after a long pause, "Good-bye, Cousin."

She turned and walked down the hill toward the hotel.

Behind her, the man lay quiet on his hilltop, watching the African sky with pale frightened eyes.

The Frightened American

BY BILL KNOX

The silver shape of the big BOAC jet whined low and touched down with a momentary squeal of rubber on tarmac, its transatlantic journey over.

New York to Prestwick, in Scotland—Cam Gordon stood by a window in the airport lounge and watched the four-engined Boeing taxi toward the terminal. Minutes later, the first of its passengers began to head across the short, rain-battered distance between the plane and the Customs area.

He grimaced, considering again the staccato briefing given him by Mr. Deathstone, the Scots lawyer who'd telephoned him the previous evening.

"Marcia Bristow—about twenty-five, daughter of John Bristow, an American. Bristow should have flown back to New York by Saturday's plane and was due to return to his State Department job on Monday. Instead, he telephoned his daughter on Saturday and asked her to wire him an immediate credit of ten thousand dollars. He couldn't fly home until this was done. The girl was sensible enough to contact some friends. Meet her, and give any help necessary."

That was all the angular Scots solicitor had known—or would tell—you never knew which with Deathstone.

Cam strolled from the window and waited by the airport newsstand while a considerable cross-section of the world passed by—air crew of a dozen different lines, passengers who chattered in a variety of tongues and accents.

At last, the porter he'd spoken to earlier appeared, guiding one of the new arrivals toward him.

"Miss Bristow?"

The girl nodded. "Yes. You're . . . ?" She was blonde, good-looking in the big-boned yet graceful way of so many American women. Her sole luggage was a small pigskin suitcase.

"Cameron Gordon, Gordon Investigations." He took over the suitcase, swung it effortlessly, and suggested, "My car's outside. We can talk there."

She followed him out to the parking area and remained silent until the suitcase was in the trunk of the dark green Mercedes and they were settled in the front seats.

"A private detective wasn't my idea," she said at last. "But, well, it looks like I'm going to need help." The girl took the offered cigarette and glanced at him over the flame of the lighter. Cam was younger than she'd expected—about thirty, dark-haired, with the kind of face which appeared carved rather than molded. "You know what's happened?"

Cam nodded. "To a point. Once you got this message from your father you decided to come straight over. You've got the money?"

"In travelers' checks." She let the cigarette burn, staring out the window at the rain beyond. "My father's a pretty level-headed character, Mr. Gordon. But he sounded in a panic—and he doesn't stay away from his job without some darned good reason. He's in a hotel in Ayr—that's just along the road a piece, isn't it?"

Cam turned the ignition key, and the Merc purred to life. "Best thing to do is go straight to him," he declared.

The hotel was large, and not far from the sea front. John Bristow was in his room—and when he opened the door, he gave a wide-eyed gasp of surprise.

"What the— Marcia! Come on in."

Cam followed the girl into the room. John Bristow was in his late forties, with the same broad-boned features as his daughter. A wide band of adhesive dressing covered one side of his forehead.

"Who's this?" The man bristled as he realized his daughter wasn't alone; then his eyes showed gathering panic as Marcia made the introductions. "Look, Mister, I don't know why you're here—or Marcia, for that matter. But there's nothing that needs your attention. Nothing, understand?"

"Isn't there, Dad?" The blonde girl stepped between them, one hand on her father's arm. "I've got the money—but I don't have to be a mind reader to spot that something's wrong, and my guess is you need help. If it isn't police-type help, then Mr. Gordon could be the answer. What's happened? All you'd say was that you were in some kind of a jam."

Bristow chewed on his lower lip. "It's— Look, Marcia, the only help I need is the money. What do we know about this guy, anyway?"

"Nothing," agreed Cam. "I could be the man in the moon for all you know."

Marcia shook her head. "He can be relied on. I saw your office—they arranged the details."

Bristow groaned. "They know about this?"

"Grow up, Dad." A hint of annoyance entered the girl's voice. "I needed somebody's advice. I'm as worried as you are—maybe more. At least you know what's happened."

The man pondered. "All right, honey. Sit down, Gordon—but remember, this goes no further." He slumped on the edge of the bed and drew one hand gently across his forehead. "I'm in a jam, and it's my own fault. A couple of guys have me over a barrel, and there's nothing anyone can do about it. I couldn't come back, because they've got my passport and return air ticket—as security until they get the cash."

"Security for what?" asked Cam.

"Their silence." Bristow shrugged. "It's the old story of a tourist landing in trouble, but in a really big way, Gordon. I got a skinful of liquor." He shrugged dejectedly. "I've been on vacation for a couple of weeks, living here but moving around—golfing mostly. Friday night, I went out, had one or two drinks too many, and met a guy called Seulman—he said he was an English businessman. Well, I told him it was my last night, and that I was celebrating the end of a darned good holiday. We talked a little, then he said he was going on to meet some friends who were waiting down by the harbor. They'd rented a sea-going launch and were having a couple of weeks' salmon fishing."

"The boat's name?"

"*Scheherazade*—we went along, and I met the other two characters aboard. Don and Ernie were their names. Ernie had glasses and a gold front tooth. Well, it was pretty dark when we sailed out, and we fooled around with some fishlines for a spell—first time I'd ever tried it. Then Ernie said the salmon weren't biting, and why not a game of poker. . . ."

"I can guess the rest." Cam sighed. "You won for a spell, then began losing. Next thing you knew, they were holding your IOU for a small fortune."

Surprisingly, the man shook his head. "No. I was two hundred of your pounds up when Seulman howled I was faking the deal. We had a fight, and the next thing I remember is coming round again in the cabin. I—I'd this cut on my forehead, and it was bleeding a little. But I was covered in blood, and so was Seulman. He was dead, lying in a pool of the stuff. Don and Ernie said I'd hit him with the whiskey bottle."

His daughter gasped, her face pale with horror.

Bristow gazed at her, bit his lip, then went on. "I guess I panicked after that. Pleaded with them to say it was an accident. They agreed to dump the body and say nothing, but it would cost me ten thousand bucks, and they'd need my passport and ticket as security."

Cam gave a low whistle. "What did they do with him?"

"Tied a hunk of iron ballast round his feet, dragged him out of the cabin, and threw him over the side— I stayed in, but I heard the splash. Look, Gordon, it's ten thousand bucks or a murder rap—"

Shakily, Marcia Bristow lit a cigarette. "What do you think, Mr. Gordon?"

"Nasty. Very nasty." Cam's voice was low. "When's the money to be handed over?"

"Soon as I get it," said Bristow. "They're phoning this afternoon. Gordon—you said you'd keep your mouth shut. No cops—I guess all I want is to get back on that plane."

"You're sure he was dead? Did you feel his pulse?"

Bristow grimaced. "I was in no state. But they said the guy had croaked, and I saw the blood."

"What happened to the clothes you were wearing?"

"I washed the shirt. The jacket was the most stained. It's in my case, but it'll have to be dumped. Gordon—" he swallowed—"I didn't fake the deal. I swear it."

Cam nodded. "All right. First of all, I'll take care of the jacket. Roll it up in a newspaper or something, Bristow. Then give me till five tonight to try and find a way out. Stall them off, tell them the money isn't through yet, that you'll need another day or so."

Reluctantly, the man agreed. A few minutes later, Cam was lashing the Merc along the road to Glasgow. He headed back from the city at four thirty, stopped off at Ayr harbor, then returned to the hotel room.

"Mr. Bristow, what's your blood group?" There was a faint twinkle in his eyes.

"Group B. Why?"

"Uh-huh. This man you killed—did he look like a rabbit?"

Bristow gave a growl. "What's so darned amusing, Gordon?"

"I wondered." Cam grinned openly. "Because he bled like one. I took a chance and had a friend of mine check these bloodstains on your jacket. There's a spot or two of Group B human blood. The rest is rabbit blood. There's a very simple test-tube routine which can do everything but tell you the rabbit's first name. I don't think you killed anyone, Mr. Bristow. I think you've been conned."

A sudden new hope flared in Bristow's eyes. "You mean I can tell them to go to hell?"

"You could," agreed Cam. "But I'd rather you didn't. You're probably not the first 'murderer' who's sneaked back to the States with his tail between his legs and a hole in his bank balance. But one man's evidence is useless in a Scots court. We need corroboration. The *Scheherazade*'s moved. She's lying at Troon now, a little way along the coast. But my guess is these boys are still operating this area—Let's give them another chance."

Cam's preparations didn't take long, and included a talk with the local C.I.D. By nine that night a cheerful young man wearing a hearing aid and flashing a well-filled wallet was on a slow pub crawl around the town, celebrating more than a little, his Scots-Canadian accent loud and clear.

At the fifth spot, a busily gay cocktail lounge near Burns's Statue Square, the spider's web began to spin. A tweed-clad arm knocked over his drink; then an English voice apologized. "Hey! I'm sorry—I'll get a refill."

Cam turned, to meet the beaming, apologetic gaze of a man with glasses and a gold front tooth. Ernie took his time. Two drinks later, satisfied with Cam's tale of being a Scot home from Canada—"a few more days and I fly back to Toronto"—the gold tooth gleamed an invitation.

"Couple of pals of mine are going out fishing," he remarked, ordering a bottle of whiskey, wrapped. "We're making a night of it. Like to come along?"

"Sounds interesting," agreed Cam. "They won't mind?"

Ernie's car, a small black Renault, was outside. They drove through to Troon, parked the car near the harbor entrance, and walked to the outer basin.

Aboard the *Scheherazade* a very much alive Seulman made them welcome while Don started up the engine. The launch headed out, pitching a little as it met the open sea, then creeping up-coast. After about half an hour they stopped, moored in six fathoms, and went through the pantomime of fishing while dusk gave way to darkness.

Cam caught a couple of rock cod, took his turn as the whiskey bottle was passed around, then complained, "This is getting dull. . . ."

Seulman agreed. "We could have a few hands at poker."

The game started fair and square, and the bottle kept passing. Then the cards began to scamper in Cam's direction—two full houses, a run, a pride of kings. The others cursed his luck and increased the stakes.

By eleven twenty, his winnings were £220 and the deal was now blatantly rigged in his favor. Suddenly Seulman rose.

"You're a lousy cardsharp, mister. You asked for this—" He lumbered around the table, then made a dive forward, fists swinging.

But it was Ernie who used the cosh.

Cam drifted back to consciousness a few minutes later, the smashed neck of the whiskey bottle in one hand, Ernie and Don staring at him and beyond to where Seulman lay in one corner of the cabin, a pool of blood by his head. Cam felt his own shirt front, and found it dark and sticky.

"He's dead—you killed him!" declared Ernie.

Cam staggered across. "Lemme see," he mumbled.

The two men pushed him away. "Leave him," said Ernie. "You're in a spot now, stranger."

"How . . . I don't remember. . . ."

"You went crazy," said Don. "O.K., he went for you first—but you didn't need to kill him."

Cam gave a life-sized gulp. "Look, fellows—he—it could have been an accident, couldn't it?"

Don raised an eyebrow. "Meaning?"

"You could keep quiet about it. Get rid of him."

"That's a risky thing," pondered Ernie. "Risks are expensive."

"I'll pay," volunteered Cam. He fumbled in his pockets. "You could have a check—name the price."

Ernie shook his head. "Got your passport?"

"Not with me. Look, if I put up security till I get the cash, will you take care of . . . of him?"

"And keep quiet," agreed Don.

Cam edged around till he was barring the way to the wheelhouse above. "Well, now, that's nice of you." He unhooked the 'hearing aid' midget transmitter. "Tell your pal he can get up off the deck. The pitch is finished, boys. You've just made your radio debut, with a launchload of police listening at the other end. They should be on their way over right about now."

In direct confirmation, a boat engine growled to life not far across the darkened water.

The three men rushed him, Seulman rising from the dead in jack-in-the-box fashion. Ernie came first, and gobbled in rainbow agony as he got a hand-edge blow on the side of the neck. Don was next—but he halted as a searchlight beam hit the cabin. He looked at Seulman, who had also frozen, and they shrugged.

John Bristow and his daughter stood in the departure lounge at Prestwick Airport.

"You saved my bacon, Gordon," said the American grimly.

Cam was content. "Seulman and his boys should get about five years apiece. Your statement and the rest adds up to enough evidence to satisfy any court."

Radiant, the girl joined in. "You told us about the rabbit blood, Cam. But what made you first guess there was something phony?"

"Fishy, not phony," corrected Cam. "Your father said they went line fishing for salmon. In open salt water?" He shook his head. "Never in a thousand years—not here, anyway."

Bristow shook hands. Father and daughter walked toward the Customs entrance, then Marcia hurried back.

"Thanks." She kissed him in a way that made his hair tingle.

"It's a pleasure," murmured Cam. After all, Deathstone's check was already in his pocket. . . .

The Dynamics of an Asteroid

BY ROBERT BLOCH

Honestly, some of the patients you get are a scream. Positively a scream!

Not that I'd want any other kind of work—where else can you make up to twenty dollars a day, and all you do, really, is sort of play nursemaid for a couple of hours? Compared to a hospital or working in some G.P.'s office, it's nothing at all. But the *types* you run into!

Take this one I had a few years ago— I didn't tell you about him, did I? He was a hundred years old.

One hundred years *old!* Can you *imagine?* No, I'm pretty sure of it, the way he talked and all. And to hear him tell it, up to three months ago he was dressing and feeding himself and handling everything in the house out of his wheelchair. Of course, he ordered what he needed over the phone and the hotel sent it right up, meals and everything. But think of that, one hundred years old and all alone in a wheelchair, and he did everything himself!

Of course, you might guess it just to look at him. He'd been some kind of professor of arithmetic or mathematics, whatever they call it, but that was when he was young. Imagine, sixty years ago or so! And then he was in this accident and his left side was paralyzed and he went into a wheelchair. Sixty years, that's a long time to live in a wheelchair. Dr. Cooper, he was handling the case, just stopping in once a week, he said it was amazing.

But the old boy was tough, I got to say that for him. Just one look at him was enough to let you know. Of course when I was put on the case he was in bed already, but sitting up. And when he sat up you couldn't tell he was paralyzed at first. He had a big bald head and a bulgy forehead and his eyes were sunk way back, like they sometimes get. But he wasn't shriveled or even very wrinkled.

He'd stick that head out and his face would move from side to side, but all the while those little eyes would stare at you to make sure you were listening. He talked a lot. Talked and wrote. He was forever having me mail stuff for him. A lot of it went abroad to foreigners in colleges over there—professors, I guess. And people in the government over here, and fellas like this Einstein before he died.

That's what I wanted to tell you about—he wrote to Einstein! Did you ever hear of such a thing in all your life?

At first he didn't talk about what he was doing, at least not very much. But he kept getting weaker and weaker and along about the last month he couldn't write. And of course it was hard for him to sleep. Dr. Cooper was all for giving him hypos but he wouldn't take them. Not him! He was tough.

But some nights he'd call me in—I slept in the other room on the couch—and he liked for me to read to him. He got all kinds of crazy-sounding magazines: scientific ones, I guess. And some of them were in German and French and I-don't-know-what-all. Of course I couldn't read those, and when I tried to read the regular English ones he got mad because of course I didn't know all those two-dollar words.

So mostly he had me read the papers. And that's where the crazy part started.

Take like the crime news. You know, there's been a lot of killings lately, all these G.I. murderers and that. And I'd get to reading about them and all of a sudden he'd be laughing.

At first it bothered me. I thought he was just plain *se*-nile. The way they get sometimes, you know.

But once, about two weeks before he died, he was listening to me read about one of those crime syndicates: I mean where they all gang up and plot like blackmail extortions and things.

And he gave this chuckle of his and he said, "Strange, isn't it, Miss Hawes?"

So I said, "What's strange?"

And he said, "To think that it's still going on. It takes one back, Miss Hawes. It takes one back."

I said, "You mean they used to have gangs like this when you were—" I stopped real quick, because I'd almost said, "alive."

And the funny thing happened, because he finished the sentence for me and *he* said, "alive?" Then he laughed again. "Yes, they had gangs when I was alive, and master criminals and workers behind the scenes. I was one myself, although you may find that hard to believe. Just as it may be hard for you to believe that I died over sixty years ago."

Then I knew for sure he was getting *se*-nile. And it must have showed on my face.

"Perhaps you might be interested in my story," he said. And of course I said, "Yes," even though I wasn't. To tell you the truth I kept right on reading the paper all the while he was talking, but I wish now I'd listened a little more because some of it was real wild.

So he kept on rambling about how it was when he was a young man in college or university or wherever, and he was studying all this fancy mathematics stuff, and then he got out and he couldn't get a job.

I guess he finally got to teaching for a sort of a small private school and then he was a tutor, like, for rich kids over in England.

And he wrote some books but nobody paid any attention because he was ahead of his time, whatever that means.

Well, to make a long story short, I gather he wanted to get married and his girl turned him down for a richer fella, and he just went all to pieces. That's how he became a criminal, to hear him tell it.

And, to hear him tell it, he was a real big shot. He was like one of those supercriminals you hear about; never did anything himself but just gave advice. He would plan things for the rest to do and get a commission.

He said he had a logical mind and because of all that studying he did, he knew just how to organize things. Pretty soon he was working for gangs all over Europe, too, and he made a fortune. That part I can believe, because even now he was living in this big hotel suite and he hadn't worked for over sixty years, being in a wheelchair and all.

But all the while he told me this he kept working in names and dates and places that didn't make any sense to me, and I just couldn't be expected to pay too much attention.

Finally he saw I wasn't listening and he shut up. That suited me, except that I wondered what he'd meant about him dying, like he said.

A couple of nights later that came up again. I was reading about some doctors out West, keeping somebody alive massaging the heart during an operation—you know. They did it over at Sinai a few months ago, didn't they?

Anyway, he said, "Doctors! Call themselves medical authorities and they don't know the first thing about life. If I'd listened to them, I'd be dead and buried these sixty-odd years past."

Well, it just happened I was pretty tired, and I guess I must have dozed off right in the middle of what he was saying. But I remember him starting out with this story about how he got tangled up with the police and some detective was out to get him, only he got him first. And they had a big fight somewhere, I forget the name, and he was left for dead. Only he wasn't dead, he was just paralyzed.

This was over in Europe someplace, and he decided to stay there when he got patched up. He had plenty of money put away in a dozen different banks, and nobody was looking for him; being crippled up, he was glad to get out.

Besides, this detective was supposed to be dead and he was wanted for killing him if he ever showed up. So it was a good idea to retire. After that he just moved around from place to place all over Europe. Once he thought he'd go back home, but the funniest thing happened, to hear him tell it—the man he was supposed to have killed wasn't dead after all, but still alive. And if he went back it would start all over.

So he stayed dead, as far as anyone knew. I guess he came over to this country from where he lived in Germany, when the Nazis got started there.

"It's a strange experience, being dead for so many years, Miss Hawes," he said. "But I see I'm boring you—"

That's when I knew I must have dozed off. I apologized all over the place, but he just chuckled. Didn't bother him a bit.

No, that's not all. Wait a minute, there's one thing more I want to tell you about. That's this crazy business about the asteroid.

You know what an asteroid is? Neither do I. Some kind of a planet, I guess—only he wasn't even talking about a real one, but just a fake one. Called it a man-made sat-something. Oh, yes, satellite, that was it. A man-made satellite.

It was the newspaper that started him off on it. I was reading him this story—he was pretty weak, you know, and Dr. Cooper said it wouldn't be long—when all at once I noticed he was sitting up.

He hadn't sat up for nearly a week, and he wasn't eating very much of anything any more, but here he was, sitting up straight. And he said, "Would you mind reading that over again, Miss Hawes? Slowly, please?" He was always very polite like that, I will say that for him.

So I read it over, and he began to chuckle again, and he got the funniest look on his face. It wasn't exactly a smile, but you know, like that. His cheeks were all sunk in the way they get before the end, but for a minute I'd swear he looked positively young again.

"I knew it!" he said. "I knew they'd do it! That's the news I've been waiting for."

Then he began to talk a blue streak. I said, "Please, you know Doctor Cooper said you mustn't exert yourself. You must rest."

And he said, "I'll have a long time for resting, now. And in peace, I trust." And he kept right on talking.

Now I don't know how much of this he was making up, because it sounds so utterly ridiculous, but of course he *did* send those letters out and he'd get answers, too. They all knew him, all these scientists.

But the way he told it, after the time he fell and nearly died, he decided to reform. He wanted to do something for the world, I guess, and he got to studying his mathematics again. He said he'd written this book with the crazy title—I remember that part all right—it was called *The Dynamics of the Asteroid*. And it was about these moon rockets and satellites.

"Yes, that's right, Miss Hawes," he told me. "Over sixty years ago. No wonder nobody took it seriously; I was ahead of my time. And I spent years of pioneering work simply trying to get a hearing from the proper authorities in the field. Bit by bit, I managed."

The point is, I guess he kept working out these theories of his and writing to scientists and feeding them ideas, like this Einstein and a whole lot of others. He didn't want any credit, just so long as they would work on his notions. And after a long time, they did. He said he had this idea for building a space platform or an artificial whatchamacallit all these years, and he pounded away and pounded away and even sent diagrams.

In Germany he made experimental models or whatever they do and donated them to universities and the government—but he never let them use his name. All he wanted was to do some good for humanity.

"It was the least I could do to atone, Miss Hawes," he said. "I wanted, in my small way, to help man reach the stars. And now, I see, the work has borne fruit. What more reward could I ask?"

Of course I knew enough to humor him; it was the least I could do for the poor old fella, the way he was. So I told him how wonderful I thought it was and how he ought to be getting *his* name in the newspapers, too, along with these other big-shot scientists.

"That can never be," he said. "And it no longer matters. My name will live only as a symbol of infamy." Whatever *that* is.

Well, I don't know how we ended up, but it was the same night, quite late, that the crisis came.

I'd been sleeping on the sofa in the other room when I heard him sort of gasping and I went into the bedroom quick and took one look and then called Dr. Cooper.

By the time he got there, though, it was all over. It wasn't what you call a painful death. He just got delirious and then went right off with just a short coma. Heart gave out, Dr. Cooper said.

But for a few minutes, there, while he was delirious, he came out with some of the most awful stuff. It was as if he was another person —probably the way he'd been when he was a criminal back in the nineties or whenever, if he'd told me the truth.

He kept cursing away at somebody or other: this detective fella, I guess. He wasn't so much mad at the fella as he was jealous because the detective was famous and he wasn't. You see, like I told you before, he was supposed to have killed him, only he revived and got away. And now the poor old guy acted as though he was right there in the room—and did he swear!

Then he started to wrestle with him: you know how it is when they go out of their head. Only I figured it out that he thought he was back fighting with him at the time when he was left for dead.

They were fighting on some cliff, and there was a waterfall or something—this was in Germany or the Alps or around there, I guess—and this detective was using jujitsu and he threw the old guy off into the water and he hit his head and bounced and swam away. But the detective didn't notice because he was climbing up the cliff himself in order not to leave any footprints, so people would think he was dead. Oh, it doesn't make any sense, but that's the way it came out.

Then, just before the coma, he was sitting up in bed after all this wrestling around, and I was trying to hold him down. But he didn't even know I was in the room, you see—he just saw the detective.

And he said, "Keep your glory! Keep your cheap notoriety and your fame! I'll die unhonored, unmourned, and unsung, but in the end I triumph. Your name will live as the hero of a ten-penny romance. My deeds will bring men to the stars! One thing you must admit—there's nothing elementary about *my* deductions—"

Real crazy stuff, I tell you!

And then he went off into the coma and died. Just like that. But can you imagine, such a mixed-up business?

I wonder how much of it was really true? I mean, about him being a master criminal and reforming and then helping scientists invent these space platforms. I never heard of that book, *The Dynamics of the Asteroid,* or whatever.

Maybe I'll look it up sometime. I wish I knew the name of that detective he hated so much; that would help.

But I've got *his* name, anyway. Irish. Moriarity, he called himself—Professor Moriarity.

Castle in Spain

BY JULIAN SYMONS

San Avalo is a dot on the map of Spain some twenty miles from Corunna, in the northwest corner of Galicia. Don Easton went there because a friend said that it was the most beautiful village in Spain, and added contemptuously that no travel agent had ever heard of it.

Don's tendency to wanderlust was aroused, and his pride as a travel agent was stung. Within a month he was on his way to Galicia, which the Spaniards used to call Finisterre, or world's end.

Galicia may not be the world's end, but it is certainly not easily accessible. The nearest big airport is at Lisbon, three hundred miles away, and the sea route to Vigo is used mostly by ships that lack tourist accommodation. Don took the train to the French-Spanish frontier and then changed to the bus, which is often the quickest way of getting about in Spain. He had already decided that if San Avalo was to figure on the Easitravel list it must be as part of a coach tour.

Traveling by bus, he might well see other good stopping places.

He sat in the bus station at Bilbao, reading a day-old English paper. There was not much news in it—a mother had left her month-old baby on the steps of the Soviet Embassy with a note asking the Russians to take care of it, Mel Charles had been declared unfit to play for Arsenal, a financier named Richard Baker had jumped his bail on a fraud charge. He put down the paper with pleasure at the sound of English voices.

A tall dark young man and a short, fair girl came in. The young man carried a heavy suitcase, the girl a lighter one.

"Has the bus for Santander gone?" the young man asked an attendant in atrocious Spanish.

Don answered him. "I'm catching it myself. And here it is." He took the case out of the girl's hand and lifted it onto the bus. The label was old and torn. It bore the name Boyd, with an address scratched out but still visible: EL CASTILLO DE ORO, SAN AVALO.

"You know San Avalo?"

A quick look, of some indecipherable kind, passed between the two. Then the girl spoke.

"I don't know it, but Roly does. He says it's nice."

"Rugged but beautiful. My uncle Justin lives out there, and I went out to see him once last July. He lives in a castle."

"The golden castle," Don said. "A nice name."

"It looks golden, too, with the sun shining on the turrets. But my word, it's cold and dank in the winter."

"Are you out here on business?"

"Sort of a holiday," the little woman said. She chirped like a bird. "March isn't just the time you'd choose for a holiday on this coast, but Roly's got a new job—he's an engineer—and they gave him a few days before he started."

"So you're going to stay with your uncle?"

"You'd better ask Roly. He says we're not. By the way, my name's Jenny Boyd, and this is my husband." She added demurely, "I'd love to see the castle."

"You don't know what you're saying, darling." Her husband shivered. He was perhaps in his early thirties, a hungry-looking man with a hard mouth but a ready smile. "Once was enough. Uncle Justin's eccentric, and I mean eccentric. He lives in this great barracks, with some old crone of a housekeeper. Doesn't smoke, doesn't drink, never looks at an English newspaper. He's no fun, let me tell you."

"That's enough about us," Jenny said, adding with a curiosity so childlike that one couldn't take offense at it, "What do you do, Mr.—?"

"Easton." Don told them what he did, and said that he was breaking his journey in several places, but would reach San Avalo eventually. Should he look up Uncle Justin?

Roly laughed. "Do, by all means, but I can't vouch for your reception. He keeps a shotgun handy to discourage strangers if he's feeling inhospitable."

There was something odd about the conversation, but Don couldn't think what it was. They parted in Santander, and within half an hour he had forgotten them.

He remembered again, and remembered the oddity, when he came down into the valley where San Avalo nestled, on a day rawly cold but beautifully sunny. The village was as pretty as a picture postcard, with its single street and three shady plazas, and the Hotel España, with a restaurant terrace overlooking the sea, and steps down to a private beach, was delightful. Don did some hard bargaining with the proprietor, Señor Mendoza, and made a block booking for July in the following year. Then he mentioned the castle.

"El Castillo de Oro," Mendoza said. He took Don out to the terrace and waved a hand. The castle stood on a promontory above the village. At this moment, with the sunlight gleaming on its towers, the place really looked as though it were made of gold.

Don described the Boyds. Mendoza had not seen them, but he knew their uncle, the Englishman who was *loco,* an old man with a beard, who sometimes shut himself up for weeks in the castle.

"For weeks? What about food?"

What indeed, Mendoza said rhetorically. Certain it was that at these times neither he nor the housekeeper he had brought out from England came down to the village. At these times, the villagers believed, he was not merely *loco,* harmlessly mad, but *dementi, maniaco, furioso.* A demon no doubt possessed him. At such times the village girls who worked at the castle were told not to go there. More than this, there were ghosts in the castle.

"Ghosts? What sort of ghosts?"

That Mendoza could not say, but certain it was that Juanita, one of the village girls, had heard voices speaking in some of the rooms, young voices, not those of the mad Englishman.

Don brooded over this information, and over the oddity that had struck him, while he ate an excellent paella. He made a telephone call to Martin Burns, his assistant in London, partly to confirm that he had made the San Avalo booking, but chiefly to ask for some information. An hour later Martin rang him back. Don had been playing a hunch, and the hunch was right. He left the hotel, called at the office of the Guardia Civil, and walked up to the castle.

He took the main road out of the village, walked along it for a mile, and then turned onto a rough track. The castle loomed ahead of him. As he walked the sun died, the sky darkened. The castle's color changed from gold to black. It looked less romantic than sinister as he walked past a big iron gate into a courtyard. Around him, the place was still. He walked toward the big iron door.

"Stop." The voice was rusty, like an unused key in a lock, but unmistakably English. "Stop, or I shoot."

The voice came from above. Don looked up. A fierce old man with a long and dirty beard glared at him out of a narrow window. The rifle in his hand was steady. Don stopped.

"Who are you? What do you want?"

"My name is Easton. I met your nephew, and he suggested I

should call on you." It was not quite the truth, but it would serve.

"The worthless scoundrel has not even called on me," the old man said, but he lowered the rifle.

"It is a long way from the village."

"Wait." Don stood in the courtyard until he heard a creak of bolts. The old man said, "Come in."

The hall he entered was so dark that for a moment he could not distinguish more than the outlines of the figure who faced him. Then he saw the matted white hair, the intense stare of dark eyes. He followed down a corridor into a room where oil lamps and a meager wood fire gave a minimum of light and heat.

"I am a recluse, Mr. Easton, but I do not wish to appear inhospitable. Will you take a glass of wine?"

"Thank you."

The old man went to the door. "Henrietta," he suddenly bawled. "Wine."

A little old woman entered the room, a black shawl over her head and black gloves on her hands, so bent that it was hard to see her face. She carried a silver tray with a decanter and glasses on it.

The old man poured the wine. "This is a friend of my nephew Roland. He came here last summer."

She muttered something. Don said, "And you have seen nothing of him this time? Or of his wife?"

"Nothing. It was his only visit." The eyes glared fiercely. "And what is the news of the world? We see nothing, hear nothing."

"You haven't a radio?" Don sipped the wine. It was strong and sweet.

"I abominate them. What do I read or hear but filth? Theft and adultery, display of the body, children deserted and given away to the godless—"

His voice died away. The old woman cackled. Don said quietly, "It's no good. Give it up."

"What do you mean?"

"You've made too many mistakes. I know who you are."

The old man said in a high voice, "I am Justin Boyd."

"Justin Boyd never existed, nor his housekeeper. Your name is Richard Baker, and you are wanted for fraud charges in England."

There was a small pistol in the woman's hand.

"It's no good," Don repeated. "I've talked to London on the telephone and got a description of you both. You're his wife. And I told the Guardia Civil I was coming up here, and who you were. They'll be coming to look for me."

"There'll be no violence," the man said. He put his hand over the woman's wrist, and twisted. She cried out and dropped the pistol. "I never really thought we could get away with it."

The housekeeper straightened up and took off the shawl, revealing bright fair hair. She said in the chirping voice of Jenny Boyd, "Of course we could have got away with it if he hadn't stuck his nose in. You should have fired that rifle."

"It would have made no difference," Don said. "It was an ingenious idea, to create a separate identity out here in Spain, ready for a getaway, so that Richard Baker and his wife turned into Justin Boyd and his housekeeper, but you made too many mistakes. First, leaving the label on the suitcase, then telling me that you'd only visited your uncle once, in July, and saying in the next breath that the castle was cold and dank in winter."

The man stripped off the wig and pulled away the beard, to reveal the darkly handsome face of Roland Boyd. "That was a mistake."

"When I came here and learned that the mad Englishman shut himself up for weeks at a time without seeing anybody, I had a hunch that at these times you might not be there at all. When I heard that there were ghosts speaking in different voices I guessed somebody might be masquerading as Uncle Justin. But the worst mistake of all was the one you made just now."

"What was that?"

"When you mentioned the child given away to the godless. I read about the baby deposited on the steps of the Soviet Embassy two days ago. How could you know about it if you never saw a paper and had no radio?"

"All right," Roland Boyd or Richard Baker said hopelessly. "All right."

"But you were foolish from the start," Don said. "Relying for your hideout on a castle in Spain."

(*Untitled*)

BY FRED LEVON

This story shall have no name. I could call it *The Snob,* or *The Frustrated Murderer,* or even *The Story without a Title,* but I shall not name it at all. It is far more fitting that way. You will soon see why.

My wife is English. We met in London during the "blitz" and were married at her home. Since the war we have resided in New York—at Peter Cooper Village, on the lower east side of Manhattan—which is not particularly British in any way. Millicent, however, has never seemed to mind and I really believe she has been happy in America, content with her choice, never seriously longing to return to her homeland. And the only discernible way in which she has carried something of England across the ocean and into our present lives has been through her subscriptions to a few British periodicals, such as *The Tatler* and *Punch.*

It was two years ago that the episode of which I write began. I was at breakfast with Leslie, our four-year-old daughter. Millicent had just returned from getting the mail.

"Well, look at this!" she exclaimed, indicating an article in one of her magazines. *The Englishman in America,* it was called, and the author was Charles Cort-Kittershaw. "Why, it must be cousin Charles!"

I had met Charles only once but I remembered him vividly. A generation older than Millicent, he was a tall, slender, gray-haired individual who took pains to accentuate a natural resemblance to Anthony Eden. I could recall his stiff, unsentimental wish that we would be happy in our "sudden" marriage, his shock to think that Millicent would soon be an ocean away, his hope that this did not mean she would abandon England entirely. And then, learning that I am a writer, his brief inquiry into my work (chiefly mystery fiction), his apparent decision that I ranked with the contributors to the "penny dreadfuls," and his all-too-plain dismissal of me as of no consequence. Charles also indulged in writing, but only, he carefully explained, of nonfiction. And although his work showed considerable skill it was to him more a diversion than a source of income. Belonging to the only really wealthy branch of the clan (his family controls the Empire White Flag Fleet of transatlantic liners), he had never been obliged to depend upon the proceeds from his small literary output.

"Oh Lord!" Millicent sighed, looking up from her reading. "It's our Charles, all right. And he all but names us. What an annoying snob!"

I took the magazine. The article was undoubtedly droll and amusing, but reading it through American eyes and recalling the patronizing manner of the author, I was unable to suppress a degree of resentment.

"Do you suppose he came across *Garden of Weeds* and recognized himself in Hamilton Drude?" I referred to my most successful detective novel, which had reached England the year before. "I wonder if he considers this some sort of revenge?"

Millicent pondered for a moment; then she said, "Charles is capable of anything. He's clever with his writing but also a bit cruel. Any offense you may find in his work is strictly intended."

She laughed, and Charles was temporarily dismissed.

Dismissed, that is, for about four months—until one evening in October, when the telephone rang. I answered with the customary "Hello."

"Edward, is that you?" The accent was crisp, undiluted by much time away from home. "This is Charles Cort-Kittershaw, Millicent's cousin. We met once, you know."

"Yes, of course. How are you?"

"I'm fine. Catherine and I are staying in Connecticut. I'll explain it all in a moment. Is Millicent there?"

I put her on and they spoke with that forced courtesy which stems from family ties bound by duty rather than by affection. Charles and Catherine (his wife) were in America for an indefinite stay while he acted in some official capacity involving the family steamship company. In a remote section of Connecticut they had found a haven which they felt had some charm, and Charles commuted two days a week to the office in Manhattan. He deplored the trains. Catherine found the climate ghastly. They begged that we drive up as they longed to see someone "from home."

Millicent took the number and promised to call back.

"It's a dreadful chore," she said, after hanging up, "and he annoys me almost as much as he does you, but it *would* be a bit sticky to just say *No*. . . ."

"There's no need to refuse," I told her. "Let's make a weekend of it."

So the result was that the three of us—Millicent, Leslie, and I—drove to Connecticut on a Saturday morning about a year and a half ago.

The Cort-Kittershaw "haven" was a huge and rather stark affair set in a park of ancient yews and unclipped hedges. The vast grounds flowed to all sides like the wild moors at Wuthering Heights. One felt that surely, nearby, there would be a brook and a stable of horses and perhaps, at any moment, a fox hunt in full cry hurdling the gorse.

A pair of enormous dogs galloped out to meet us.

"Wouldn't you know!" Millicent whispered.

Leslie found an instant fear of the animals and climbed into the safety of my arms.

"Hello, Charles," Millicent cried as our host appeared at the door. "Call off your beasts—they have my daughter terrified."

"Nonsense," said Charles, "they are as gentle as lambs. How are you, Millicent?" And to me, "Hello, Edward."

The house was a museum of fine woodwork and stiff, pedigreed antiques. Although kept in excellent condition there was no hint of recent alteration, modernization of plumbing, or any of the newer conveniences of the kitchen. In spite of the seasonable cold, most of the windows were open.

Almost immediately Catherine served tea and freshly made scones (pronounced, you may be sure, without the *e*). All her china was from England, and she had also brought over a butler and maid, not wishing to risk what she called "inferior domestic help." Proud of her cooking, however, she preferred to cope with the kitchen unaided. She is desperately lonely, I thought.

Having neither toys nor playmates to distract her, Leslie soon became bored and fussy. It was clear that Charles disapproved of this. Millicent gave the child her pocketbook, a concession generally reserved as a last resort.

Inevitably, the conversation turned to friends and family.

"How is Uncle Cliff?" Millicent inquired and then quickly added, in order to dispel any suspicion of unfairly poaching on the family's nobility, "He's really not an uncle to me, but he's always been my favorite."

Uncle Cliff was everyone's favorite, one of those rare and wonderful people with a capacity to be universally admired. Being the widowed Duke of Burbridge, he resided alone in the clan's one feudal castle, an enormous turreted structure with mullioned windows; but not being a member of the steamship wing of the family, he was obliged to allow tourists to troop through his home behind a paid guide.

"Uncle Clifford's quite well," replied Charles, to whom the man was authentically an uncle. "He's developed pernicious anemia, you know, but he's taking liver injections and seems to be back in good health."

"Yes, we had heard," Millicent said. "According to my information, pernicious anemia can be quite benign under proper management. And how is Roger?" Roger was Clifford's only child, a bachelor now in his forties.

"Roger's in Canada," said Catherine. "He's taken some obscure post that requires him to travel a good deal. He may come to Washington next year. Perhaps we'll see him then." Looking to Charles, she added, "*If*, of course, we are still here ourselves."

"Yes," sighed Charles, with the air of one suffering an indignity.

Catherine's roast beef and Yorkshire pudding were excellent, but dinner was an uncomfortable meal. The room was drafty and the conversation was strained with Millicent's unease over Leslie's restlessness. Despite a blazing fire, the library in which coffee was later served was not much more pleasant. Rising impulsively, Catherine insisted that we see her herb garden before the evening settled into darkness.

Millicent and I followed her and stepped between painfully geometric beds of healthy, fragrant plants. In her pride Catherine's face opened with the first real happiness we had seen it reflect. Suddenly, through the murmur of our admiring utterances, Leslie's cry reached us.

"It must be the dogs!" Millicent said, running for the house. But the child had broken a teapot and sat on the floor among the fragments, frightened and in tears. Charles, tight-lipped, stood over her.

We apologized profusely, blaming ourselves for allowing Leslie to remain up so late after the day's journey. Catherine begged us not to think again of the accident. Charles, however, remained unconsoled and spoke little during the remainder of the evening, his face showing a rather startling ugliness of mood. Millicent withdrew with the child, and shortly thereafter we all retired.

Breakfast next morning was again cold and awkward. It came as only a mild surprise when Millicent announced: "Charles, Catherine, I hope you won't mind if we leave now. Leslie seems to be coming down with a cold and she so easily develops fever. I think we ought to get her home."

Catherine forced a promise that we would return, and we left.

The trip home was uneventful. We listened to the Sunday radio programs and Leslie, who had awakened in terror during the night, napped on the rear seat.

Back in New York, Millicent revealed her duplicity. "I didn't want to tell you there because you would have made a row, even though it would have been justified." She showed me Leslie's arm, which bore a large and discolored bruise. "She says that Charles shook her and called her a nasty child—yesterday when she dropped the teapot."

My heart turned with pity for the child and in fury at Charles. My first impulse was to call back in protest over his behavior. Millicent implored me to allow her to handle the matter by mail. "There is something unforgivable about cruelty to a child," she agreed, "and I shall not ask you to see Charles again."

But in the end I could not resist putting the matter into a story I was then writing and which was to appear in a magazine I had seen on the Cort-Kittershaw coffee table and to which Charles apparently subscribed. I titled the piece "Suffer Little Children," certain that it would catch his eye. And with this childish retaliation I allowed the matter to rest.

A few months later Charles, who had clearly also succumbed to an impulse at reprisal, had a piece in the *Review* in which he was critical of the "lax" standards of discipline used by parents in America.

"He rather forced the point, don't you think?" Millicent asked.

"I'm sure he wrote it purely in spite. It's a wonder he could sell it at all."

"He's probably under contract with the *Review* to do a series about Americans. He's only distorted it a little to suit his purpose."

She shrugged, and again the Cort-Kittershaws were dismissed, both of us confident that we had seen the last of them.

But in this we were wrong. After months of silence Catherine called and spoke to Millicent, whose responses changed from chill politeness to sorrow to concern. "Well, I'll see. . . ." she promised, and cradled the phone.

"Roger was killed in an airplane crash," she explained, her face lined with sadness. "You remember, he was Uncle Cliff's only child. Catherine and Charles went to England for the funeral and returned just a few weeks ago. Catherine says she's terribly worried about Charles, that he's been acting strangely since they got back. She begs that we come up, to put her mind at ease. There's really no one else to whom she can appeal. . . ."

I said nothing, not knowing what to say. Millicent, close to tears, fell into a chair and looked to me for aid.

"Well," I decided, "if it upsets you, let's go. In times of need a family should forget its grievances."

So again, last month, we drove to Connecticut. After debating the issue we took Leslie with us, repeating the cliché about bygones.

Charles did indeed look changed. Although not thinner or ill in appearance, he spoke and gestured with a new nervousness, as if eager and expectant. Clutching a cane, he limped on a swollen, unshod foot.

"My podagra," he mumbled, his face a pantomime of anguish. "I'll have to walk with a stick for a bit."

"His gout," Millicent whispered. "He's a little proud of it. So traditionally aristocratic, you know."

The Cort-Kittershaws spoke first of the funeral and of Uncle Cliff's great grief. "I really don't think he'll recover from it," said Catherine. "He feels that all is lost and there is no future for him. Everyone's terribly alarmed. He won't see his doctors and an old nurse gives him his injections. In the latest letter we learned that his anemia has increased and that he's weakening steadily."

"He's closed the castle," Charles added, "although he doesn't have a bob. We're all trying to help. Catherine's sending tins and foods that are hard for him to get and I . . ." His voice trailed away, his thoughts apparently elsewhere.

In spite of Charlie's hyperkinetic behavior, however, it was Catherine who caused us the greater concern. Looking frequently to her husband, she spoke distractedly, clutched her hands together, and snapped impatiently at the blameless dogs at her feet. She arose twice to make tea, and Millicent finally went with her to the kitchen.

After a long interval the tea appeared, with Catherine far more relaxed. Shortly thereafter Millicent suggested that we leave, indicating with a gesture that our mission had been accomplished.

As we donned our coats Charles limped into the library and emerged with a package. "I wonder," he asked hesitantly, "don't you go down the West Side Highway in the city?"

"Yes," I replied, "is there something we can do for you?"

"Well, if you wouldn't mind awfully, this is something for Uncle Clifford and I thought if you could drop it off with one of the chaps at the steamship office it would go to England on the next crossing, which leaves tomorrow. I don't think I'll get into town this week, because of my foot."

I assured him that I didn't mind and took the package. He instructed me where to make the delivery, and we left.

"Poor Catherine," Millicent said in the car. "She's never had children and feels her loneliness now, surrounded only by her beautiful china and art treasures and those cold, untouchable antiques. She's filled with terrible premonitions and fears. The maddening thing, of course, is that Charles is incapable of tolerating weakness or showing sympathy. She needed a good cry and feels better now for it."

I asked when they planned to return to England.

"Not for a while yet, I'm afraid. Although they hate it here they're obliged to stay for several years. Apparently a group of them take turns at the New York office and this was inescapable."

Millicent turned to look at Leslie in the rear seat. "Oh Lord!" she cried, "look at what Leslie's done!"

I stopped the car to inspect the extent of the damage. Leslie had opened the package Charles had given us for delivery. It consisted of a dozen small vials of the type put out by pharmaceutical houses, and from the labels (which read *Liver Extract* and *Vitamin* B_{12}) it was clearly the medicine for the Duke's pernicious anemia. The child had succeeded in opening two of the vials and had spilled their dark brown contents on her dress.

"Well," I said, when the mess had been cleaned up, "there's no need to worry Charles over this. I'll see if I can't replace these two through the druggist and I'll take the package to the pier tonight."

The pharmacist was very obliging. Not demanding a new prescription, he produced two identical bottles. "Do you want the others replaced, too? I notice the cellophane collars have been removed from all the caps."

"Does it make any difference?"

"Not for immediate use. But if it's going to do a good deal of traveling the stoppers may work loose."

"Well, we'd better not take any chances. Is this hard to get in England?"

"Liver and B_{12}?" He frowned. "No, I don't believe so." He took out ten more bottles. "Well, here's your even dozen."

In the car I searched again, turning up the rear seat and looking over the floor and into the crevices. There was no sign of the cellophane collars to which the druggist had referred. I drove to the pier on the west side and delivered the package, newly tied and labeled.

When I returned to Peter Cooper Village, Leslie had been bedded for the night and Millicent was preparing a late supper.

"Who would inherit the dukedom?" I asked, "if Uncle Cliff were to die?"

She considered it for a moment. "Why, Charles, I suppose. Now that Cliff's only child is dead, I suppose Charles is next in line. Why?"

"And he would return to England immediately, would he not, to take over the estate?"

"Probably. Why?"

I told her about the cellophane collars that were missing from the vials. "I'm sure Leslie didn't remove them. That leaves only Charles and Catherine."

"My God, whatever for?"

I suggested the obvious. Millicent recoiled in disbelief. "It's too monstrous!"

"Well, I don't see how we can ever know. Unfortunately, I poured out the old bottles at the pharmacy. But why should Charles go to so much trouble to supply something so readily available in England when there are other things Uncle Cliff needs more?"

"Catherine *does* send other things—tins and foods," Millicent said, groping, "and now that Uncle Cliff isn't seeing the doctors I suppose these drugs are no longer easily available to him through the National Health Service. And Charles, looking for something Cliff needs . . ."

"But this package is going alone, on a special trip. Is it really so urgent? Is it possible that Catherine has found Charles tampering with the duke's medicines, and can't quite appease her conscience?"

"Oh dear," Millicent cried, "how will we ever know?"

"Well, at least we can be sure that the present supply is the genuine article, and if you want, you can take over sending a few packages yourself."

"Yes, let's. But how can we stop Charles from sending his?"

"I don't know," I said reflectively.

I slept on it, restlessly. And during the next day I evolved a plan.

Seeing my physician over a minor complaint, I asked in passing for some "information for a story." Pernicious anemia, he assured me, is quite adequately treated with Liver Extract or Vitimin B_{12}. If, however, the injections are replaced by plain water (colored, say, with vegetable dye), the patient will appear to become refractory to his therapy and ultimately die.

And then we had a letter directly from Uncle Cliff. In response to a card from Millicent he wrote that he had been quite stunned by his son's death and had suffered a few bad weeks, but was glad to report that during the last fortnight he had felt much better. He had decided to reopen the castle to tourists now that he felt up to it. He hoped that Millicent and her family would come for a visit.

But what about Charles, you ask?

Well, I doubt if the Cort-Kittershaws will be vacationing in England next year.

You see, I decided to write up this narrative, altering very few of the facts and names—not enough to make it unrecognizable to Charles. I am sending it to another magazine to which he subscribed. The editors are a decent sort and quite partial to my material. I have asked them to make an exception and schedule this for immediate publication, for personal reasons. They are intrigued by the implications. Is there a real Charles Cort-Kittershaw, they ask?

Well, that will remain my secret.

And Charles'.

If he is blameless, then this is entirely a piece of fiction and no harm will be done; but if the assumptions I have made strike uncomfortably home to Charles, I am sure he will not dare to make any further moves.

For I think I understand Charles fairly well. I can now see the deep insecurity which he hides behind his poses, his literary conceit, his snobbery. I pity the loneliness that he and Catherine share, and yet fail completely to share. I can sense his desperate need to be admired by those of whom he approves. And I think he will find in this story the irony of his own false dreams, his striving for something which will now probably not be attainable—at least, not for many years.

For this narrative and Charles Cort-Kittershaw will both share one deficiency—a deficiency which may be an asset to a fiction story, but to Charles will represent a bitter disappointment.

That deficiency is, as you have already seen, that neither the story nor Charles will have a title.

The Frantick Rebel

BY LILLIAN DE LA TORRE

"What! Boswell!" cried the strapping virago to whom I had just been presented—"the friend to Liberty! Come to my arms! I must infallibly kiss thee!"

Though I am not by custom averse from the kisses of the Fair, I own that the proffered caress daunted me. The nymph who had offered it was taller than myself, vast, and antient; she had the hawk's profile of a red Onondaga, and a piercing, maniacal dark eye. Before I could protest, I found myself engulphed in draperies and soundly bussed on both my cheeks.

"The friend of Liberty," she cried, "is the friend of America, and the friend of America is the friend of Patience Wright."

Her voice boomed like an orator's in the dusky halls of the Chelsea China Manufactory.

Dr. Sam: Johnson snorted.

"As for thee, Sam: Johnson," cried Mistress Wright, "surely

monarchist that thee is, a kiss is far from thy deserts; but I will kiss thee in token of Christian forgiveness."

Dr. Johnson started back in horror. The potter's freckled boy snickered; the potter yielded to a fit of coughing. As the proffered kiss was bestowed upon the rigid philosopher, I could only stare at the extraordinary creature we had encountered. Friend to Liberty and friend to America I had always been; I glory in the appellation; but at that juncture I was not forward to publish my sentiments. 'Twas at the height of our unfortunate struggle with our fellow subjects 'tother side of the water, and I suppose in all London no other could have been found, besides this mad American, who would shout out rebellious sympathies in a voice that could be heard with ease clear to the Surrey side of Thames.

Dr. Johnson had come down to Chelsea, not to bandy words with a rebel, but to try out his newest clay in the potter's kiln. Setting his little brown scratch-wig straight and working his lips in silent disapproval, he withdrew to his work-room with what dignity he could muster. Being for the nonce potter's devil, I followed, leaving Mistress Wright engaged in kissing the potter's boy, presumably for being in his humble way also a friend to America. I pondered much what such a flamboyant rebel might be up to in London.

I was soon to learn, and from none other than the head of the secret service. Mr. William Eden came himself to Johnson's Court, begging with agitation my learned friend's assistance.

" 'Tis Patience Wright the wax worker," he groaned. " 'Tis certain she's a spy, yet we can do nothing with her. Her wax-works are all the rage, and she is so great with her Royal Highness the Princess Amelia, and with even higher Personages, that we cannot lay a finger on her. At the Palace 'tis all 'Patience' and 'George' and 'Charlotte,' she being a Quaker by religion and a Republican by sympathy; and I have it from the highest authority, the woman has had the impudence to rate his Sacred Majesty to his face about the American war. Upon this she was banished the Palace; but Queen Charlotte still inflexibly protects her, the while she communicates to Franklin in Paris."

"Foh," said Johnson, "what does a madwoman know that could advantage our enemies?"

"She is not so mad but there's method in it," said Eden, biting his lip, "and as to what she knows, she knows enough at this moment to foil all our scheams and lose us our colonies forever."

Johnson: "Then she must be prevented from communicating it."

Eden: "Yes, Sir, 'tis a matter the most serious. When you have heard all, I know you will lay aside your every occupation in order to serve your country."

Johnson: "Well, Sir, say on."

Eden: "Sir, the scheam was laid down by one whom I shall call General B——. 'Tis for a military campaign of the first importance, which shall divide the rebellious colonies so that we may reduce them at our leisure. Now General B——, though a brilliant soldier, is in hours of ease a rake and a man of pleasure. No sooner, therefore, has he come to town, but he takes into keeping one Miss Fleay, late of the stage, and sets her up in a house in Chelsea, hard by the pottery. Down goes Miss Fleay to Chelsea with her cook and her odd boy and her waiting-woman—and Mistress Wright, if you please, goes along to teach her modelling, at which the lady has a dainty hand. Miss Fleay thought the kilns of the pottery the attraction held out by Chelsea—but now it appears as if the presence of General B—— was the true loadstone."

Johnson: "Well, and so Chelsea was all one idyll of true love and modelling in wax."

Eden: "Aye, and thence comes our danger. In an ill moment, General B—— communicated his scheam to his companion, whose loyalty is above doubt; only to find too late that Mistress Wright, the frantick rebel, had over-heard all."

Johnson: "If the secret's out, how can I or any man mend the matter?"

Eden: "Miss Fleay took steps at once. She attached herself so closely to Mistress Wright, that the American was totally unable to communicate with anyone; having meantime sent an urgent message to me, revealing the situation. We immediately placed the spy under the closest surveillance, and I do assure you that she has as yet neither communicated nor attempted to communicate with anyone outside the household. But this cannot last; she must send a messenger to Franklin at Paris, or go herself, within this eight days, if this intelligence is to advantage the rebels."

Johnson: "Sir, I am no bailiff; I cannot undertake to watch this lady. I am deep in experimentation with clays; my friend Boswell is newly come to town for a frisk; you must seek elsewhere for a watch-dog."

Eden: "Nay, Dr. Johnson, the lady is encompassed by watch-dogs. Miss Fleay has augmented her domestic staff; Mrs. Wright's waiting-woman is one of my people, and the coachman, and the gardener's boy."

Johnson: "Then what do you ask of me?"

Eden: "Sir, in the words of the satirick Juvenal, *Quis custodiet ipsos custodes?* We must have someone on hand who cannot be bought. Furthermore, the lady has a wild and fertile invention, beyond the ken of any mere watch-dog. I would have you match wits with her, and intercept her communications no matter how slyly they are put forth."

I was eager to accept the commission: "Pray, Sir, let us do it. 'Twill be better than any frisk, and not so dull neither; and as to the clays, 'tis but a step to your kiln at the pottery."

Dr. Johnson scowled; the ranting republican of the pottery was clearly before his eye. But Mr. Eden added his perswasions to mine and Dr. Johnson, appealed to in the sacred name of his King, consented to sojourn in Chelsea till the dangerous week was past. For better obfuscation, 'twas given out to the gazettes that Dr. Sam: Johnson and Mr. James Boswell were gone down to Oxford upon a literary errand.

Mr. Eden's coach set us down in Paradise Row, Chelsea, without more delay. We found the frantick American calmly modelling the head of a Cherokee Sachem, pulling and pinching the softened wax.

Her companion in the gracious panelled room was a lady, to whose charms I incontinently yielded my heart—Miss Flora Fleay, late of Drury Lane, tall, agreeably formed, with a countenance in which strong sense and caressing manners mingled. She greeted us with a suspiration of relief, Mistress Wright with a calm inclination of the head.

Seated hand in hand by the fire, an antient pair in Quaker garb greeted us not at all.

"Your servant, ma'am," says nearsighted Sam: Johnson, bowing to the aged lady.

"My old father and mother," said Mistress Wright, pointing towards them with a hand from which trailed plain ruffles rather the worse for draggling in wax. "Don't be ashamed of them because they look so—" the pair in question heard this extraordinary remark without moving a muscle—"they were good folks, they turned Quaker—"

I looked at the subject of this discourse. They were wax figures.

"They turned Quaker," Mistress Wright was rattling on, "and imbued me with their most excellent principles. I shall call thee Samuel."

"As you will, Mistress Wright," said Dr. Sam: Johnson wryly.

"Pray call me Patience. And thee, friend Boswell, what is thy name?"

"James."

"James, I desire thy better acquaintance. Don't despise these good folk, they did well by their children, they would never let us eat meat, and that is the reason why we were all so ingenious. Thee has heard of the ingenious Mrs. Wright from America, I suppose?"

Dr. Sam: Johnson scowled like a thunder-cloud, as he did at every affectation of singularity; but Mistress Wright continued her discourse unabashed:

"And as to strong spirits, I do contemn 'em, holding that nothing so operates to void phlegm and clarify the intellects as prime lemonade, in a glass of which I desire you'll join me."

I thought the lady's offer rhetorical; when to my surprise she absolutely extracted from her capacious pocket a pair of lemons, and loaf sugar in a twist, and then and there compounded for the gratified philosopher a glass of his favorite regale. Dr. Sam: Johnson assisted at the mysteries with complaisance.

I seized the opportunity with raised eyebrow to question my agreeable hostess. She nodded encouragingly in reply:

"Not out of my sight a moment since the General departed."

The secret, then, was still safe; our task to keep it so yet lay before us.

Dinner passed without incident, save that Mistress Wright, eating vast quantities of beef-root, favoured us with a discourse in support of abstaining from meat and monarchy. Only Johnson's desire to serve his King prevented him from denouncing the eccentrick American.

Dinner done, we returned to modelling in the parlour. Miss Fleay did me the honor to embark upon the task of reproducing my features; features which, she said civilly, 'twas an absolute duty to transmit to posterity, being indeed, I flatter myself, though not beautiful, yet strong and characteristick.

Mistress Wright had a mind to Dr. Johnson—"Dear creature, I must have his head"—but the Sachem was to be finished first. The hawk face was nigh completed by bed-time, but being yet to be coloured, looked something ghostly, like a Roman busto. We left it haunting the mantelpiece as we retired. With Mistress Wright went her woman, Mr. Eden's agent, a rosy pretty-faced creature with the powerful person of a grenadier, to lie in the truckle-bed and keep the American spy under her eye till morning. Dr. Johnson carried me with him for a late stroll about the garden. On the back step sat the gardener's boy. At the locked front gate the gardener was consoling his vigil with a short pipe of tobacco. Our charge was safely surrounded till morning.

The morrow was Dr. Johnson's day at the Pottery. With more misgivings than I liked he consigned his charge to me, and stumped off towards Cheyne Walk with the gardener's boy carrying his basket behind.

I passed the day most agreeably in sensible feminine society. Much to my contentment, General B—— never appeared (and I may say that through all this adventure we never laid eyes on the rakish General). Miss Fleay devoted herself assiduously to her modelling, and the moulded wax began to take on something the semblance of James Boswell. Mistress Wright had forgotten the Sachem. She took a freak to form a candle like an effigy. She fetched a roll of wax from her apartment, where Eden's agent was, finally, getting her sleep.

"Foh, how that woman sleeps!" cried Mistress Wright, little dreaming that her companion had devoted the night, not to sleep, but to surveillance.

Warming the wax by the fire, she began to pull and pinch it into the semblance of a blackamoor page. 'Twas a quaint and pretty thing, and when 'twas done at the day's end I longed to possess it. But 'twas not for me. The wax-worker wrapped it lovingly in a roll of silk, and carried it carefully off. I followed; except when retired, the lady was my charge. I found her tendering it, a folded billet, and a coin to the odd boy.

"Ma'am," said I, twitching the billet from the boy's hand, "allow *me* to be of service. I will myself take this billet in charge." I scanned the superscription: "To Joshua Fennel at the Cross Keys."

The sharp eyes measured me; the lady shrugged:

" 'Tis no matter. The boy may carry the gift, and my message by word of mouth."

I gave permission with a nod.

"Say from me," Mistress Wright instructed the boy, "I desire my gift may give him light for his business."

"With permission, ma'am—" said I, and boldly unfolded the billet.

'Twas not sealed. Perusing it took but a moment. Mistress Wright desired that her gift might give him light for his business, and remained his true Christian friend.

As I scanned the missive, Dr. Sam: Johnson turned in at the gate, followed by the freckle-face potter's devil carrying the basket.

"What's to do here," says he, "and whither goes the boy?"

He indicated our messenger, now scuffing his way without hurry down Paradise Row.

"He carries a specimen of Mistress Wright's workmanship," said I, "and a message from her mouth. We have thought best to retain the written billet."

Mistress Wright smiled serenely. Dr. Johnson, scanning the billet, bellowed like a bull.

"Stop him!"

It was the freckle-face potter's lad who caught him. I was close on his heels, and had the candle out of his hand in a trice.

Mistress Wright's smile was not quite so serene; but with a fair grace she returned to the fire in the sitting-room. We left her under Miss Fleay's eye, and retired with Mistress Wright's pretty candle.

" 'Tis a shame," said Dr. Johnson, regarding it, "and yet it must be done."

He shattered it. It would have cast light on the rebels' business indeed—at its core was a rolled missive:

"Pray acquaint Mr. Franklin at Passy that a new British thrust will be launched—"

"This secret is not ours," said Johnson, and to my inexpressible disappointment cast the paper into the fire.

Mistress Patience's demeanour matched her name. She conceded us the first trick, and sat serenely by the fire patting and pulling her Sachem into shape. We'd a fine dish of jugged hare to our dinner. As we relished it, Mistress Wright, eating roast potatoes, denounced us as no better than Society Islanders, that eat our fellow-creatures.

"Ma'am," says Johnson, his mouth full of hare, "you frantick republicans would upset the order and subordination of nature. And with Heaven's help, I shall myself endeavour to forfend the day."

"Thee will fail," said Mistress Wright cheerfully; "for ingenuity, he who is full of meat is no match for him who is nourisht with sallets; more especially when his cause is just."

Dr. Johnson choaked with indignation and jugged hare.

Mistress Wright carried the Sachem's head early to her chamber; her woman was at her heels. All retired betimes.

I was waked from my first light sleep by a knocking at our door. 'Twas the pretty-face grenadier, in a taking.

"Sir, she's dead. She don't breathe. Pray, pray, come to our chamber."

We struck flame to the candle, huddled on our cloathes, and ran to Mistress Wright's bed-chamber. There was the disarrayed truckle bed, as the woman had risen from it. In the shadow of the bed-curtains a figure lay motionless.

Johnson held the candle to the still face, the lappets of the nightcap falling on the high cheek-bones and sharpening the look of the nose. He touched the cold cheek. The head rolled sidewise—and kept on rolling. 'Twas severed from the trunk!

"Tschah," said Johnson, "this trick is as old as time."

He stripped back the cloathes and revealed the rolled bolster. The waxen Sachem's head fell to the ground and shattered.

"She's slipped between your fingers, woman," said he sternly to the distrest secret agent. "We must find her before she gets clear away."

"Nay, Sir, I have only nodded a moment; she cannot be far."

We ran down the stair. In the morning-room a light shewed. At Miss Fleay's writing-bureau, engaged with pen and ink, sat Mistress Wright. She had been taking refreshment, for the half of a lemon was at her elbow, and her start as we rushed in precipitated to the floor a glass half full.

"I rejoice, ma'am," said Dr. Johnson cordially, "to see that you are safe. You have given us all a turn. Pray, ma'am, allow me to escort you to your chamber."

Mistress Wright hesitated; then a second time conceded defeat. She deliberately tore into strips the written paper before her, and tossed it into the fire.

"Your most obliged, Sir," said she statelily, and laid her large well-formed hand on my friend's wrist.

The next morning the forgiving Quakeress addressed herself to the design of "having Dr. Johnson's head." She proposed to possess herself of this desirable item by means of a life mask, the secret of which she was famed to have brought to a fine art. As upon her late lamented decease her secret died with her, I will endeavour to gratify the publick by detailing her proceedings.

To begin, then, the sturdy philosopher was denuded of his upper garments and placed supine upon a couch. The application of hog's lard followed, an operation which my friend only endured with much mumbling and grumbling. He redoubled his complaints when the fair artist inserted in his nostrils two stout straws to afford him breath during the remainder of the process. Now a thin grout was swiftly plastered over his countenance, stilling his mouth and sealing his eyes in the operation. Mistress Wright worked swiftly and silently. Thinly and evenly covered with grout, the face looked ghastly as a spectre; and Mistress Wright proceeded to chill my marrow the more by swathing the corpse-like jaw with such a fold of linen as is commonly used to bind the jaws of the dead in their winding-sheets. I shuddered silently.

Dr. Johnson lay like a Stoick as succeeding layers of grout were laid on, till the mask was so thick it lost all human form.

And three minutes after the last smear was applied, all was hard and ready to remove in two neat pieces.

"Faugh," said Dr. Sam: Johnson, sitting up, red in the face and glistening with hog's lard. " 'Tis too much like being buried alive; yet I rejoiced, in my prison, that my friend Boswell was by to effect my release if need arose."

"Sir," said I, acknowledging the tribute, "you may rely upon my vigilance."

"I design to do so," replied Johnson as Mistress Wright retired, "for today is my day at the Pottery. Pray be more wary than last time."

Shamefacedly I promised, and pursued Mistress Wright belowstairs.

I was privileged to see Mistress Wright test her handiwork. This she did by closely pressing into the mould a thin shell of softened wax, working it into every crevice. With a kind of handle of wax she withdrew a perfect waxen mask of my revered friend's features.

"Bravo!" I cried. "The likeness is speaking! Pray, could not you gratify me with a copy?"

"Thee shall have it, James," promised the hearty Quakeress.

So saying, she summoned her woman to assist her, and disappeared with her into her own domain.

That morning saw the completion of the waxen busto of James Boswell; and I do verily believe that as fair Miss Flora's hand shaped my image in the pliable wax, so the same image was impressed upon her heart, erasing therefrom in some measure the gaudy figure of indiscreet General B——. Once I thought good to oversee the proceedings of Mistress Wright; but I found her calmly seated in her own apartment, applying the colourings of life to the waxen mask of my friend, while her woman sat stolidly by; so I returned to more congenial company.

At dinner Johnson was not by; but shortly after, I saw his familiar figure sitting in the wing chair by the fire, holding a book so close before his eyes as to brush his very eye-lashes. Mistress Wright's woman went to her dinner. It was with pleasure that I saw Mistress Wright take the opposing chair by the fire, with a cordial word that my friend, absorbed in his book, neglected to answer. I was free to walk in the garden with Miss Flora.

What was my surprise, then, as we came round the house, to see Mistress Wright, unattended, slipping down the walk with a covered basket on her arm. As I followed, I was still more thunderstruck to see Dr. Sam: Johnson approaching from the direction of Cheyne Walk. He met her as she left the gate.

"Well met, Mistress Wright. Allow me to relieve you of your burden. Whither do we carry it?"

Her countenance changed no more than the waxen Sachem's which it resembled.

"To the Pottery, friend Samuel."

He bowed and handed her with courtly mien. I was glad to make one in the expedition, having been a prisoner in the house since our vigil started.

I shuddered as we passed Dr. Driffield's private mad-house, euphemistically denominated "the Academy." We turned into Lawrence Street, passed the sign of the Cross Keys, and came to the Chelsea China Manufactory.

The potters looked their surprise at seeing Dr. Sam: Johnson so precipitately returned; but among the mixing-rooms he had a cubicle of his own, and thither we turned our steps. The fire still burned on the hearth to give us warmth. Mistress Wright set down her basket, which Dr. Johnson officiously undertook to turn out. 'Twas filled with rumpled old gazettes.

Dr. Johnson carefully uncovered the white unblemished wasp's-nest shape, and set it to one side, scanning each gazette with care. Though he could detect no scribbled word, he prudently consigned all to the flames. Now for the first time I saw Mistress Wright's Red-Indian composure broken. She snatched ineffectually at his hand; the tears started in her eyes as the flames took the gazettes, and we saw the brown spidery writing start up with the heat.

"I thought so," said Dr. Sam: Johnson with satisfaction. "Lemonade indeed! You have been writing with it, ma'am, not quaffing it; and I counsel you to turn your attention to good roast meat, if you expect to prevail at this game."

"I will do so," said the angry rebel between her teeth, "and I will prevail."

I heard with satisfaction the instructions issued to the freckle-face boy for preserving the mould that should gratify me with a busto of my illustrious friend; and then we walked back towards Paradise Row in the falling twilight.

At home a new wonder awaited me. I entered the drawing-room with my illustrious friend, in his snuff-colour suit and second-best wig; and there, in second-best brown suit and best wig, holding the book to his eyes, he sat in the wing chair by the fire! I looked from the Johnson at my elbow to the Johnson by the fire, and realized how I had been duped by the wily rebel and her wax-works. But for my wilier friend, I had permitted to happen the catastrophe we sought to avoid!

Sternly admonished, the waiting-woman sat up through the night, and Mistress Wright was for the nonce muzzled. On the morrow, it seemed, she took Dr. Johnson's advice; for when Mistress Wright joined us at table for the mid-day meal, her woman whispered me that she had spent the morning dressing a roast duck!

"So, ma'am," I rallied the lady, "you have become converted to our way of thinking, and have drest a succulent roast duck, which no doubt we are now about to sample."

"No, sir," replied she readily, though I thought she looked put about, "for nothing less than sweet charity would I require a fellow-creature to give up its life. 'Tis for a poor man, lies ill at the Cross Keys."

"I applaud your benevolence, ma'am," says Johnson, "and desire to imitate it. Come, let us all go down to the Cross Keys."

Accordingly the duck was fetched in its basket, covered by a linen napkin.

"Ma'am," says Johnson, peeking and sniffing the tempting aroma, "pray tell me, how have you stuft this tender fellow-creature?"

He probed at the filled cavity with his finger, and tasted the fragrant stuffing.

"This is too bad of thee, Samuel!" cried charitable Mistress Wright. "Think of the poor man!"

"He'll not grudge me a bite," says Johnson coolly, and pulled out a handful of dressing. Something came with it—a billet, folded small and tied with pack-thread. Johnson's smile became broad.

"Fie!" he cried. "How came this waste paper to mar such a dish!"

He tossed it in the fire, where it spluttered and flared to nothing in an odour of burning grease. Mistress Wright turned on her heel and left the roast duck to an inevitable fate.

There was no poor man ill at the Cross Keys, so much we learned of Eden's agents; neither had Joshua Fennel ever been heard of. Dr. Sam: Johnson muttered to himself upon this intelligence, and resolved to go no more to the Pottery until the matter was safely concluded. It fell to my lot to carry his commissions to the potters.

"At Dr. Johnson's service, Mr. Boswell," said the master potter, "and pray say to him, we deeply regret the accidental destruction of his mould, and desire he'll soon commission another—"

"Destruction!" I cried. "Is the mould destroyed, and no copy taken off?"

"Aye, with a pox on Josh and his clumsy fingers."

"He deserves," I cried, "to be soundly swinged."

"And swinged he shall be, when once I can lay my hands on him. Pray say so to Dr. Johnson."

Upon receipt of this bad news, Mistress Wright was eager to set about making a new mould; but Dr. Sam: Johnson incontinently refused.

"No, ma'am; you'll stop up my eyes no more."

Mistress Wright thereupon sulked; she sat with folded hands, and would not partake of the convivial punch which Miss Fleay that night brewed. Casting off care in the presence of my penetrating friend, I sped the hours in gallant drinking of healths; Miss Fleay and I were merry together; I felt the shadow of General B—— totally withdrawn, and longed to take his place with the lady that night. But, foxed though I was, duty restrained me; I left Miss Fleay to the punch, and Mistress Wright to the care of her woman, and followed my respected friend to our chamber.

He scowled upon me; I felt an uneasy sense of having exceeded prudence. I slumped on the bed.

"Resume your coat, sir," said he, "and stand up, if you can. I am uneasy for the safety of our secret, and mean to keep watch tonight."

We tiptoed down the stair and took up our stand in the garden under the American's window. A light shewed, and two figures moved in the room. The curtains were drawn; in a little the light was extinguished. Then nothing, only darkness. A great drowse fell upon me. I cannot say how long I floated in it, but I know I was brought back with the jerk of a thumb in my ribs. Down the vine that rose to the window was clambering the figure of a man.

We closed in upon the spot where the intruder must take to the ground; when with a savage leap the dark figure hurled itself down from above our heads, dashed us momentarily to the ground, and made off towards the stables.

In a trice Johnson had recovered himself, pulled me to my feet, and reached the stable door in time to see the man leap to the bare back of Miss Fleay's own horse and ride out at the opened door. There was nothing to do but follow suit. Johnson must have got the General's horse—I marvelled at the agility with which he kept his seat on the mettlesome creature, holding to the halter with one hand. I followed riding loose and reckless on a less fleet creature.

There was no sound in Paradise Row save the sound of galloping hoofs. For the moment the stranger had the start of us. Then we began to gain. At the corner of Cheyne Walk the rider ahead passed under the street-lamp, and we saw the hawk-like profile and the piercing eyes—'twas the Quakeress herself in male attire! Though she rode with reckless skill, we were still gaining as we galloped in a string up Cheyne Walk. There were lights in the private mad-house; I shuddered to think of the wretches incarcerated there.

"This is too dangerous," shouted Johnson over his shoulder. "If we cannot confine the frantick rebel one way, we must try another."

Before I could divine his meaning he had flung his pocket knife boldly through the closed window of Driffield's Academy. It brought the attendants to the gates in a trice; they were after us, hallooed on by Johnson, as we overhauled our quarry at the foot of Cheyne Row.

Johnson pulled down the horse she was riding. She sat erect and impassive as the mad-house attendants came level with us. Then the boldness of Johnson's scheam, so suddenly formed in his mind, became apparent.

"Alack, gentlemen," his Lichfield burr was suddenly strong, "I fear we have arouzed you late. This frantick wife of mine—" Patience Wright suddenly looked full at him with startled gaze—"this frantick poor creature should have been consigned to your care at a more reasonable hour, but that she suddenly gave us the slip at the ordinary and escaped in my attire as you see—"

I looked at her garb. It was indeed Dr. Johnson's second-best brown.

"Pray conduct us to Dr. Driffield."

I saw defeat in the American's eye; but I reckoned without her bold slyness. Narrowly watched by the attendants, and with one of us on each side, she was conducted through the portals of the madhouse, and the heavy door swung to behind us. Dr. Driffield received us, rubbing his fat hands.

"Hark ye, Doctor," said Mistress Wright, cool and collected, "a word in your ear. I am your debtor for delivering me, for yonder husband of mine—" impudently indicating Johnson—"is mad as the wind, and a sly madman he is. Coming hither to consign him to your care, he found means at the ordinary to deprive me of my attire and confine me. I gave him the slip in a suit of his cloathes, but he was nigh catching me, and it had gone hard with me but for a fortunate chance—in a fit of madness he flung a missile through your window, and so it chanced that your keepers have laid him by the heels. I beg you'll not credit his sly lies; for yonder lies his missile—" she nodded to it where it lay on the floor—"and the better to assure you he's mad indeed, he imagines himself in his phrenzy to be one of London's most famous men."

Johnson was indeed inflating himself to thunder out a denial of this impudent fabrication.

"Sir," he began, "I am Samuel Johnson—"

"Is it likely?" counters this impudent American. "Has Sam: Johnson a wife? Nay, is Sam: Johnson in London? You know from the gazettes he is gone to Oxford."

Dr. Driffield, alas, proved to be a great reader of the gazettes.

"True, ma'am," says he.

"I am Sam: Johnson," said my friend calmly, "and there are weighty reasons of state why this mad-woman must be confined."

"Be perswaded, sir," I cried, "this is indeed the Great Lexicographer, and I am James Boswell, at your service."

Unfortunately our midnight dash had discommoded my vitals. I hiccupped. Mistress Wright turned to me with scorn.

"What, Thomas!" she cried. "Is this the part of one who has been in my service, man and boy, for fourteen years! Take care, sirrah, you'll lose my favour. You have been bought by this old reprobate, 'tis clear—"

The hiccup did my business. Dr. Driffield used his own nose, and put me down for the drunken serving-man she made me seem.

"Away with them, men," says he.

"I'll not stir till this woman is confined," cried Johnson stoutly.

The fat doctor looked on him sourly. The American woman might have got clear off, had she but let well enough alone. But when one of the hulking mad-keepers laid a doubtful hand on her arm, she lost her head.

"Touch me," she cried defiantly, "at your peril; the Queen is my friend."

"You see," said Johnson to the mad-doctor, "her brain is addled."

Driffield looked from one to the other of us in perplexity.

"They're all mad," he decided. "Let them be confined."

I stared aghast as my revered friend was seized; while Johnson held the American spy in a grip of iron. Clearly so long as she was confined he had no care for us.

For four-and-twenty hours I saw my friend no more. Dawn came on, and with it thoughts as painful as the head they filled.

The sun was high when one of the mad-keepers gingerly thrust some hard bread and a bowl of water between the bars.

The hours dragged on. As my head cleared from the fumes of the punch, I began to feel a savage hunger. I would gladly have devoured Mistress Wright's roast duck, secret writings and all, if I could have come by it. The thought of the duck recalled to me the task we had set ourselves, and I rejoiced that even at this cost we had found a way to confine the frantick rebel with her secret still undivulged. Let her remain under restraint until the moment of danger should be past.

Nevertheless, I had scarce resigned myself to a like fate for myself and my friend. As my head cleared, I resolved to strike a stroke for freedom. When the burly mad-keeper returned at sun-down, I was ready for him.

"What say you," said I perswasively through the bars, "to a handful of broad pieces?"

I saw in his eye that the mad-keeper could be bought; but he was wary.

"You've never a handful of broad pieces about you," he muttered, measuring my garb.

"True for you," said I; "but hark'ee, friend, my master has a purse of golden guineas in the keeping of the landlord of the Cross Keys; how if I was to come to him and say, my master sent for 'em? We should have the dividing of 'em between us."

"Done," said the mad-keeper instantly, and added slyly: "We'll go together."

I could hope for no better. The mad-keeper instantly set me free, and led the way through a tangle of out-buildings towards Lawrence Street and the Cross Keys. I kept ever alert to give my conductor the slip; but he pressed along with his arm linked in mine, and I was a prisoner still. Before the Cross Keys we halted.

"We must not enter together," said I with firmness. "The landlord will scarce yield the bag of guineas if I come with an accomplice at my elbow. Do you go in and bespeak a pot; I'll follow, get the swag, and join you as if by chance."

"Ye'll make off, ye mean," rasped the mad-keeper with a cunning look. "No, no, me lad; *you* go in, and I'll follow. And look ye don't get out of my sight."

I shrugged, and went in.

"Hark'ee, landlord," I began to speak quietly and hastily to the thin needle-nose little man at the bar. But for him the smoky dark-panelled room was empty. He looked at me with disfavour. I saw in his eyes as in a mirror how I must look, rumpled, pasty-faced from punch and lack of sleep, and my heart sank. Over his shoulder I saw the door open, and in came the mad-keeper. He grinned evilly at me, and took up a post of vigilance on the settle by the fire.

The landlord listened to my muttered plea without change of expression, and then shook his head. He absolutely refused to send a messenger all the way to Whitehall. He seemed apprehensive that I was the advance guard of the running smobble.

"Then pray, landlord," I shifted my ground, "pray let the pot-boy be sent no further than Miss Fleay's in Paradise Row, I'll engage he'll be well paid for his trouble."

The landlord continued to look at me, impassive.

"The lady affects me," I lied desperately. " 'Tis an *affaire du coeur,* 'pon honour, landlord, do but befriend me, you'll be well rewarded, pray let me have ink and paper and the pot-boy to carry my billet."

The sharp little face suddenly split in a wide smile. There was not a tooth in the grinning gums.

"Faith, lad, if 'tis the heart is in it, I'll befriend thee," lisped he, "being myself a great sufferer from the tender passion."

He set paper and pen before me. As I dipped the quill, he set himself with relish to peer over my shoulder and enjoy the composition of my *billet doux.* I ground my teeth, and wrote:

Honour'd Madam:

He who loves you better than life, acquaints you that our time is ripe, for my schoolmaster Mr. J. is detained in Cheyne Walk, at the Academy, whence he will scarce come off with ease. Pray be circumspect, for should Eden hear of this he would enlarge him instanter.

You take my meaning. I am detained at the Cross Keys by a bailiff—[The landlord glanced at my mad-keeper, and then back to me, and shook his head commiseratingly, as if to communicate the sympathy of a fellow-sufferer equally from bailiffs and the tender passion]—but I will take what means I may to give him the slip and come to you, whereby we may have the consolation of one another's company.

Thine till death,
J.B.

The pot-boy was rouzed from the kitchen inglenook, and off he went for Paradise Row. I returned willy-nilly to my mad-keeper, and told him the first tale that came to my head, that mine host had sent for the keys, and the guineas should shortly be ours. The man scowled into his pot.

Now up comes mine host, and with a wink to me, sets out to ply the sullen mad-keeper with liquor, lacing his pots with gin with the liberal hand of a friend to lovers. Four pots later the boy returned with a verbal message: "The lady bids me say, she takes your meaning, and will deal with your schoolmaster." The mad-keeper was too owlishly drunk to do more than blink foolishly. A few moments more, and his head dropped to the table. With a broad grin full of gums the landlord jerked his head in signal, and I was off in a trice. I came into Cheyne Walk just as Sir William Eden descended from his carriage at the mad-doctor's door. Soon my learned friend was once more at liberty, no whit the worse for his Academic sojourn, he having borne it as a philosopher.

That day week, all danger past, we were once more at Dr. Driffield's door, and the frantick American, still wearing Dr. Johnson's second-best brown, was in her turn enlarged.

"No hard feelings, ma'am," said Dr. Johnson; "we have gained time, and time fights for the King."

"I'll kiss thee farewell," replied Mistress Wright, smiling, "in token of Christian forgiveness."

Dr. Johnson, magnanimous in victory, bore her Christian salute with a good grace.

We saw no more of the American wax-worker; but as Christmas came on we had a message from her.

"I am to say from the lady," said the messenger, "she desires it may cast light upon your business."

We stared upon the message, a slab of such petrified grout as had formed the ill-fated life-mask of the Great Lexicographer.

"This is an Egyptian message," puzzled I as the messenger withdrew. "I can make nothing of this."

"It comes with the candle-message," mused Johnson. "We shattered the candle; are we to shatter this as well?"

Boswell: "Will it shatter like wax?"

Johnson: "The mould was shattered. The mould . . . Stay, Mr. Boswell, you oversaw its making, pray detail to me the manner of it."

Boswell: "Well, sir, she smeared your face with grout, and braced it with a fold of linen—"

Johnson: "A fold of linen! Why did I not hear of this?"

Boswell: "Nay, sir, you were by."

Johnson: "I was by! Deafened and blinded with grout! *'Twas the message!"*

Boswell: "Nay, sir, the linen was blank."

Johnson: "Blank! Tschah! 'Twas writ in secret ink. The Americans have had the secret after all!"

Angrily he dashed the slab to the hearth. It shattered. Folded within lay a strip of linen protecting a slip of paper. The paper was from that day's gazette:

"We are advized from New-York, that Lieutenant-general John Burgoyne—"

"Of course," remarked Johnson, "Gentleman Johnny Burgoyne. Who else would take a lady of Drury Lane into keeping while great events depended?"

"—Lieutenant-general John Burgoyne with 6,000 men has surrendered to the rebels near Saratoga in the Province of New-York. This stroke has much heartened the rebels, and 'tis thought that his Majesty the King of France will now conclude an alliance. . . ."

Johnson threw down the item in disgust, and picked up the linen. Written on it in a curiously rusty-looking stuff was a letter from the American spy:

Sir,

Pray accept of my acknowledgements for the help Dr. Johnson lately rendered the glorious cause of Liberty, in transporting with his own hand, the mould which carried that most necessary communication to Mr. Franklin, into the hands of my accomplice the potter's boy. The comedy of the mad-house served to keep the minions of the King amused until the boy had made the best of his way out of the country. How well he did his part, this glorious victory of Saratoga attests. With the blessings of a great and grateful nation, I am,

Sir,

Your oblig'd humble servant,

PATIENCE WRIGHT

[By growling against the rebellious Colonists, the Great Cham invited at my hands this fictitious come-uppance dealt him by a factual American spy. The Chelsea scene suggested the China Manufactory, which Johnson frequented, and the mad "Academy," which he did not.]

The Man Who Hated Scenes

BY ROBERT ARTHUR

We were somewhere west of Chicago, rocketing through flat Iowa farmland at a velocity that sent the coffee slopping over the edge of my cup. It was early—so early that I was the only one in the dining car, except for the very neat little man who sat opposite me. I didn't know his name, but we had chatted over a drink in the club car the evening before, and it had been natural for me to invite him to sit with me when he entered the diner a moment after I did.

"I can never sleep on a train," he complained. "So I thought I'd get dressed and have some breakfast." His accent was English.

"Same here," I told him. "Going all the way to New York?"

"All the way to Europe." He poked at the scrambled eggs the waiter had put in front of him.

"England?" I asked.

"No, I left England long ago. I like a warm climate. My nerves are upset. I'm going to spend a quiet winter on the Riviera. . . . I *did* order shirred eggs, didn't I?"

He had. I'd heard him say it as he handed the order to the waiter. A sleepy chef had sent in scrambled eggs instead.

"I should send them back." The little man sighed. "I detest scrambled eggs. But I do hate a fuss." He looked at me plaintively. "Even a little one. I just can't bear a scene of any kind."

He began to eat as the car made a lurch which forced me to mop coffee from my saucer with a napkin.

"You can imagine," he said, between bites, "what a dilemma I was placed in when I learned that my wife was deceiving me."

"Dilemma?" I repeated. He nodded.

"Oh yes. She thought I didn't suspect. I was deeply hurt by her unfaithfulness. At the same time I couldn't bear the idea of the scene that would take place if I spoke to her about it."

He pushed aside the eggs.

"I guess I'll just have coffee." He poured it carefully from the silver pot. "You see, all my life I've made it a strict rule to avoid excitement. My nerves—I get so upset whenever there's any fuss. . . ."

He added cream to the coffee, very precisely, and then put in exactly one and a quarter teaspoons of sugar.

"I suppose you'd call it a very British eccentricity," he went on. "But luckily I inherited a good deal of money and money is a wonderful insulator—it keeps at a distance all kinds of annoyances that the average man can't avoid. So I've never objected when I've been overcharged or anything like that—it's easier to pay and remain calm."

He looked at me appealingly with large, liquid brown eyes. "You do understand, don't you?"

To be polite, I answered that I did.

"I was sure you would." He seemed happy at my reassurance. "Then you can understand what torment I went through, trying to decide how to break up my wife's affair with our chauffeur without precipitating a scene."

My face must have expressed something which he misinterpreted, for he hurried on.

"Oh yes, the chauffeur. Of course Charles wasn't a typical chauffeur —he was young, and very good looking. But that didn't excuse it, naturally."

He smacked his lips.

"Very good coffee. It makes up for the eggs. But I was telling you about my wife. You see, she was a swimmer before our marriage. Almost made the Women's Olympic team last time. I'm fond of swimming myself—there's nothing that soothes the nerves more than a long, leisurely swim—and that's how we met. At a resort in Florida.

"I was bowled over the very first time I saw Marilyn—my wife. She was doing some exhibition dives from the high board into the hotel pool. In a white bathing suit, poised far above me on the end of the board, she seemed to me like a goddess—Diana turned mermaid instead of huntress.

"We hit it off from the beginning. In a month we were married. Then we went on a world cruise—luxury liner, of course. We had a wonderful time together. We both liked good living and fine service, and I could afford it. We saw all the romantic spots of the world— the Taj Mahal, Bali Bali, everything.

"Then we returned to my home in California—a big mission-type place outside of Santa Barbara. It's a beautiful spot—looks out over the Pacific from a cliff, with the waves breaking in white foam on the wide beach. Delightful climate—not too cold, but not always sticky hot.

"I had a staff of very good servants, my financial affairs were handled by an investment firm, and so there was really no need for me ever to leave my home. It gave me the seclusion my nerves required, and besides, I had everything there that I wanted.

"Including a swimming pool—the ocean was too cold. I believe my swimming pool is one of the biggest private pools in California. Fifteen feet of water at the deep end, all heated and filtered. Wonderful swimming any time of the day or night, any month of the year.

"Marilyn loved it. We splashed about for hours every day, then I would lounge in the sun and watch her practice her diving—she'd made me promise she could try out for this year's Olympic team. Sometimes we'd send the servants away for the day and swim nude. It was genuinely idyllic, in an age when all graciousness seems to have gone out of life."

He sighed, poured more coffee, then went on. "Then after a few months Marilyn seemed restless. I realized that our life, idyllic as it was, was perhaps too quiet for her. So I decided we'd go to the Riviera for six months. We dismissed all the servants and were shutting up the house when I had my upset.

"It was the result of world conditions, my doctor said—I simply became too overwrought by the news from Korea, from Europe, from China. Naturally, we couldn't go to Europe. I spent a few weeks in a very good hospital—a rest home, really, where the soothing quiet and attention did wonders for me. And Marilyn was solicitude itself. She came to see me every day, read to me, or just sat with me and enjoyed the sunshine.

"Then, when the doctor said I was well enough to return to my home, she didn't rehire the servants—they had other positions. Instead she engaged a chauffeur, who took us for long drives during the day, and Marilyn cooked and cared for me herself.

"On the days when we didn't go driving, she would practice in the pool and I would sit watching. At night I retired early, using sleeping tablets to get me to sleep. Marilyn was always solicitous about seeing that I took my pills, saying that if I wanted to get better a sound night's sleep was the best medicine in the world.

"So for some weeks I continued to improve. Then one night about one in the morning I woke up feeling wretched."

The little man sighed.

"Is there anything worse than insomnia?" he asked. "I suppose there is, but surely it's among mankind's greatest curses. At any rate, I lay there, tossing and turning. Finally I called for my wife to bring me another sedative. She didn't answer. At last I got up, turned on the light, and went into her room. She was not there.

"At first I thought she must have got up for something. Then I saw her bed was still made; it was almost two and she hadn't retired yet. A little alarmed, I began to look for her. Then, when I reached the downstairs living room, which opened on to the patio, I heard voices.

"I opened the patio door. The voices were clearer. I heard the sound of splashing too. I understood at once. My wife and Charles were swimming together in the pool.

"It was pitch black—they had, of course, not turned on any lights. But I could hear them laughing and talking in low voices. I heard them climb the diving tower, and dive together into the deep water. They came up, wrestling and playing.

"I stood there, heartsick, holding on to myself with an effort. I almost rushed out and confronted them. But I could not bear the thought of such a scene. So instead I stood and listened. They swam for another half hour, then went across to the servants' wing where Charles had his quarters.

"It was almost daylight before my wife came to her room."

The little, almost unpleasantly neat man paused. He looked thoughtfully into his coffee cup, then across at me. Far up ahead of us the locomotive gave a long whistle which spread out across the empty Iowa farm-land like ripples on a lake.

"The next day," he said, "I engaged a firm of detectives to make inquiries about Charles. They reported that he was a swimmer who had teamed with Marilyn to do exhibition diving the summer before I met her. Then of course the answer was obvious. When I became ill she had sent for him to come—to solace her loneliness, shall we say? Then as I grew better, she had conceived the idea of making him our chauffeur.

"You can see now why I called it a dilemma. Here I was just recovering from a nervous illness. A scene, a quarrel would undo all the work of weeks of convalescence. In any case, I could scarcely have faced such an explosive situation; now of all times it was impossible for me to confront my wife, to send Charles away, to do what another man would have done instantly. It was a weakness, but I could not overcome it.

"Instead, I dissembled. I pretended that I knew nothing. I waited, racking my brains for a way to let Marilyn know that I knew, but to do it in such a manner that no scene would take place. If I could just manage it delicately enough, I was sure, there need be no fuss, no emotional storm.

"But the days went by and I could think of nothing that would not mean a violent break. Each night Marilyn and Charles swam together secretly in the pitch-black pool. Each morning just before daylight she would come at last to her room and slip into bed, not guessing that in the room beyond I lay awake, in a torment of indecision.

"Then, just as I had almost given up hope of a peaceful solution of the matter, it came to me. I saw how it could be done. Quietly, without fuss.

"Marilyn wanted to go to a moving picture in Santa Barbara—something new which had received favorable reviews. I urged her to go; I ordered her to go, and said Charles must drive her, as I did not like her driving alone at night.

"She saw me to bed, saw me ostensibly take my sleeping tablets, then she left. I heard the car drive away with young, handsome Charles at the wheel; then I rose again. I dressed and went downstairs. I knew they would be back late, whether they went to the moving picture or not.

"I had plenty of time. I arranged a hint that would let them know, upon their return, that I was aware of what was happening, and retired to my room, feeling sure the affair would not continue longer.

"It was midnight when I heard them return. It was a very dark, sultry night—just the night for a swim. Marilyn did not even come to her room, but went with Charles to his. Then, a few minutes later, I heard them laughing softly as they emerged and went toward the pool.

"It was inky dark—once Marilyn stumbled and I heard her giggle as Charles caught her, and in the darkness kissed her. Then there was a moment's silence as they climbed the diving tower, then the high board creaked as they both stepped out on it. I heard it creak again sharply as they dived off into the pool, Marilyn first and Charles right behind her in the little game they enjoyed so much. It was too dark to see a foot in front of you, but of course to swimmers of their skill that made no difference. They always swam in the dark, lest I should wake and see the lights, and I rather imagine it added to their fun."

The train lurched around a curve. My napkin fell to the floor. When I had picked it up, my companion was staring out at the empty fields that raced upon us.

"And your hint," I felt compelled to ask, "did it succeed? Did it break up the affair?"

"Eh? Oh yes." He seemed to bring his attention back to me with an effort. "The affair was ended that night."

Apparently he was going to leave it at that, but I could not resist asking the obvious question.

"The hint I left for them?" he repeated. "It was quite simple when I finally thought of it. Before they got back I just drained all the water out of the swimming pool."

Love Will Find a Way

BY DAVID ALEXANDER

When you see an avalanche roar down a mountain, you believe in God.

Not the new God of peace and compassion and forgiveness, but the old, fierce God of wrath and vengeance, whose eyes were lit with lightning and whose voice was thunder in the hills. Only such a God could make a mountain tear itself apart.

We were on the topmost ledge of the peak the Swiss call God's Staircase, standing outside the log-girded summit house, when we heard the first low rumblings of disaster. In the beginning there was only a faint patter as tiny pebbles bounced from ledge to ledge, and then the sharp staccato of a stony hailstorm, and finally the rending crash as tons of tight-packed snow exploded into a lethal torrent. Boulders that were old when dinosaurs walked the earth were belched up suddenly to skip and hurtle and pound as they broke the mountain's granite face.

For half an hour, for thirty minutes that were all eternity, the three of us—my wife Linda, the Swiss guide Keller, and myself—stood there suspended in awesome space as the terrifying tidal wave swept by within a hundred feet of us. Fragments of rock and shards of ice-hard snow were spewed into our faces, but none of us moved. We simply stood there staring at this unbelievable spectacle. When the old, forgotten God returns to show his might, you do not turn away.

When the thing was finally over we saw that half the topmost shelf, the shelf on which we roosted precariously, had been sheared away. All the other ledges had disappeared and we knew at once that there was no way down. We would almost surely die here in a little log house suspended a mile above the earth.

We thought of the pleasant village beneath the clouds and of the laughing, rosy people, buried now forever beneath a new mountain made of rubble.

God's Staircase is the most peculiar peak in all of Switzerland—but I should not use the present tense. It *was* the most peculiar, before the avalanche sliced half of it away. It stood remote from other mountains. From a distance it resembled a slender spindle thrusting up into the clouds, or a gnarled finger pointing to Infinity. On three sides it had been sheer, slick rock, with no handholds, no footholds. A mountaineer, however foolish and daring he might be, would never have attempted to scale those sides. The fourth side afforded the easiest climb in Europe. Even fat old ladies encased in rigid corsets could conquer the fourth side of the mountain without undue exertion. That was why the villagers compared it to a staircase.

In some remote age of earth a slowly grinding glacier had made a serrated design on one side of the mountain, so that it resembled a jagged saw blade. There was a pattern of ledges, some narrow, some comfortably wide, from top to bottom. Climbing God's Staircase had always been an amusement rather than a feat. There had been little difficulty in moving upward—or downward—from ledge to ledge.

Now the avalanche had struck, it was impossible to move either up or down.

The three of us were stranded in eternity as effectively as spacemen in a runaway rocket.

I can remember now how Schweder, the fat innkeeper, had warned us against the climb. In the spring, he said, the mountain clears its throat and someday it will cough and the whole village will be destroyed. Keller, our guide, had laughed at him and chided him for being an old woman.

"There has been no avalanche in the memory of the oldest man," he said. "It is safer to scale the peak than to climb your creaky stairs, Innkeeper."

I had not wanted to make the climb. I have never been a physical man and I have had little exercise since I was a child. I can see no point at all in knocking a small ball over acres of ground, even though this appears to be the sport of Presidents. It seems to me to be sheer cruelty to make bloody holes in animals with bullets or to rip the mouths of fish with jagged hooks. I am a novelist, you see, a novelist and a poet. I am most at peace with myself in my book-lined study in a quiet old house. I am entirely happy only when I am putting words on paper. That is why I am scribbling in my journal now, despite the unendurable pain, despite the gnawing hunger in my gut, despite the fact that Death stands here beside me, hovering like a white-faced nurse, waiting patiently. A writer must always write, even at a time like this.

When we came to Switzerland I certainly entertained no idea of climbing a mountain. It was Linda who insisted that we should scale God's Staircase. Linda is a strong woman and a determined woman. She is also a very physical woman. She nearly always finds a way of doing exactly what she wants to do.

Linda and I had been drifting further and further apart in recent years. We had come to Europe on a kind of second honeymoon in the hope of saving our marriage. I suppose that basically the trouble was our lack of mutual interests. Linda seldom reads books, although she makes an effort to read the ones I write. She loves the outdoors and excels in sports. She plays tennis and golf and rides to hounds and it seems to me that she has spent more time in the summers swimming in water than she has spent walking on dry land.

The walls of my study are decorated with delicate and charming Japanese prints by Hiroshige and Sharaku and Hokusai and many other masters. Linda has expressed admiration for only two of the beautiful prints in my large collection. She likes a portrait of a rearing horse by Harunobu and a wrestling scene by Shuncho. The rest of our home belongs to Linda. At least she has appropriated it. The walls of the living room and dining room and halls are cluttered with prints of beefy men, whose faces are as crimson as their coats, mounted on leaping horses.

Linda says that our widely different interests are not the real cause of the trouble that arose between us. She says my gnawing jealousy is the true reason. It is a fact that I am jealous of Linda's admiration of other men. I have no proof that she has ever been unfaithful to me. Still, there have been ugly stories linking Linda with Benson, the golf professional at the country club, and with young Aldrich, who is usually her partner in mixed doubles, and even with the gross and fattening Gaines, who is a Master of Foxhounds, whatever that may mean.

Linda says I criticize her too much. It's true that her eating habits used to annoy me almost as much as her strenuous physical life. I do not see how a woman can possibly retain a figure as lovely as Linda's and still eat heavy meals of meat, potatoes, and rich desserts. I have always been a spare eater myself. A single lamb chop, a green salad, and rice pudding for a sweet used to comprise a feast for me.

Now that I am on the verge of starvation I confess that my mind is swimming with dreams of the rich and heavy food that Linda fancies. Oddly enough, now that there is no possibility of gratifying the fleshy appetites these unholy lusts overwhelm me. I do not deeply regret the books and poems I did not write. I regret that I was not a glutton and a lecher while I had the chance of gratifying the hungers of the body. Human beings like to think that in their final hours they turn their minds to God and dwell only upon matters of the eternal spirit. This is false. When you know that death is near, that it is inevitable, you become an animal. Your mind is occupied entirely with yearning for the most primitive pleasures of the flesh.

When they feed me my ever-decreasing rations, I wolf them down like the slavering mastiff Linda once owned wolfed down raw meat. That dog was the beginning of the trouble between Linda and myself. Linda threatened to divorce me when she discovered that I had poisoned the disgusting beast. Now I am little better than the dog. I exist from morsel to morsel that Linda and Keller give me. Sometimes I whine and beg for more. When Linda is near, I reach out a clawlike hand to touch her wasting body and an overmastering, though impotent, desire burns in me. Yes, I have become an animal. Even in this extremity, Linda and the guide named Keller have managed to cling to some shred of human dignity. Both still have hope, I think, but hope died in me long ago. Because of my broken leg, I am completely dependent upon them. They must do everything for me. I know they have given me more than my share of the scant supply of tinned food with which the summit house was stocked against an emergency like ours. Now the food is gone. Half an hour ago I was fed the last of it.

Even now, Linda does not despair. When I sobbed and begged for just a teaspoon more, she had to tell me that the rations were completely exhausted, that she and Keller had given me the last. When I finished the last food I will ever taste, Linda put her thin arm around my shoulders and tried to comfort me.

"Don't worry, darling," she said. "There has to be some way down the mountain. I will find the way before it's too late. I promise you." She managed an almost cheerful little laugh. "Love will find a way," she added.

Linda's habit of uttering clichés as if they were original and witty remarks used to grate on me.

Now I said, my voice so weak I could barely whisper, "Do you really love me, Linda? Did you really love me all the time?"

She gave my shoulder a squeeze and said, "Of course, you foolish darling. And I love life. I do not want to die. I am going to find a way to live."

I dozed off into one of my fitful sleeps after writing the above. In reading it over, I see my narrative is wandering, and I wish to be coherent, for there is at least a chance that the journal will be found some day. Pain and hunger do something to the mind. It is difficult to think clearly, to set things down in their proper order. But I will try.

As I have said, it was Linda who insisted upon climbing the peak called God's Staircase. I refused point-blank and we arrived at another of the small and silly crises that have been too frequent during our married life. Linda stated that she would make the climb, even if I did not go. I could not tolerate that, of course. She would be alone on the summit with Keller, the guide, and he was the physical type of man I have always heartily detested, a stocky, ruddy fellow with fair hair and bright blue eyes. I had seen Linda looking at the Switzer covertly, the way she always looks at male animals who appeal to her.

And so the three of us made the climb, despite the landlord's grumbled warnings.

I suppose the climb was an easy one, as Keller had said. Yet by the time we were halfway up I was choking for breath and my body was slimy with sweat. My wife and Keller seemed to find the ascent only a mildly exhilarating experience. Neither was even breathing hard. They tried to conceal their annoyance at the slow progress I was making, for I was holding them back, of course. At last we thrust our heads through low-hanging snow clouds and reached the final shelf at the top of the peak. I dropped down, completely exhausted.

It was a few moments later that the mountain began to "clear its throat" as Schweder, the landlord, had predicted. Within seconds the bellowing thunder of snow and rock began.

When it was finally over I stood for moments dazed by shock. And then I screamed at Keller, "How will we get down? How will we get down again?"

Keller examined the havoc carefully before he answered. Then he shook his head and said, "There is no way down."

I became hysterical. My voice was little more than a womanish screech. "You have to get us down! We can't just die up here!"

Keller looked at me with contempt. He threw out his arms and gestured toward the village that was hidden beneath the snow clouds.

"We are better off than the ones down there," he said. "They are already buried. My father and my mother and my sister are all buried in the village."

I could waste no pity on Keller and his lost relatives. Our own predicament was too urgent.

"But we're alive!" I cried. "You must find a way down. You're our guide and it's your duty to take us down safely!"

Linda spoke softly, as if she were conversing with herself. "There has to be a way," she said. "There's always some way out."

Keller was exasperatingly calm.

"It has begun to snow," he said. "The clouds hang very low and there is fog in the valley. There is no way down, and there is no way up, either. No rescue party could try to scale this peak now. But there is a chance. There is the little plane from the military post, the one that has the funny windmill on top of it. It is possible it can land on this ledge and take us off. But not now, and not tomorrow. Not until the weather clears. And no one can say when that may be. No one knows when the snow and fog may disappear in these mountains. Perhaps a few days from now. Perhaps a few months."

"We must signal somehow," I said. "We must. . . ."

"There is no use," Keller interrupted. "No one could see our signals through the clouds and fog and snow. And they will be quite busy down there for many days digging out the bodies. But it could be worse. We have shelter in the summit house. There are cots and blankets inside. There is a stove and firewood. We guides have stocked the place with tinned food, bought out of the small fees we earn from tourists. It will last a while if we are careful. We can melt snow for water. My fellow guide and friend, Jan Brucker, knows we made the climb today. He is taking a party up Thunder Ridge, miles from here, and he will have missed the avalanche. He will tell the military post we are on God's Staircase. When the little windmill plane can fly, they will search for us."

"And when will that be?" I screamed. "When, Guide, when?"

The Switzer remained calm. "I cannot answer that," he said. "Perhaps the little plane will come in time, perhaps not. It all depends upon the weather. We must use what rations we have most carefully. By the way, there is *schnapps* inside the log house, too. You are trembling. You can use a glass."

His tone infuriated me. I was even more enraged by Linda, who put her hand on my arm and spoke to me as if she were a patient mother soothing a squalling child.

"We will find a way," she said. "There is always some way. Keller has been climbing this peak for many years. He knows every detail of the mountain, the way you know every detail of your Oriental prints."

Her words drove me mad with fury. In this life-and-death emergency she relied entirely upon the strength and resourcefulness of this stocky blond stranger. She looked upon her husband as a helpless, puling, effeminate man, good for nothing but such precious pastimes as collecting Japanese color prints.

Linda's words goaded me to an act of ridiculous bravado.

"*I* will find a way down!" I yelled at them.

And I began to run forward over the slippery rock, toward the path we had ascended, the path the avalanche had crushed. When I reached the precipice, I looked down. The clouds parted for a moment and I could see the sheer, awful drop. But I had to make a gesture, I had to impress Linda, who was calling after me in a frightened voice. I had to dare a thing the phlegmatic Switzer refused to attempt.

I saw that just below our shelf, before the naked plunge of almost vertical cliffside, there was a slight protuberance of rock, heaped over with the rubble of the landslide. I was sick and dizzy, but I began to lower myself carefully and slowly over the precipice, seeking a foothold in the debris of broken rock and snow. It was a completely futile risk that I was taking, for even if I found a foothold just below, there was no possibility of my proceeding farther.

My left foot touched something that seemed solid, but the rubble parted under me like quicksand and my whole leg was sucked down into the pile of snow and rock. And then the boulder itself gave way and went plummeting down the mountain and my kneecap was banged against the hard side of the peak, and I was dangling by my fingertips, it seemed. A sickening pain stabbed my leg from ankle to hipbone, and I screamed.

Keller managed to lift me back to the ledge. He examined me and found my leg was broken. I am a small, slight man. Keller had little trouble lifting me in his arms and carrying me into the log house. He placed me on a rude bed. I was still screaming in my agony. There was a little cache of medicines in the log house, as well as food and firewood. The Switzer found a syrette of morphine and injected the narcotic into my arm. Then he took pieces of firewood and the coiled rope from his belt and devised a splint of sorts.

I cannot tell you how long ago that was. I am sure that Linda and Keller have kept track of time, but I am afraid to ask them how long we have been here. I only know that they say the snow and fog still screen the peak where I lie dying.

The little log house is partitioned into two sections. Linda sleeps in here with me and sometimes she sits beside my bed, holding my hand, assuring me that she will find a way. But she spends more and more time in the other room with Keller. Perhaps that is because I am too weak to talk much to her.

I can hear Linda's footsteps now. She is coming toward the door. Perhaps she has found more food. Oh, please, God, please! Make Linda bring me food!

Linda did not bring food. When I complained, she told me there was none to bring. Instead she gave me an injection of morphine. She told me it was the last syrette. When the effect wears off, I will be left to suffer unendurable pain, and to starve to death. . . .

. . . I have waited awhile before continuing this record. I tried to sleep. But I have become immune to morphine, it seems. To please Linda, I closed my eyes and breathed heavily. She thought that I was sleeping as she tiptoed back to Keller's room. She left the door open a crack, and I could hear them talking. Perhaps the pain and hunger have sharpened my sense of hearing. I could hear them quite clearly, although they spoke in low voices, fearing to awaken me.

Linda said, "Keller, will the helicopter come in time?"

"The what?" asked Keller dully.

"The helicopter. The little windmill plane."

There was a long silence before Keller spoke. "I will tell you truthfully," he said. "The little plane will come, but I do not think now that it will come in time. We are very weak. We have been here a long while and all the food is gone. And we gave most of what we had to your husband. No, I do not think our lives will outlast the fog and snow that keep the little plane away."

Linda spoke very softly. "I have found a way, Keller. We must not die. I have a plan that will save our lives."

Linda told Keller of her plan. I listened in amazement. It was so obvious, so simple. I could not understand why she had not thought of it before. She is such a clever woman, equal to any emergency. Now that I know Linda has a plan, I am hardly conscious of the searing pain in my leg or the gnawing hunger in my belly. I can even smile. There is nothing I have to do now but wait. . . .

. . . I have not waited very long. I can hear Linda coming toward my door. I wonder if she will tell me of her plan, of the way that she has found. No, of course not. She will think it much better to have it come as a surprise to me.

There is no need to tell me. I have heard them talking and I know exactly what they are going to do.

They are going to eat me.

About the Authors

A Kentuckian by birth, DAVID ALEXANDER is a New Yorker by adoption. For ten years he was managing editor and columnist on the New York *Morning Telegraph*, America's oldest theatrical and sports daily. At one time he enrolled for an intensive thirteen-week course at the New York Institute of Criminology and graduated with highest honors in a class that included professional policemen and practicing investigators. He has been praised by federal and city police for his accurate depiction of professional police work.

In the days when people were still listening to radio, ROBERT ARTHUR was writer-producer-director for *The Mysterious Traveler, Nick Carter,* and *The Shadow*. He was winner of a special award for one of his stories in *Ellery Queen's Mystery Magazine,* and of two Edgars for the best radio mystery of the year. He was one of the earliest members of Mystery Writers of America, and the originator of the MWA writing course. He lives in New Jersey.

A retired physician, JOSEPHINE BELL has spent much of her life in the two careers of writing and medicine. After studying medicine at Cambridge University and graduating with honors, she continued study at University College Hospital in London. In 1954 she retired from medical practice to devote her full time to writing. Miss Bell lives in Surrey, England.

ROBERT BLOCH is best known as the author of *Psycho*. Born in Chicago, he lived for many years in Weyauwega, Wisconsin—but he lives now in a haunted house in Hollywood, where he writes motion picture scripts and television thrillers. It is said of him that he has scared more people out of a week's growth than Bluebeard, Lugosi, Karloff and Chaney combined—though on a typewriter.

A familiar name to mystery fans, an active worker with hopeful mystery writers, HERBERT BREAN in 1964 is perhaps most gratefully known for his book *How to Stop Smoking*. Mr. Brean started in the news business, reporting and writing, before he graduated from college. He has been with the United Press and the Detroit *Times*, and presently writes for *Life* magazine. The writing workshop given by MWA each fall is conducted by this editor of the *Mystery Writer's Handbook* (text for the course), and somehow, with all this, Mr. Brean still finds time to add titles to his list of suspense novels.

GLADYS CLUFF was born in a Michigan blizzard, was raised on a sunny California orange ranch, recovered from an early pottery-and-epic-poetry fever ("after the Greek") and abandoned a series of "educational distractions" with relief to marry a Stanford law student and produce three daughters and six grandchildren. A Greenwich Villager now, she has written radio serials and historical dramas, articles, plays, verse, and short stories—and has just finished a first (adult) novel at the age of seventy-two.

It was not until she was forty that LILLIAN DE LA TORRE conceived the idea of combining mystery with history, and even then it was quite by chance that she created her well-known character, Dr. Sam: Johnson. Since Miss de la Torre can trace her ancestors to Pizarro's Conquistadores, the Minute Men and the Green Mountain Boys (and those who "just missed" the *Mayflower*), it was not surprising that she should possess a historical bent. Her first story was the indirect result of her studies in eighteenth-century literature, which provided her with a spur-of-the-moment point in a family discussion: that detective heroes should be believable, vital human beings. Since the first story that this conversation inspired, Lillian de la Torre has written a good number of short stories and some plays, including *Goodbye, Miss Lizzie Borden*.

The son of writer parents, MICHAEL GILBERT decided early to follow law. Lack of funds forced him to take up schoolmastering for some time, but while teaching he took a law degree at London University. Shortly thereafter the war intervened, and Mr. Gilbert served with the H.A.C. in North Africa and Italy. He was captured in January 1943 by the German parachute regiment, was imprisoned in North Italy near Parma, and then escaped when the Italians surrendered. After the war he returned to London, completed his training as a solicitor, and entered the Lincoln's Inn firm of which he is now a partner. He has written novels, short stories, radio and television scripts, a play and a study of the Tichborne case.

A Rochester, New York, boy (1930), EDWARD D. HOCH served with the Military Police in Korea after attending the University of Rochester. Formerly in the publishing business (with Pocket Books, Inc.), he is currently in the public relations department of Hutchins advertising company in Rochester. His list of short stories and novelettes exceeds 150, and his work has been reprinted in several countries abroad.

JAMES HOLDING is an example of the mystery-fan-turned-writer. He graduated from Yale, worked for the BBDO advertising agency for twenty-eight years, retiring (recently) as vice president and copy chief of the Pittsburgh office. He read mysteries until one day he decided he would sit down and write one. Since then he has written over thirty mystery short stories. Mr. Holding is also something of a traveler; he has been to many parts of the world, including several trips to Africa.

Born in 1928, BILL KNOX was the son of a well-known Glasgow journalist. He followed his father's line of work, becoming a copy boy at fifteen and the youngest reporter in Glasgow a year later. The number of cases he covered as a crime reporter in Scotland is enough to make any researching mystery writer's mouth water. He became engaged in one of Scotland's biggest murder trials, that of Peter Manuel, born in America and believed responsible for eleven killings—and after two years on that story Mr. Knox was asked to cover it twice daily on television, something new to Britain then. In 1959 he began working for Scottish television, for which he is presently a news editor. Mr. Knox lives in a suburb of Glasgow with his wife and three children.

Though fiction writing is not a full-time profession for FRED LEVON, over the past seventeen years he has written several mystery stories and one mystery novel (*Much Ado About Murder* received an MWA scroll in 1956), as well as a considerable amount of nonmystery fiction. He is forty-four years old, the father of three girls, and a New Yorker.

JAMES McKIMMEY was born and grew up in Nebraska, served in World War II, and then, while attending the University of San Francisco in 1948, sold his first story. After that he devoted his time to writing, and has now published ten novels. He lives on a cattle ranch near La Honda, about fifty miles south of San Francisco.

The team of Frederic Dannay and Manfred Lee—who, as everyone knows, are ELLERY QUEEN—has edited fifty books and written fifty-three more, including those first published under the pseudo-pseudonym of Barnaby Ross. A conservative estimate has placed their total sales in various editions at more than 60,000,000 copies. Ellery Queen has won five annual Edgars, including the Grand Master award of 1960, and both the silver and gold "Gertrudes" awarded by Pocket Books. In 1964, the editing team celebrates a twenty-third anniversary with *Ellery Queen's Mystery Magazine.* Ellery Queen's recent fictional successes are *And on the Eighth Day* and *The Player on the Other Side.* They will, perhaps, go down in history as Anthony Boucher described them in a *New York Times* profile: "Ellery Queen *is* the American detective story."

JACK RITCHIE and his wife Rita have isolated themselves on Washington Island in Wisconsin to prove that writers *can* earn a living just by writing. Though they don't collaborate as writers—they write in different *genre*—they combine forces to make writing possible for each of them, with Jack writing from 4 A.M. till 9 and his wife from 9 till noon. Mr. Ritchie has yet to write a novel, but his increasing popularity as a story writer suggests that when he does it will probably be a good one. "Ritchie," by the way, is a concession to confused spellers; the name is originally Reitci.

Since he was seventeen, HENRY SLESAR has been earning his living with a typewriter, turning out advertising copy for a number of agencies. In 1955 he began to write fiction and since then has produced and sold innumerable short stories, many of which have been adapted for television and motion pictures. He was born and raised in Brooklyn and now lives in Katonah, New York. He is an ardent jazz fan—and vice president and creative director for Donahue and Company, Inc. The author of several novels, his first, *The Gray Flannel Shroud,* won an Edgar for the best first mystery novel of the year when it was published.

Working as a research chemist in South Charleston, JOHN F. SUTER finds that his job with Union Carbide gives him too little time to do the writing that he would like to do—but a perfect source of technical information for authentic backgrounds. (It would seem that scientific curiosity runs in the family: one of the Suters Jr. is currently an aeronautical engineer on the Saturn rocket project.) When he is not defending the "much-maligned state of West Virginia," Mr. Suter finds time also for photography, bowling, travel and amateur archaeology.

JULIAN SYMONS began writing poetry at an early age, edited a poetry magazine for three years before the war, and has published two books of poems and many critical articles in English and American magazines. He has written a weekly article ("Life, People—and Books") for the Manchester *Evening News* as well as mystery reviews for the London *Times.* He has been a copywriter and advertising executive for a London agency, and is the author of a number of biographies and nonfiction books as well as numerous suspense novels, the latest of which (*The End of Solomon Grundy*) is to be published in the fall of 1964.

Born in New York City in 1903, LAWRENCE TREAT graduated from Dartmouth College and Columbia Law School, became a member of the New York bar, practiced six weeks and retired to the more congenial occupation of writing suspense novels and magazine stories (light love and mysteries). He started writing for the detective pulp magazines of the thirties and early forties and then turned to books, of which he has since written seventeen. Mr. Treat pioneered the police procedural novel in 1945 with *V as in Victim,* and is presently doing a series of short story procedurals for *Ellery Queen's Mystery Magazine.* Several hundred of his short stories are published, and he has written for radio, television and ballet. Mr. Treat is a director and the treasurer of MWA—as well as a frequent traveler and a summer idler at Martha's Vineyard.

Format by Mort Perry
Set in Linotype Times Roman
Composed by York Composition Co., Inc.
Printed by York Composition Co., Inc.
Bound by The Haddon Craftsmen, Inc.
HARPER & ROW, PUBLISHERS, INCORPORATED